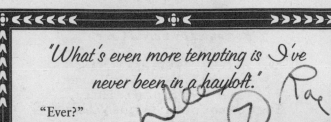

"What's even more tempting is I've never been in a hayloft."

"Ever?"

"Ever."

"Well, it's an experience every young woman should have. Now go climb the ladder and I'll make very certain you don't fall down."

But he kissed her again, and before she knew it, she was like a languid rag doll in his arms as he guided her toward the ladder. Dizzy, she turned and began to climb, knowing he was watching her from just below.

When Will was standing at her side, she gave him a curious glance.

"Horse blankets," he explained. "Some are for warming, some for cooling, some for flies. These are newly washed, and I haven't folded them away in their bins yet . . . what a perfect opportunity."

And then he gave her a gentle push backward, and she grabbed hold of him and pulled him down with her. He covered her mouth with his, slanting his head, tasting deep within her. She moaned, arching into him, then gasping when she felt his hand at her waistline, beneath her t-shirt.

He kissed h

a yes or no gas

"Yes. Oh, p

Ever After at
SWEETHEART RANCH

EMMA CANE

A VALENTINE VALLEY NOVEL

AVONBOOKS

An Imprint of HarperCollinsPublishers

This is a work of fiction. Names, characters, places, and incidents are products of the author's imagination or are used fictitiously and are not to be construed as real. Any resemblance to actual events, locales, organizations, or persons, living or dead, is entirely coincidental.

AVON BOOKS
An Imprint of HarperCollins*Publishers*
195 Broadway
New York, New York 10007

Copyright © 2015 by Gayle Kloecker Callen
ISBN 978-0-06-232342-2
www.avonromance.com

First Avon Books mass market printing: May 2015

Avon Trademark Reg. U.S. Pat. Off. and in Other Countries, Marca Registrada, Hecho en U.S.A.
HarperCollins® is a registered trademark of HarperCollins Publishers.

Printed in the U.S.A.

10 9 8 7 6 5 4 3 2 1

To my agent, Eileen Fallon: thanks for sticking with me through all the ups and downs of this crazy publishing business. I know I can always count on you.

Acknowledgments

I owe a debt of gratitude to so many people for their patience in answering questions as I researched this book: Jim and Angie Callen, M.J. Compton, Alee Drake, Sam Herwood, Elisa Konieczko, Martin Masarech, M. Reed McCall, J. Lynn Rowan, Susan St. Thomas, and Holly Weeden. Another big thank-you to the Packeteers, the Purples, and my husband, Jim, whose help and advice keep me sane. Any mistakes in this book are certainly mine.

Ever After at
SWEETHEART
RANCH

Chapter 1

Lyndsay De Luca stood near the picture window in her living room, staring down at the paperback book in her hands, her eyes stinging with tears of joy. The sun glimmered across the cover, a picture of a distant ranch and mountains with a lone cowboy riding his horse in the distance. She let her trembling fingers trace the title, *A Cowboy in Montana,* and then her own name up above, embossed, with letters as large as the title. This was *her* book, a book that would be on store shelves across the country in just a month. Soon, readers would be swept away into a story she'd created. She could make them laugh and maybe cry, and escape into a world of happily-ever-afters . . .

She'd also finally have to tell her friends and family about the secret she'd been keeping. Her day job as a middle school math teacher was very public, and she'd always liked having her writing as something private she did for herself. If her family had known, they'd have constantly asked when she was going to start submitting her work, or if she'd heard back from an editor. She had enough pressure at school and hadn't wanted any more, interested and supportive though her family might be.

There was another reason she was leery about her revelation, and that reason was now playing catch on Mabel Street, outside her window, with her fourteen-year-old nephew, Ethan.

Will Sweet.

She heard a sharp rapping, and, startled, she glanced up to see him in the center of her picture window as if he'd been framed there, sunlight burnishing his hair. She felt her breath catch and her mouth go dry.

Grinning at her, his eyes narrowed from the sun, Will spoke through the window with a muffled voice. "You still coming with us to the game?"

She nodded and called, "I'll grab my purse and meet you out front."

After pulling on a sweater and sticking a Windbreaker in her purse, she stepped through the door and paused to watch Will throw the ball back to Ethan. If Will caught her staring, he wouldn't think much of it. He was used to being the center of attention every time he entered a room, with his easygoing charm and killer good looks. He had sandy blond hair that lightened in the sun, and since he made his living as a cowboy on the Sweetheart Ranch, owned by his family, he was outdoors all the time, that tall, lean body honed and chiseled from years of outdoor work. His eyes were a changeable hazel, fringed with thick lashes and full of merriment. The cleft in his chin might as well have winked at each woman he passed, and he had a model's hollow cheeks. Occasionally those cheeks bore the scruff of a day-old beard, as if he couldn't be bothered shaving that morning.

"Think fast!"

She flinched as Ethan jumped in front of her, pretending to throw the ball.

"Aunt Lynds, you fall for that every time," he said, shaking his head.

After pulling her door shut, she punched her nephew playfully in the upper arm, because she was no longer tall enough to wrap an arm around his neck. Ethan was almost as tall as his dad, and his hair had slowly been darkening over the years until now it was a light brown. He had the De Luca brown eyes and his dad's laid-back manner.

Laughing, Ethan led them down the street toward the rec league softball game, tossing his ball and catching it. Lyndsay fell in beside Will. He smiled at her, then inhaled deeply of the spring air, exhaling with a sigh of satisfaction. You didn't live in Valentine Valley, Colorado, without loving the outdoors.

She studied him surreptitiously, admiring the fit of his baseball t-shirt, which sported the logo TONY'S TAVERN—her brother's place. There'd been a time in high school when she'd harbored a secret crush on Will. But he'd dated her girlfriend Brittany, and

Lyndsay would never have intruded on that. Then Will had gone and done something so nice that it had struck her heart. It had been Valentine's Day—a big deal in Valentine Valley—and Lyndsay's boyfriend had just dumped her. She'd been wrapped up in her problems and accidentally spilled her books from her locker into a heap on the floor. Will had stopped to help her pick them up, and couldn't have missed her bad mood. At lunch, there had been carnations on sale, red for romance, pink for flirting, white for friendship, and he'd gone and bought her a white one, just to cheer her up. And it had worked, but it had also made her notice how kind he was, how good-hearted—and hunky. Soon she'd battled a brief and guilty crush on him. That crush had been forgotten when Brittany had died in a terrible accident.

Lyndsay had long ago put him out of her mind—

And onto paper. She winced, then smoothed over her expression when Will glanced at her. Ethan lobbed the ball to Will, who caught it and tossed it back, along with some good-natured jibes.

Somehow, without noticing it *at all*, she'd made the hero of *A Cowboy in Montana* a lot like Will. She'd created Cody by taking the characteristics of some of her favorite celebrities and "randomly" picking sandy blond hair and hazel eyes. She hadn't thought anything of it until last week, when a blogger had asked who she'd based her hero on. At first, Lyndsay had answered that Cody was her own creation, but then the blogger had mentioned a scene that Lyndsay had previously written in revisions after her editor had asked for a "grand romantic gesture" by the hero. And the realization of what she'd done had slammed hard into Lyndsay—that scene was a version of something Will had done for Brittany. Cody . . . was a lot like Will.

She didn't want to believe it at first—couldn't let herself accept that she'd made such a foolish mistake. She'd long since moved past what she'd thought of as a schoolgirl crush. Over the years her heart might have given an occasional kick when Will had been around, but she'd put that down to admiration for the man he'd become.

Now, watching him amuse her nephew, aware of that soft spot she'd always felt for him rising right up through her chest into her throat, she had to face facts. It was really true—she'd made Will Sweet the star of her romance novel.

Maybe he'd never realize it. What were the odds he'd read a romance? No one else would guess either. Different name, different state—although her hero was a cowboy. . . .

Though the shadows were starting to lengthen and a chill began to seep from the ground, Will still thought of it as a beautiful late-spring day in the paradise that was Valentine Valley. And he would be spending the evening playing softball with his friends, like he was a kid again.

Walking with Lyndsay really was like he was

back in school, hanging out with the De Lucas. Lyndsay'd been a friend as far back as he could remember, but it wasn't as if he was blind. She'd always been gorgeous, and so smart that he used to enjoy watching her question their teachers or lead a discussion group, so confident in her abilities, eager for every new challenge. But Tony had made it very clear that his sister had been off limits. Will had been focused on Brittany then, and sorrow now pierced him gently before he pushed it away to focus on Lyndsay and Ethan bantering.

"Just think how sad your life will be in high school this fall," Lyndsay told her nephew, "when you won't get to see me every day."

"You mean I won't have to hear from my friends how you're taking it easy on me."

Lyndsay rolled her eyes. "Oh please."

"Sounds like a good deal to me," Will said. He enjoyed watching the two of them together, had heard more than once how grateful Tony was that Lyndsay was there for Ethan, especially after the divorce—the divorce that had separated Lyndsay from her best friend as well as her sister-in-law.

"I didn't take it easy on him," she explained. "Occasionally he'd 'flunk' a test just to prove that to all his friends."

"You flunked tests?" Will eyed the teenager.

Ethan spun slowly to walk backward, still tossing the ball in the air effortlessly. "Just once or twice. I did it for Aunt Lynds's reputation."

She gave an exaggerated cough around the words "Didn't study," which made Will chuckle.

Ethan's grin grew cocky, and he slowly spun and faced forward again, watching the ball and just assuming cars would see him coming. On their small-town streets, that usually happened.

"You know, you didn't need to escort me," Lyndsay called to her nephew.

To Will's surprise, she glanced at him as if she was embarrassed.

"I can find my way to Silver Creek Park, you know," she added.

"I know, but you always forget about the games," Ethan said with a shrug. "And then you're mad at yourself. I don't know what keeps you so busy that you forget important stuff. And Will decided to come with me so we could keep playing catch."

Will elbowed her playfully and was surprised when she gave a nervous start. "So what are you doing on Monday evenings that you can't even check a calendar?" he asked.

She actually turned red, and for a moment, he wondered if she had a guy she had to keep hidden. Which was ridiculous in this day and age. And she'd never made a secret of the guys she dated. They'd all been men comfortable in a suit—doctors, engineers, accountants.

"Grading papers," she finally answered. "I don't finish my workday at three, you know."

"Me neither," Will answered. "Guess we have that in common."

She didn't meet his eyes, leaving him utterly clueless by her cute—but baffling—behavior.

Ethan turned to walk backward, and he and Will started tossing the ball to each other. At Silver Creek Park, they left Lyndsay and headed toward the dugout. Will could have sworn she sighed with relief. Stranger and stranger . . .

Lyndsay put Will out of her mind and scanned the people scattered through the stands for friends to sit with. Nearby, she saw a big banner that hadn't been there last week, stretched across two poles and stuck into the ground, in perfect view of the stands.

THE VALENTINE VALLEY HISTORICAL SOCIETY
NEEDS YOU!

Vote for Mrs. Rosemary Thalberg for President!

On the left side of the banner was a picture of Mrs. Thalberg wearing a confident smile. Her hair was dyed a flattering red, and her tasteful makeup gave her the appearance of being in her sixties instead of seventies. The woman herself was overseeing the placement of the last pole, making suggestions to her grandsons Nate and Josh Thalberg, who both kept glancing toward their softball team with longing.

"What do you think?"

Lyndsay's recently renewed best friend, Kate Fenelli, was walking toward her. Still wearing her law firm work clothes of tailored slacks, multicolored top, and blazer, Kate radiated happiness. Her short blond hair was windswept around her head, and her laughing eyes were a violet hue that always made people take a second look.

Ten years ago, when Kate's marriage with Lyndsay's brother, Tony, had fallen apart, neither of them had even told Lyndsay they were having problems. The breakup had ruined Lyndsay's friendship with Kate and strained her sibling love, but you didn't break up with a brother over something like that. Of course Tony hadn't been talkative about his problems—he was a guy.

Kate, on the other hand . . . nine years had gone by, but last fall their friendship was repaired. Kate had quit her job with a powerful Denver law firm and moved back to Valentine Valley to buy into a small, local firm. And somehow, she and Tony had rediscovered their love and were getting remarried in two months.

"I didn't know about an upcoming vote for the historical society," Lyndsay remarked to Kate.

"I'm surprised a banner was necessary," Kate said, crossing her arms over her chest and examining it almost critically. "After all, wouldn't a mailing to the historical society members accomplish the same thing?"

"That's right, you were gone nine years and don't know. Every resident in town is a member of the historical society, automatically."

Kate blinked at her. "Now that's interesting."

"Keeps everyone invested in the town's history and tourism. The society puts out a great newsletter."

Kate eyed Mrs. Thalberg. "Are the widows the driving force behind that, too?"

"Oh, they're part of it all right, but it isn't their 'baby,' like the Valentine Valley Preservation Fund is. But the two groups certainly go hand in hand."

"And you just know all about this stuff from living here?" Kate asked.

"Nope. Remember, my dad has been dating Mrs. Thalberg for a few months now. I get to hear all the gossip."

"Uh-oh," said a deep male voice behind them.

Lyndsay jumped, recognizing Will. She could have kicked herself for the reaction. She didn't like having secrets that made her nervous. Glancing over her shoulder, she saw Will frowning at the banner.

Kate smiled at him. "So you're against political promotion?"

"'Course not, but don't you remember who's running for reelection?"

He glanced from Kate to Lyndsay, who tried to think up an answer but floundered.

"My grandmother," Will answered patiently. "She's run unopposed for a couple years now."

"The democratic process at work," Lyndsay said lamely. "Will she be upset?"

"Probably—not that that matters. Anything the widows do usually upsets her."

Lyndsay eyed him with sympathy. For as long as she could remember, the widows of the Widows' Boardinghouse hadn't seen eye to eye with Mrs. Sweet, the elegant, patrician owner of the Sweetheart Inn. Lyndsay often thought Mrs. Sweet could be brought down a peg or two, but a grandson probably wouldn't think the same thing.

"What's their feud all about?" Kate asked him.

Will shrugged. "They don't talk about it. My dad did tell me there was something about a Beautiful Baby contest in the sixties, and one of them or the other cheated. We think it goes back farther than that. It all seems kinda weird."

Lyndsay and Kate exchanged a smile. "That usually sums up the widows," Lyndsay said. "Although not usually your grandma," she hastened to add.

Will gave her his white-toothed grin, the one that sent feminine hearts fluttering in concentric circles out around him. And now she'd become just as affected?

"My grandma prefers the term 'eccentric,'" he said. "Hey, I gotta get back to the team before Mrs. Thalberg sees me and starts asking my grandma's stand on their upcoming historical projects."

Lyndsay held back a laugh as he pretended not to see Nate and Josh waving at him from where they stood at either banner pole, adjusting it an inch one way or another for their grandmother.

"Will's such a goof," Kate said, shaking her head as they went to sit in the stands. "Did you know he was going to ask me out on a date last fall if Tony and I hadn't gotten back together? He actually asked Tony's permission!"

"You can't be surprised." Lyndsay shielded her eyes to watch as the Tony's Tavern team took to the field. "He's running out of women of legal age to date in Valentine Valley."

Will Sweet never had a serious emotion in his life, his dating history being the perfect example. He was a serial dater, never with one woman for long. Not that the women complained all that much— and Lyndsay knew them all, living in a small town like Valentine Valley. He treated his dates well and attentively until it was time to end things, usually in a month or two. But there were women in Aspen, Carbondale, and Basalt, too; otherwise, he would have long ago run out of dates.

Although a year younger than Tony, Will had been one of his best friends, so he'd been at her house a lot growing up, eating snacks after school while killing time before football or baseball practices. Tony had extracted a promise from her that she could never date any of his friends because it would put him in the middle when they broke up. Oh, he'd had a double standard all right, since he'd dated Kate, then married and divorced her. It had been awful on the friendships involved, so he'd been proven right.

She'd laughed at her brother then for laying down the law, but inside she'd taken him seriously.

Now Will was playing shortstop, always in the

thick of the action, and Lyndsay didn't have to hide watching him play. Oh, and her brother was out there somewhere, too, center field.

"Did you ever date Will?" Kate asked.

Lyndsay almost betrayed herself by stiffening, but she caught the reaction in time. "Nope."

She and Will had absolutely nothing in common—she was a math teacher who played trumpet in a small jazz band and wrote books. Talk about geek. He was a cowboy whose love of the outdoors carried over to snowboarding and mountain biking, but he was a reckless daredevil. Once she'd gone on a ride with her brother and him, and she'd ended up walking halfway down the side of a mountain leading her bike because she couldn't keep up.

"I thought you said he'd dated everybody," Kate said skeptically.

"Only those women interested in him. We don't all fawn over him, you know."

"Defensive much?"

Lyndsay gave her a frown. "No, Counselor, just stating a fact."

"And you're perfectly happy with that dentist from Carbondale, right? We had a good time double-dating at Wild Thing."

Lyndsay hesitated, then admitted, "We broke up a couple weeks ago."

Kate gasped. "Oh, Lynds, I'm so sorry! You'd been together awhile, hadn't you?"

"Eight months."

"Are you okay?"

"It was a mutual thing, no big deal." But Lyndsay kept her eyes on the team at bat, not wanting to admit the truth—that she'd ended things and left the poor guy brokenhearted. The confusion and disbelief in his eyes still made her flinch every time she remembered it.

She'd been just as confused, but she'd known one thing—she hadn't fallen in love with him, and at thirty-three, if she wasn't feeling a long-term commitment, then what was the point?

Deep inside, a part of her scoffed at the all-or-nothing mentality, but she didn't want to look closely.

"Tell me he didn't go right to another woman," Kate demanded.

"No, he's got kids. He takes his time."

He'd taken a lot of time with her, and she knew he'd been more and more serious. And she'd practically run screaming for the hills. What the hell was wrong with her?

Will made a spectacular catch and passed the ball at lightning speed to first base, which made three outs. Lyndsay clapped and cheered along with half the stands, and she was glad for the distraction.

He was pretty easy on the eyes. Last year, Will had been part of "The Men of Valentine Valley" calendar, used to raise money for the Valentine Valley Preservation Fund. He'd been featured in the month of June, playing baseball, shirtless. And he'd been in the group shot for July, all of the men in swim trunks. Will had been front and center in the hot spring up behind the Sweetheart Inn, hazel eyes smoldering, sandy hair dark and curly with moisture, water dripping down his incredible six-pack abs, as steam rose around him—them. There'd been a whole crowd of local guys, she'd reminded herself at the time, including her brother.

Kate eyed her closely as the applause died away. "You seem . . . okay about it."

It? Oh, the breakup. "I guess I am. I wasn't in love with him."

"Then I feel better. So you're ready to get back out in the dating world?"

Lyndsay shrugged. "I've got a lot going on right now." Like a book about to publish, a Facebook fan page to create, a website to finalize, papers to grade . . . and deciding on the perfect way to tell her family about *A Cowboy in Montana.* "I'll take my time."

But Kate still radiated suspicion.

"I'm starving," Lyndsay said brightly. "Want a hot dog?"

"Okay, thanks. Want me to come?"

"I can carry it. Be right back."

Lyndsay felt both relieved and guilty at the need to distract her friend. But by the time she got back, Kate's grumbling stomach seemed to erase her memory about guys, and they enjoyed a couple more innings of the game—

—until Mrs. Sweet arrived, her chiffon overskirt

floating on the spring breeze as she walked cautiously, regally, over the grass. Her broad-brimmed hat shielded her narrowed eyes from the sun as she stared at Mrs. Thalberg's banner.

Lyndsay glanced at Kate to see her pressing her lips together, as if to keep from laughing.

"This is about to get ugly," Lyndsay said solemnly—then winked.

Chapter 2

But it didn't get ugly right away. Mrs. Sweet sat down in a chair provided by granddaughter Stephanie Sweet, whose blond hair was up in a ponytail pulled through a ball cap. Steph was home for the summer after her first year of college. She was also Will's baby sister, so, of course, she started shouting his name when he was up at bat. Mrs. Sweet clapped politely when he made it to first base.

Lyndsay noticed that Mrs. Sweet wasn't always staring at the ball field; she was looking toward the dugout, where more chairs were grouped. Lyndsay realized that all three widows were watching the game, as well. Her own father, Mario De Luca, was sitting in the middle of them, at Mrs. Thalberg's side. He was tall, bald above a graying fringe of hair around his head, with broad working man's shoulders and a bit of a belly, now that he'd settled into semi-retirement. She wondered with loving exasperation where his hat was, as his head gleamed in the setting sun.

She still was surprised about her dad dating again after all these years. Her parents had tried for a long time to have kids and were far older than all her friends' parents. Her mom had died of cancer when Lyndsay was only nine years old, leaving a void in her life that well-meaning friends and family could never really fill. But her dad had been a hero, the rock of the family, becoming both parents for his children. A self-employed plumber, he'd been able to adjust his schedule around their school field trips and sporting events. They'd had dinner together every night. Never once did she remember her dad dating. Last holiday season, she saw him with the widows. Knowing he played poker with them and taught Sunday school with Mrs. Thalberg, she hadn't given it any more thought than that. But soon, he was only with Mrs. Thalberg, the widow of a rancher, and when Lyndsay had finally asked if they were seeing each other, he'd confirmed it. She was happy for him. Mrs. Thalberg came to the occasional family gathering, but mostly she and Lyndsay's dad just enjoyed each other's company. Her dad insisted that Mrs. Thalberg wasn't about to leave the Widows' Boardinghouse, where she'd spent years living. It was on Silver Creek Ranch land, which her family owned. And Mario insisted he liked having his own place.

Her dad must have felt her stare, because he suddenly waved an arm at her, and she waved back.

"I love your dad," Kate said softly, her voice warm with feeling.

Lyndsay glanced toward her friend, whose expression was suffused with love, and whose eyes gleamed with unshed tears.

"Gees, stop that," Lyndsay said gruffly.

Kate cleared her throat and blinked her eyes. "I just can't believe he'll be my father-in-law again soon. I'm so, so lucky." She slid her arm through Lyndsay's. "And we'll be sisters again."

Now it was Lyndsay's turn to feel her eyes sting. "Can you just stop this? There's no crying at baseball."

Kate giggled. "I think it's actually 'in' baseball. It's from that movie *A League of Their Own*, right?"

"Whatever. Let's just watch the game."

But the drama between the widows and Mrs. Sweet loomed like an impending storm. Lyndsay heard the murmurs, saw the glances from the stands toward the elderly ladies, and it would have been funny if she hadn't had to choose sides.

She didn't *have* to choose sides. All she had to do was vote. Privately.

"So what's with the crowd?" Kate asked, glancing around, her forehead furrowed.

Lyndsay sighed. "Mrs. Sweet arrived."

"I see that, but so what?"

"She's the reigning president of the historical society and running for reelection."

"Ahh," Kate said, nodding. "Will they come to blows?"

Lyndsay grinned. "Who can say? The historical society had an 'incident' "—she used air quotes—"earlier this year. The museum asked Mrs. Sweet if she'd lend memorabilia about her famous mother."

"The silent movie star!" Kate said enthusiastically. "I remember hearing about her. Didn't she and Mrs. Sweet's rancher dad meet in Glenwood Springs, when she was passing through by train, and he'd brought his cattle to be sold?"

"Yep, love at first sight and all that. They're the ones that built the Sweetheart Inn as their home. Anyway, there's a collection of movie memorabilia the museum wanted to borrow, but Mrs. Sweet worried it would get damaged or lost, so she refused and ended up creating a permanent display at the inn."

Kate shrugged. "I can see both sides of this argument."

"Needless to say, the widows—already touchy about anything associated with Mrs. Sweet for mysterious reasons—had a fit on behalf of the museum. And Mrs. Thalberg running for president must be the result."

Kate pointed toward Tony's team dugout. "Look at the way the guys and Brooke are staring at the widows and Mrs. Sweet. I feel really sorry for all the grandkids involved."

There were a lot of Sweets and Thalbergs on the team, but only one female—cowgirl Brooke Thalberg.

At last the game was over, with Tony's Tavern squeaking out a win over the True Grits Diner. As Lyndsay climbed down from the stands, she noticed that the Thalbergs and Sweets stayed overly long in the dugout. Feeling amused, she wondered if that was deliberate on their parts to avoid the brewing election controversy.

"Hi, Lyndsay!"

She turned and saw Sean Lighton, wearing a True Grits Diner t-shirt, walking toward her. He must have been a little out of shape, for beneath his damp, curly brown hair, his face was still red from the game. He was new in town, a web designer and, as he himself put it, "a geek in the great outdoors."

She thought he might be pretty amusing when he relaxed a bit. "Hi, Sean. You're playing for True Grits, huh?"

He looked down at his chest and gave a chagrined smile. "The restaurant is a client. I thought, what the heck. It's a good reason to be outside." Then he glanced past her, and his expression fell. "Have a good night, Lyndsay."

As Sean walked away, she turned around and saw Will striding toward Kate and her, loose-limbed and broad-shouldered. Giving Lyndsay a nod, he moved past her to kiss his grandma's cheek and stand between her and the looming banner with Mrs. Thalberg's cheerful face. Lyndsay noticed he used his killer smile even on his grandma.

"Thanks for coming to the game, Grandma," Will said.

"Of course, dear." Mrs. Sweet eyed him with fondness. "It's a lovely evening."

Will put an arm around his sister Steph's shoulders. "Hey, kid, maybe you should join the team one of these days."

"Some of us often work evenings," Steph said.

Will spread his arms wide. "And I don't? Those dams have to be moved for the hay irrigation morning and night. I don't see you out in the fields."

"I'm going to be a pastry chef and bakery owner, thank you very much," Steph said.

"I don't see the *current* pastry chef and bakery owner. Did she work so you didn't have to?"

"She might have," Steph admitted sheepishly.

The owner of Sugar and Spice was Emily Thalberg, Steph and Will's long-lost half sister, with whom they'd been reunited a few years back. Emily was now married to Nate Thalberg.

Lyndsay winced in sympathy as she realized that the coming war for president of the historical society put Emily directly in the middle, with Mrs. Sweet as her grandma and Mrs. Thalberg as her grandma-in-law. But who was Lyndsay kidding—the whole town was going to be in the crosshairs. Lyndsay watched Mrs. Sweet's pleasant expression fade as she studied the banner again.

"Now, Grandma," Will said in a cajoling voice, "all's fair in an election."

Mrs. Sweet sniffed. "I've never had to resort to such . . . tactics to earn the vote of each citizen."

"There's a first time for everything," Will answered. "Do you want to respond somehow, or just run on your record?"

Lyndsay bit her lip to keep from laughing, knowing what Will must wish would happen.

"I will give it thought, William, thank you."

Will looked over his grandma's head, and Lyndsay saw that the widows were approaching. To her surprise, Will caught Lyndsay's eye and mouthed, "Help me!"

She pressed her lips together though they twitched with laughter, then raised her hands helplessly.

"You heading home?" Kate called.

"Not yet," Lyndsay said, gesturing at the approaching conflagration.

"Oh dear," Kate murmured.

The three widows were like a force of nature, each very different from the other. Where Mrs. Thalberg was a practical rancher's widow, Mrs. Palmer was the flighty wild child of the group, with her outrageous makeup, tarot-reading skills, and patterned homemade dresses—tonight's was a child's print with baseballs, bats, and mitts—and a big blond wig upon which perched a ball cap. She had pom-poms in one hand and a massive purse in the other. Mrs. Ludlow, with her pressed slacks and simple white blouse, could be anyone's grandma, and she moved with slow and steady speed behind her walker. When Mrs. Ludlow offered a genuinely warm smile to Mrs. Sweet, Lyndsay remembered that Mrs. Ludlow had ever been the peacemaker.

"Eileen, how good to see you in the park, enjoying the fresh air."

Mrs. Sweet leaned forward to kiss Mrs. Ludlow's cheek. "Connie, dear, we all only wish we could be as health conscious as you."

Will seemed to notice Lyndsay's surprised expression at all the congeniality. Why did he keep looking at her? It was making her think he knew her secrets.

"Apparently," Kate whispered, "not all the widows have a problem with Mrs. Sweet."

"Poor Mrs. Ludlow—a divided loyalty can't be easy in this town," Lyndsay pointed out.

Ignoring the other widows, Mrs. Sweet spoke directly to Mrs. Ludlow. "I'm surprised to learn of Rosemary running against me like this." She gestured to the sign. "Rather ostentatious, isn't it?"

"It gets the point across," Mrs. Thalberg said.

Mrs. Sweet's gaze was glacial as she said, "You could have spoken to me if you had a problem with how I run the historical society."

"Amazingly, it's not supposed to be a monarchy," Mrs. Thalberg said in a pleasant voice. "I did voice my concerns, and I was ignored."

"Ignored?" Mrs. Sweet echoed coolly. "I don't know what you're talking about."

"It's hard to hear us common folk when your head's up in the clouds," Mrs. Palmer said, her Western accent strong.

Lyndsay looked around for the woman's grandson, Adam Desantis, but noticed that he and his wife, Brooke, were nowhere to be seen. Not that she blamed them.

Lyndsay's dad approached and gave Mrs. Sweet a big smile. "Good evenin', Eileen. Guess Rosemary's going to make the race interesting this year."

"So she is," Mrs. Sweet answered. "I will have to run the race in my own way."

"Bring it on, Eileen," Mrs. Thalberg challenged, her expression brimming with confidence.

"Grandma, how 'bout we go for an ice cream?" Will asked, sticking out his elbow to Mrs. Sweet. "You always took me for ice cream after my games—time I returned the favor."

"Very well, William. Perhaps you will be a good sounding board for my election ideas."

Will hesitated only a fraction of a second, but Lyndsay noticed it. She almost felt sorry for him.

"Of course, Grandma. Sounds like fun."

The two of them, along with Steph, walked off together, leaving the widows to stare after them.

Wearing matching frowns, Mrs. Thalberg and Mrs. Palmer studied Mrs. Ludlow.

Mrs. Ludlow held up a hand. "I've already told you, I am not getting in the middle of any altercations. The election is a democratic process—let us treat it without emotion."

"Without emotion?" Mrs. Palmer said, aghast. "When have we *not* had emotion with Eileen?"

Mrs. Thalberg glanced at Lyndsay and Kate, still avidly listening. "We can finish this discussion in private."

"I'll drive you ladies home," Mario said, then gave his daughter a kiss on the cheek. "Have a good night, babes."

"Hey, Mom!" Ethan called. He was playing catch with his father on the other side of the stands. "You coming?"

Kate looked at Lyndsay. "Come on and walk home with us. We can have our own ice cream."

"No, but thanks. Gotta grade papers." *And write.* The next book was due to her editor in two months, and she still had a couple chapters to go. Lyndsay raised a hand good-bye as Kate left to join Tony and Ethan.

She turned to start around the far side of the stands and came to a sudden stop. Will was still there, talking to a middle-aged couple. They seemed familiar, but Lyndsay couldn't place them. Mrs. Sweet had already reached her car across the field and was seated inside, waiting for him. Lyndsay backed up and considered walking the long way around the ball field.

"Will, you don't have to come, really you don't," said the woman, her cajoling voice full of warmth.

"Mrs. Acker, you can't keep me away," Will said. "I always ride fence with Mr. Acker. What do you say, sir? It's our spring ritual."

And then Lyndsay remembered who they were, and a wave of sadness—and curiosity—washed through her. They were the parents of Brittany, Will's high school girlfriend, the one who'd died in a car accident.

"Will, you have your own ranch to work," Mr. Acker said.

"You tell me this every time, but it makes no difference," Will insisted. "I have two brothers who work with me, my dad, and some ranch hands. I can name my own time. So I'll see you tomorrow morning at eight?"

Lyndsay couldn't see their faces, but in the silence she could imagine Mr. and Mrs. Acker looking to each other to make a shared decision.

"All right then," Mr. Acker said, his voice thick with emotion. He cleared his throat. "See you then, Will."

Lyndsay stood with her back against the cold metal stands, waiting for what she hoped was a long enough time for everyone to have left. Then she came around the end of the stands and—

Ran right into Will.

Chapter 3

Will caught Lyndsay before she could fall back on her ass. He felt the lean strength of her arms, saw the wide shock in her deep brown eyes, and, for the first time, he noticed the tiny golden flecks hidden within. Her breasts brushed his chest, and for just a moment he held her still, stunned by an unexpected flare of desire, the need to bring her hips up against his. Her full lips shone with a touch of pink gloss, looking suddenly so kissable that he let her go and took a step back.

They stared at each other, and he couldn't help admiring the long fall of her brown hair where it tumbled around her shoulders and touched her breasts. She'd recently added highlights—when had he first noticed that?—and her bangs fluttered evocatively in spikes almost to her eyelashes. He was letting himself see her as a desirable, *available* woman—and then he had to push that thought away. She wasn't a woman like all the others—

she was Tony's sister and a longtime friend. She was probably his *only* woman friend, since ex-girlfriends and the wives of his buddies didn't count.

But this smoldering heat within his veins was telling him otherwise, and it made him uneasy. He wasn't going to let emotions overrule his good sense.

"Will?" Lyndsay said at last, the surprise in her eyes giving way to confusion and then concern. "Are you okay?"

He put on the easy grin that worked like a charm with women. "Of course I'm okay. Just curious why you were lurkin' around, eavesdropping."

A blush flamed across her cheeks. "I didn't mean to eavesdrop. I came around the corner and you were right there. It—it looked serious, and I didn't want to interrupt."

"Serious? Since when is anything I do serious?" He felt a deep sense of unease that was hard to keep hidden. What the hell was up with him?

"Well, I know, I thought the same thing, Will. How could I not?"

Her smile was tentative. He'd known her too long to see it as anything other than forced.

"Okay, sorry for startling you," he said. "Hell, you startled me, too." His own reaction to her certainly had.

"I don't want to keep you from ice cream with your grandma."

She bit her lip, perhaps to tamp down her smile, but all he saw was her lips. He thought again of kissing her—like he hadn't just kissed . . . what's-her-name . . . a couple weeks ago.

Had it been a couple weeks since he'd broken it off with . . . damn, what *was* her name, the gift shop owner from Elk's Crest? Maybe that was his problem. He needed his kisses more regular.

He glanced at his grandma's Audi sedan, where she was still waiting, her stare out the passenger window quite pointed.

"Will," Lyndsay said, "is everything okay with Mr. and Mrs. Acker?"

"Sure, they're doing as well as can be expected, right?" *When their only child is dead.* It had been sixteen years since her death, but he'd never forget the anguish, disbelief, and horror. He was long used to the tight cramp that clenched his chest whenever he thought of Brittany, and his own part in her poor parents' suffering.

"Gotta go," he said, trying not to sound stiff and realizing he was failing. "See ya, Lyndsay."

He gave a brief wave as he turned away, but he hadn't met her eyes again. She seemed to be looking too deeply into his soul.

His grandma was doing the same thing, but for different reasons, and he let his expression turn cocky as he slid behind the wheel.

"Hey, Grandma, can't believe you're letting me drive your prized Audi."

"You're not sixteen anymore, William. You drive a swather across a hay field. I believe you've proved you can be trusted."

"Gee, thanks." He tossed her another smile as he started the car and pulled away from Silver Creek Park.

"That was Lyndsay De Luca you were talking with after the Ackers."

"Yep."

"She is quite the gifted teacher. And very smart to be able to teach mathematics to budding teenagers."

He glanced at her with curiosity. "So I've heard."

"She cares about the children, too. I understand she's an advisor to the 4-H club."

"Grandma, if you're such an admirer, why don't you hire her at the inn?"

She shot him a sharp look. "You are quite out of sorts, young man. One might think you have a problem with her."

"I don't have a problem except that she seemed to be eavesdropping on my conversation with the Ackers." He gritted his teeth. Damn, why had he mentioned that?

"Lyndsay is too well raised to be eavesdropping. Which means you felt uneasy being overheard and cast your doubts onto her. Why is that?"

He sighed. "That's ridiculous, Grandma. I'm friends with the Ackers. I've known them ever since high school." Ever since Brittany had innocently decided he'd be the perfect boyfriend.

"And since their daughter's death, you've been a good friend to them," she said quietly.

There was gentle understanding in his grandma's voice, tough as nails though she was.

"Of course I have. It's the least I've been able to do after what they suffered."

"And you suffered, too, in your own way."

"We all did," he said woodenly. "When a classmate dies . . ."

With long practice, he pushed the memories aside, resurrected his smile, and pulled into a parking spot on Main Street, right in front of Just Desserts.

"Great parking spot, Grandma. I didn't even need to drop you off. Do you know what kind of ice cream you want?"

She frowned at him from beneath the brim of her sweeping hat. "Very well, William, I will consider the subject closed for now. I do believe a vanilla cone sounds lovely."

"Vanilla?" he scoffed. "That's pretty boring. I like the one with chocolate-covered cone pieces in it. Nuts, too. Now let's get in line before we have to wait all night."

"Perhaps I can move the line along by intimidating a child or two with a good long stare."

He snorted. "Their parents, too."

He grinned at her, and she gave him a slow, wicked smile in return.

Lyndsay had converted the back bedroom into an office in her three-bedroom ranch. Her desk was L-shaped in a corner, with plenty of room along one side for research books and index cards and, on the other end, her laptop. She swiveled her office chair easily down the length, trying to stare at the bright screen of her computer, but the scene just wouldn't come to life, the characters wouldn't effortlessly talk to each other. As usual when the words were slow, she gazed into the distance. The desk overlooked a wide window and a view of her garden, with its mix of annuals, perennials, and shrubs. Above that rose the majesty of the Elk Mountains, still occasionally spotted with snow up above the tree line, like someone had licked ice cream and let drops fall where they might.

But the sun had set a while back. Against the gray darkness, the dark mountains rose up like jagged teeth to take a bite of the first stars.

But she was still thinking about ice cream, which led her back to Will. He'd caught her to keep her from falling, then he'd taken a step back like he'd been trying to get away. She slid her hand down her face, grimacing, wondering what he'd seen in her expression. She'd been careful to school her features, worried about her new sensitivity to him.

And there was his conversation with the Ackers, and how it sounded like he'd been visiting their farm all these years. It kind of surprised her, and her memories fell back in time. She and Brittany had known each other from the beginning of school, although they'd never been truly close friends. In a small town, you graduated with the same people you started kindergarten with, shared lunches, and played school pranks using farm animals or manure. They'd gone to parties in the woods, and once, Will had made a swimming pool with a waterproof tarp in the back of his pickup. Brittany had been at his side in the water, had drunk beer with him by firelight, and disappeared into the woods for make-out sessions for which Lyndsay had envied her.

But her envy had disappeared the stormy night Brittany had driven off the road and slammed into a tree in her little car. She'd died instantly, but the grief had seemed to drown the whole school for many weeks. Will had walked around as if in a daze. That summer, Lyndsay hadn't even seen him at the ice cream stand or on the ball fields. He'd thrown himself into ranch work, Tony had said.

But thankfully, that fall he'd been his old self, enjoying his senior year. He must have had a girl-friend eventually, but Lyndsay couldn't remember who the first one was. Not that it mattered. They'd all been young and ready to face the world again.

But Will hadn't forgotten Brittany's parents, and that touched something deep inside Lyndsay's heart, surprising her in a way she thought he never could. After all, she'd been telling herself for years that she knew everything about him. But obviously she didn't. She rather liked knowing he could be loyal to a memory.

She'd been thinking about Will too much, ever since she'd realized that her subconscious had played a little joke, basing her hero, Cody, on Will. She'd assumed these resurrected feelings would fade away eventually, but after a week, they still lingered. Her dating life was in a rut, she was about to publish a book based on a guy she'd never even dated—so what was she waiting for? Maybe it was finally time to date Will Sweet and get him out of her system.

She knew the drill: he dated and dumped and everyone moved on without too many complications. After all, he never let a relationship get far enough for anyone to be hurt. So it was *her* turn—and it wasn't as if Tony could object. She was thirty-three years old. His friendship with Will could take the "strain."

She exhaled a long breath, feeling better at having made a decision. She'd ask Will out, and he'd say yes, because surely he was running out of women to date who didn't live two towns away. After getting a close-up view of his flaws, the flaws every man had, she'd move on with her life.

It was a logical plan, and she was all about logic.

Just before dinner on Thursday night, Will sat in the bubble cockpit of the family helicopter, the sound of the rotors muffled by his headset. Holding the steering bar, the cyclic, with his right hand, using the gentlest of touches to hover for a moment, he admired the beauty of the Sweetheart Ranch spread out along the base of the Elk Mountains north of Valentine Valley. He felt at peace, and, as he often did, he said hi to Brittany.

She'd been the one who'd sparked his imagination about helicopters in ranch work, showing him a Texas photo she'd found online and teasing him about being a cowboy in the sky. A few years after her death, he'd talked his dad into the purchase, and from his first solo flight, he'd felt close to her. In those first few months in the air, her memory finally became a peaceful one for him, and even all these years later, he felt a connection to her whenever he flew.

As he hovered over the Sweetheart Ranch, which generations of his family had built, a sense of pride in the many buildings was still a feeling of satisfaction deep in his chest. Out in one pasture, a dozen horses roamed free. The family home itself was two stories, with dark wood siding and low additions on either side. There were several barns and outbuildings, of course, but he was hovering over the field outside the hangar, a big red metal barn of a building that fit into the landscape of the ranch.

Down below he could see his brother Chris waving at him from near the hangar. Chris had left the tractor in position, and all Will had to do was land on the dolly so the helicopter could eventually be towed into the hangar.

But still, Will hovered, looking down at his brother through the round window, feeling tired before even facing Chris. He was tempted to rise up, as if he could escape, but he knew that was pointless.

Chris had a strong enthusiasm for helicopters, considering he wasn't interested in learning how to fly himself. He was a bookworm, along with being a cowboy. He liked playing sports as well as the next guy, but . . . he thought too much, over-analyzed everything. He was convinced that Will's passion for flying meant he should start a side business, going into search and rescue or renting himself out to the forest service or the power companies for surveying. No matter how much Will insisted he was all about being a cowboy and focusing on the Sweetheart Ranch, Chris seemed not to believe him.

But Will had never really told Chris—or anyone—the truth, that the helicopter was also about feeling close to the memory of Brittany. Even though that might have faded a bit over the years into a warm glow of celebrating good times rather than a tragic ending, it still seemed almost like a betrayal to be up there with anyone other than family.

At last he lowered the collective handle next to his hip and settled gently onto the dolly. He saw Chris give him a thumbs-up, but Chris knew better than to get too close. Will had the landing checklist to run through as he waited for the temperature to cool so he could begin fuel cutoff and eventually start slowing the rotors.

When at last the clutch light turned off, Will opened the cockpit door, hopped onto the dolly, and then to the pavement.

Chris was striding toward him, light blond hair gleaming in the sun that was just about to slide behind the mountains. He was shorter and leaner than Will, but there was no mistaking that they were brothers.

"So did you see the coyotes where we thought they were? The herd has been so nervous."

"I saw several near the McGuire. We'll have to head up there soon and take care of them."

Chris nodded. "I bet if you approached the Thalbergs or other ranchers in the valley, they'd pay you to look for coyote."

Will rolled his eyes and headed for the main house, saying over his shoulder, "They handle their own predator problems just fine. You can stop bringing this up."

Chris caught up to him. "But you're missing a prime opportunity to—"

"I don't have time."

"Daniel and I can—"

"Stop!" Will's voice was a little too sharp. With a sigh, he turned to walk backward so he could see his little brother. "Let it go, Chris, okay?"

"For now. Just so you know, I moved the dams on the Rigel field. Daniel took care of the Orion. We can handle things."

"Put the helicopter in the hangar, will you?"

And that was the end of the conversation. Will would be happy when Chris and his fiancée, Heather Armstrong, were married. Maybe then Chris would focus on his wife and his home and leave Will in peace.

At the house, Will entered through the mudroom, kicking off his cowboy boots and washing his hands and face in the big industrial sink.

As he was drying off, he spotted his mom, Faith, standing in the doorway, holding a glass of wine. As usual, she wore a flowing, billowy dress, like a flower child from the '60s, though she'd only been a young girl then. Her dark, frizzy hair, streaked with gray, hung soft and loose down her back. There were faint lines on her fresh-scrubbed face, but none of that mattered next to the warmth of her smile.

"How was the ride?" she asked.

"Good. Beautiful conditions," he said, dropping a kiss on her cheek as he walked past.

The kitchen lights weren't on yet, and the golden rays of the setting sun cast the room in warm, mellow tones. Crystals hanging in the windows separated the light into the occasional rainbow of color across the countertop or floor. Candles burned in lotus holders, and a statue of the goddess held the place of honor in the picture window of the breakfast nook. Will shook his head fondly at all the evidence of his mother's bohemian lifestyle. It wasn't just his mom, of course. His dad was big into Slow Food, and he was involved with the distribution of organic foods to all the restaurants in the entire Roaring Fork Valley.

He glanced toward the dining room, hearing lots of raised voices.

"We're having a dinner party," Faith said.

Will cocked his head. "Any special reason?"

"We're celebrating Emily and Nate's inclusion on the adoption agency website."

"Good reason. Do I have time for a quick shower?"

"No, you're fine." She swept past him, leaving a perfumed trail in her wake. "I'm just getting the appetizers ready. Can you carry a tray in?"

He grabbed a couple pieces of cheese before doing as his mom asked. The decibel level vastly increased as he entered the dining room, which was separated from the living room by a big stone fireplace open on both sides. Floor-to-ceiling windows overlooked the patio and the Elk Mountains beyond, in shadow now that the sun had set beyond them. He was swamped immediately by starving family members, and he set down the tray before returning for another one. Standing momentarily in the doorway, he watched them all, feeling a sense of contentment and love. Chris stood talking to his fiancée, Heather, who owned As You Like It Catering. His baby sister, Steph, had brought along her boyfriend, Tyler Brissette, who ate like he hadn't seen food in a week. Will's dad, Joe, stood talking to Grandma Sweet, both of them wearing serious expressions. The two of them always had a lot to talk about, including gossip about everyone in Valentine.

Even Daniel had brought a date, Will thought with surprise. He wasn't sure he'd ever met her before. She was dressed all in black, with dark makeup around her eyes, black hair that covered half her face, and a stud beneath her lip, just like Daniel had. Coincidence? Will would have to ask later.

And then he realized that he and Grandma Sweet were the only unattached people in the house. He suppressed a laugh. He asked if anyone else needed a drink, then went and got himself a bottle of beer.

The guests of honor stood near a laptop on the dining table, pointing at the little picture of their smiling faces on the screen and saying something about it to Heather. Nate had his arm around Emily, and they seemed to glow with enthusiasm and excitement. Nate ran the business empire part of the Silver Creek Ranch. He was a genius at investing, and he'd shored up the shaky finances of the business a few years back. He'd fallen in love with Emily when she'd moved to town, ostensibly to sell a family property. She'd ended up staying after falling in love with Nate, opening a bakery—and discovering that Will's dad was also hers.

Joe's high school girlfriend had left town and married someone else, pretending that that guy was Emily's father. Only after her mom's death was Emily able to follow the clues and discover the truth. Joe had missed out on thirty years of her life, and in the weeks after he'd first found out, he'd been sadder and more distracted than Will had ever seen. But he'd bounced back as he'd gotten to know Emily, and now she was just as much a part of the family as any of them.

Will joined Nate and Emily. "Congratulations,"

he said, shaking Nate's hand and giving Emily a hug. "Why don't you show me this website? Read the info out loud so we can all hear."

Everyone gathered around as Emily read with an excited voice. She had their dad's blue eyes, adding her own tint of strawberry blond hair to the family's various blond hues. Only Daniel had their mom's darker hair.

"It took us a while to decide how we really wanted to go," Emily continued. "Foreign adoption or private, a baby or any age child. After a while, we realized we wanted a baby and we wanted to try to make it happen here."

"So how long can a private adoption take?" Faith asked, after taking another sip of wine.

"The average wait time is eighteen months," Nate said. "Basically, you just wait until you're chosen."

"But we've already had the home visit and been approved—that's a major hurdle," Emily added. "We're even considering starting our own website for the adoption, with more details about us and our lives. They say it helps the moms decide who to choose for the adoption."

"Here's to a quick success!" Grandma Sweet said, lifting her glass in a toast. Everyone else followed suit.

After a few more minutes of adoption excitement, everyone settled down for dinner. Will grilled steaks on the patio with his dad and listened to the highlights of Joe's latest projects, from the high school garden program to the farmers' market in Silver Creek Park and the newest restaurant joining the organic food network he coordinated. Joe and Grandma Sweet even had some investments on Main Street that they kept track of. Will was glad all those interests made his dad happy, but he wasn't much like his dad. As Will kept telling Chris, he was all about the ranch. He worked hard as a cowboy, and he loved his life, whether it was riding fence or herding cattle or rebuilding the engine of the feeding truck. Every day was different, and he was outdoors—even if that meant rain or snow.

Sometimes he worried he was disappointing his dad, since he wasn't involved in the inn or any of the other businesses. But he had brothers and cousins who wanted to deal with those things. Even his mom seemed to be spreading out, recently becoming a partner in the Mystic Connection, the New Age shop in Valentine. Since she spent enough time there, he thought as they all settled around the table to enjoy their meal, he was glad she'd have a say in its future.

The conversation went from baby talk to weddings, and Chris and Heather admitted they were about to discuss wedding dates. That started a whole discussion about what kind of reception they wanted.

"Every time we think we know what we want, someone else beats us to the marriage game," Chris admitted. "Last Christmas it was Brooke and Adam, and this summer it's Tony and Kate—and this is their *second* wedding."

"It's very romantic that they're having it at the same place," Emily said with a soft sigh.

"The Rose Garden," Chris said, shaking his head.

"What, you can't get married at the same place someone else did?" Daniel demanded with pretend outrage, itching his latest tattoo.

Heather laughed. "No, it's just the Valentine Valley curse, I guess. Weddings everywhere."

"You know you are always invited to have it at the inn," Grandma Sweet pointed out.

"We know that, Grandma," Chris said, "and you're the best. We're just not sure if we want a formal or informal wedding."

"And you want yours to feel special," Faith said.

"Of course it'll feel special." Heather took Chris's hand. "I'm marrying a great guy."

Everyone around the table did the "aww" thing, and the wedding talk just kept going on and on. By the time Steph, Emily, and Heather were gushing about flowers, Will caught Daniel's eye, and they shared a commiserating glance. Will thought a guy had to be getting married to care about wedding details, but it wasn't that way with women.

Daniel's date, Chelsea—Daniel had finally remembered to introduce her—didn't have all that much to say. She worked at the Open Book and seemed as if she must read more than she spoke.

But she did speak up about the meal. "Sorry I

didn't eat my steak, Mrs. Sweet. I'm a vegetarian."

Faith frowned her worry. "I'm so sorry, dear. Daniel should have told me."

"I left a note on your desk, Mom," Daniel said. "You didn't get it?"

"Oh," Faith said, her cheeks going red. "I must have missed it. Guess you'll just have to text me next time," she added awkwardly.

"We can text you now?" Steph asked, surprised. "Since when?"

"I have to get better at all this modern technology." Faith sounded a little defensive.

Steph cleared her throat. "And on that subject, guess we'll get a chance to text even more than you thought. I'm going to sublet the apartment over Monica's Flowers and Gifts."

A frown wrinkled Faith's forehead. "Oh, I didn't realize you weren't happy."

Emily, Steph's summer boss, appeared chagrined. Tyler, Steph's boyfriend, pointedly kept eating his steak without glancing up. Will wondered if Tyler was moving in too, but he didn't ask. He knew the boy was attending classes at Colorado Mountain College, CMC. He also knew that Steph was perfectly old enough, but . . . even he was a little uncomfortable at the thought of his baby sister running off to—

"Not happy?" Steph's eyes widened, even as she grinned. "Of course I'm happy. But I'm nineteen, Mom, and I just finished my first year of college. Monica's place is empty because she and Travis just bought a house, remember?" She scrupulously kept her eyes off their grandma, who studied her with interest. "And I'm working full-time with Em, and I just . . . want my commute to be a little easier."

Will held back a snort and didn't look at his brothers. They might easily set each other off into laughter. Everyone knew a commute in Valentine Valley was a few minutes at best. Heavy traffic was a herd of cattle crossing the road from one pasture to the next.

Their dad cleared his throat, and Will wondered if he was warning his sons to keep quiet.

Joe then smiled at his youngest. "Of course we understand, honey. It's just kind of surprising."

Steph glanced around. "Probably because none of the boys have bothered moving away at all."

"Hey, we all work here," Will pointed out. "And we have our own place." Okay, they'd renovated and converted the bunkhouse. But it was away from the house.

"I don't see you eating in your own kitchen much," she shot back knowingly.

"This isn't about me, is it?" Will asked.

He thought her eyes took on a slightly pleading look, her head tilting toward their mom, who still wore a troubled frown, and he relented.

"So, Grandma," he said, after swallowing a bite of baked potato, "what's going on with the historical society?"

Grandma Sweet delicately patted her lips with her napkin and replaced it on her lap. Tonight's little hat was made of straw, and it was perched jauntily toward one side of her head. She tilted her chin up, which made the hat jiggle.

"Going on?" she echoed in that imperious way she sometimes had. "I believe an election is 'going on.'"

Goth Girl stared at Grandma Sweet, her black-rimmed eyes rather wide.

Steph choked and covered her mouth with her napkin. Will shot her an "I did this for you" glare.

"We have an election every other year," Grandma Sweet continued, elongating her words as if Will was a child.

"I know that, Grandma," he said just as slowly, "but I was with you when you saw Mrs. Thalberg's banner at the ball field. This is not just a normal election—or so your expression said." He knew she wouldn't take it well, discovering that her emotions were so obvious.

"Mrs. Thalberg's banner?" Joe asked, frowning.

Will gave his grandma a pointed stare.

"Rosemary is running against me for the presidency. She put up a campaign banner visible from the baseball stands."

All eyes went to Nate, Mrs. Thalberg's grandson, who looked like he wished he could drop a spoon and crawl under the table to find it.

"Are you blushing, Nathaniel?" Will teased.

Emily rolled her eyes, but laughter lurked at the corners of her mouth.

"I don't need to blush," Nate insisted. "I have nothing to do with any of it."

"Easy out," Daniel said, sitting back with his arms crossed over his chest.

"So you didn't know anything about it?" Will pressed.

"Well . . . sure I knew," Nate said. "She told me she was running, and I told her not to take on too much."

"She does not run a business," Grandma Sweet said coolly.

The claws were coming out, Will saw. Because of course, his grandma ran the Sweetheart Inn— with the help of her daughter, Aunt Helen, but he wasn't going to point that out. Grandma Sweet was a ruthless businesswoman, and apparently she was the same in the historical society.

"She does help run the Valentine Valley Preservation Fund," Nate responded. "And there was the Christmas market last December. I'm surprised she finds time for a social life."

"She's always found time for that," Grandma said. "And I've known her longer than almost anyone."

"And how long is that?" Will asked, truly curious.

"We both lived here and went to school together, and that is an amount of years best left unsaid."

Women and their reluctance to discuss their ages. Like everyone couldn't subtract . . .

"But were you never friends?" Emily asked poignantly, now the granddaughter to both women.

"We were childhood friends for a time,"

Grandma admitted. "But high school . . ." She trailed off briefly. "Back then, we still had our own high school here in Valentine Valley. It's the middle school now, but then . . ."

Will thought of a certain middle school teacher, whom he'd been trying not to think too much about since their run-in in the park. But to his surprise, the thought of her kept popping back up when he least expected it.

"But then?" Joe urged his mom on.

Her smile twisted a bit. "Then they were the Purple Poodles, not 'The Widows,'" she said, emphasizing their unofficial title, "and they were the outcasts of the school."

Chapter 4

Friday night at Tony's Tavern—Lyndsay rarely ever missed it. She liked the silly animal heads mounted on the wall, because someone always managed to decorate one rather inappropriately. Tonight there were colorful beads draped across an elk's antlers like it was Mardi Gras. But there were also a lot of flat-screen TVs showing sports—that brought the guys—and, of course, a pool table in the back room. The open secret was the food. Chef Baranski looked like a biker and cooked like a five-star chef. Most of Lyndsay's friends came to party, and between the laughter and the dancing, the pool and darts—and oh, the food—she always managed to unwind from a tough week at work, which was a great segue into a day of writing on Saturday. And work had been particularly tough.

"Lynds!"

She turned at the sound of her name to find her

friend Jessica Fitzjames striding toward her. Jessica drew stares, with her long, wavy blond hair bouncing around her shoulders, but during the day, she often wore it up, the better to be taken seriously as a journalist at the *Valentine Gazette*.

"Jess!" Lyndsay called back, and the two women grinned at each other.

Jessica pulled up a chair. "I saw Kate behind the bar. Is she working here again?"

Lyndsay laughed. "Nope. Now that they're engaged, she and my brother see enough of each other."

Last Thanksgiving, Kate had returned to Valentine on a two-month sabbatical from her big law firm over a disagreement about a client. When she'd been bored out of her mind, Tony had challenged her to work as a server again, something she'd done as a teenager in her family's restaurant, Carmina's Cucina. But that hadn't been enough for Kate, who'd ended up coordinating a band festival in Tony's parking lot after Christmas.

Kate arrived next and flounced into a seat with a big sigh. "Long day. I had to file some papers at the Basalt Municipal Court House. And I ended up stuck there because—oh, never mind." She took a sip from her beer bottle and smacked her lips. "Ah, that's better. Did I tell you Ethan is taking riding lessons at Brooke's riding school?"

Lyndsay listened to Kate's motherly excitement over Ethan, but her mind briefly drifted as she saw Will enter the tavern. He knew everyone, of course, kissed the cheeks of several women even as he made them laugh and flutter, stopped to talk to guys at various tables, then ended up at the bar, head bent to say something to Tony. "Sparkle" could honestly be said about Will's eyes, making the cliché true. He always looked so happy and contented, and she found she envied him. Must be nice to have exactly the life you wanted.

Maybe some of that would rub off on her when she started dating him—*if* she started dating him. It was only fair to ask him out first.

"What's that expression for?" Jessica asked.

Lyndsay surfaced out of her thoughts. "What expression?"

"Yearning," Kate said to Jessica.

Jessica nodded solemnly. "About sums it up."

"Pfft," Lyndsay said, leaning back in her chair and eyeing her friends. Should she tell them her plan?

"You were staring at Will," Kate said suspiciously.

"Of course I was. What woman isn't staring at him at some time or another? He likes to be the center of attention when he walks into the tavern. I think he's the Captain Kirk of Valentine Valley."

Jessica's eyes went wide as she stared past Lyndsay, and too late, Lyndsay glanced over her shoulder.

Will stood there, thumbs in the belt loops of his low jeans, t-shirt taut across his stomach muscles, inches from Lyndsay's face.

"Talkin' about me, ladies?"

Lyndsay opened her mouth, but nothing came out. God, she was an idiot.

Kate motioned to a chair. "Of course we were. Have a seat, Will."

He took the one right next to Lyndsay. She could feel his interested stare like a laser beam, and she told herself that was a good sign. Jessica's green eyes were wide and shiny as she tried to hold back her laughter, and Kate just exuded eagerness, like this was her much-anticipated evening's entertainment.

Will leaned a forearm on the table, which seemed to create his own little shared space with Lyndsay. "So . . . the Captain Kirk of Valentine Valley? Where do I begin?"

Lyndsay arched an eyebrow at him. "It was a joke."

"Well, I know that, darlin', but I still need some explanation."

"I'm not your 'darlin',' Will."

"Sorry, it just comes naturally."

He grinned, obviously not sorry at all.

"*Flirting* comes naturally to you," Lyndsay explained with slow patience, "one of the reasons I called you Captain Kirk."

"From *Star Trek*."

"The original series—or the new movies—and yes, I know all about it. I grew up watching reruns with my dad."

"Guess I can't be surprised—you are a math teacher, after all."

"And that makes me a geek?" she asked sweetly. Okay, she *was* a geek, but still . . .

"No," he began, using the same slow and patient tone she'd used on him, "you like math and science, so I assumed you like science fiction."

"Oh. Well . . . yes." He might still be calling her a geek, but she let it go.

"And I'm Captain Kirk."

Her face heated. "It was a joke. You like to flirt, and you certainly don't have long-term relationships with women. Captain Kirk often has a new woman every episode."

"What a stud." He arched his own eyebrow, let his voice deepen into a playful growl. "So I'm a stud."

"I didn't say that," she said. "*You* did. Not sure what that says about you."

Will glanced at Kate and Jessica, who were sharing a bowl of popcorn and watching with the rapt attention one used at a movie theater.

"I think I'm more of the Han Solo type," Will said, leaning back in his chair and straightening out his long legs.

When he crossed his arms over his chest, Lyndsay could see his biceps and forearms emphasized, and thought there might be some good perks to dating Will Sweet.

"Does that make my brother Chewbacca?" she asked, wrinkling her nose. "Although he has the right hair color, he's not that hairy. Or that tall."

Kate chuckled.

"Definitely Han Solo," Will said with conviction. "Wisecracking outer space adventurer—"

"Who does things for money." Lyndsay hiccupped a laugh and quickly sipped her beer. "You are a little . . . out there."

Will smiled, emphasizing the cleft in his chin.

"So you think of yourself as roguish and devil-may-care. I guess you forgot about the mercenary part." She leaned closer to him and let her gaze drift briefly down his chest. "Unless that means you only do women for money."

"Well, we know *that's* not true."

"Do we?" Lyndsay countered.

"Han Solo is not a gigolo."

"Then you better pick another representative, one more down to earth. And don't tell me you think you're some kind of Prince Charming." She felt another unexpected flash of yearning and hoped no one could read it on her face this time.

He cocked his head. "I'm thinking James Bond."

"You're so conceited. Or did you forget Bond leaves a lot of women behind, just like Captain Kirk? We can't say we ever saw Han Solo do that. He was all about the money."

"The new James Bond doesn't love 'em and leave 'em like the old Bond did," Will insisted.

"But he's still wrong for you. He used a lot of women to get what he wanted, you know, for whatever furthered the external plot. And I'm using the word 'used' in a literal sense. Does that make sense?"

Kate and Jessica groaned, but the sound barely reached Lyndsay. She was focused on Will as they leaned toward each other competitively.

"External plot?" he repeated, eyeing her with interest.

Lyndsay took another casual sip of her beer and forced herself to keep her gaze meshed with his. He'd pounce on any sign of weakness. "Didn't you ever take English?"

"I know what an external plot is," he said patiently. "And I took English in the same class with you. I even read books. Still. To this day."

"No!" Lyndsay countered with mock surprise. "When do you have time, since you're off saving the galaxy one woman at a time?"

"Someone has to save the day. But I don't *use* women, you said." Will nodded. "That's heartening to know about myself. So I'm not James Bond."

"And you needed someone to tell you that?" Tony asked as he approached, a towel tossed over his shoulder.

Lyndsay smiled at her big brother, who put a gentle hand on Kate's shoulder. Lyndsay and Tony both had the same brown hair—she'd lightened hers a bit—and brown eyes, though she was always wanting to cut his longish hair. They'd never had any major disagreements, had always been close, except for the short period after his divorce. Maybe that's what happened when a mom died young and left her kids to form an even closer family with just their dad.

"Hey, enough joking from you," Will said to Tony. "Your own sister called you Chewbacca to my Han Solo."

Lyndsay rolled her eyes. "No, you implied Tony was Chewbacca when you called yourself Han."

Tony frowned at his friend. "James Bond, Han Solo? What's going on with you guys?"

Will aimed a thumb at Lyndsay. "It started with your sister calling me Captain Kirk."

Lyndsay gave an exaggerated sigh. "Let's change the subject. Kate, did you guys finally decide on your reception?"

Will got abruptly to his feet. "If we're talking weddings, I'm out of here. I get enough of that at home."

"Just like Captain Kirk," Lyndsay teased. "Commitment-phobe."

"No, I'm just tired of Valentine's proclivity for weddings."

"Ooh, a big word," she said.

He leaned both big hands on the table and loomed over her, making her heartbeat go a little wild.

"My brother Chris is engaged, remember, and that's all he can talk about. I work with him all day. A guy can only take so much about flowers and favors and themes."

He straightened up, and Lyndsay was surprised to feel like she could breathe again.

"Tony, is there a game of pool in back?" he asked.

"Should be."

And the two of them left. Lyndsay let out a big sigh and sank back in her chair.

Kate arched a brow. "That was an interesting reaction."

"It's been a long day, and he can be exhausting. But seriously—the reception?"

It was Kate's turn to let out a sigh, and Jessica eyed her with interest before saying, "Trouble in paradise?"

"No, not at all," Kate scoffed. "The wedding is on schedule to be at the Rose Garden, where we first got married. But the reception is going to be at Carmina's."

"Your parents must be thrilled."

"They are, but . . . I feel like Tony is settling. We're having the rehearsal dinner here, but he would have loved to host the whole thing."

"That's sweet of him," Jessica said dreamily.

Another single girl in Valentine thinking about true love, Lyndsay thought. Jessica was a few years younger, and Lyndsay almost teased, "Wait your turn."

Lyndsay leaned toward Kate with sympathy. "Tony knows logically that there isn't room here. He'll get over it."

"I know, but . . . I'm sort of flattered he's upset he can't do this for us."

"Now it's getting a little overly sappy around here," Lyndsay said.

Kate laughed. "I know, I know. It's not like it's a major problem, I just . . . worry."

"And it's sweet," Lyndsay insisted. "I shouldn't tease you. You know how utterly thrilled I am that you two are back together again." She glanced at Jessica. "It was a long nine years, let me tell you."

Smiling, Kate said, "It *was* long. And pointless. I wish I'd done so many things differently." She suddenly focused on Lyndsay with that penetrating lawyer stare. "Don't you sometimes wish you'd done that?"

"Don't we all have occasional regrets? I'm sure you don't regret having me as your maid of honor—again. Not sure what else you're saying." Lyndsay thought about her book, and how weird it was going to be to break the news now. She wished she'd done *that* differently. But she had to talk about it with her whole family together.

And then there was her teaching career. She'd always wanted to teach, and though she loved her kids, it was still shocking and sad that she wasn't content. But what would she have changed?

"Who *else* would be my maid of honor but my once-and-future sister-in-law?"

The wording was getting to be a joke between them.

Lyndsay looked around her with exaggerated care, then leaned forward so secretively that both Kate and Jessica did the same. "There is one particular thing I'd like to do that I've never done before."

When she paused dramatically, Kate said, "Don't keep us in suspense!"

"I'm going to ask Will out on a date."

Lyndsay spoke just as Kate took a sip of her beer, and Kate coughed, covering her mouth with the back of her hand. Lyndsay chuckled and offered a napkin.

Jessica eyed Lyndsay with interest. "You've never dated him? I thought almost everyone in his dating age range had."

"I know *you* dated him," Lyndsay said, then almost wished she hadn't mentioned it. She wasn't sure she wanted to know the details of what had happened between Will and her friend.

Jessica waved a hand. "Only for a couple weeks. We never even—" She broke off, wearing a lame smile.

That made Lyndsay feel better. "Why did you break up?"

"It's not like we even had anything official enough to warrant a *breakup*," Jessica began slowly. "We just . . . went out a few times and that was that. I think we both found other people or something. I don't think we had a lot of sparks." She shrugged. "It was last year. I barely remember."

"Then it's settled," Kate said happily. "Lyndsay should date him. There were a lot of sparks at this table."

"You're right, there were," Jessica said with interest.

"Let's not get ahead of ourselves," Lyndsay said, raising both hands. "I haven't even asked him out yet. He could say no."

And then Will sauntered in from the back room, both fists raised. "Pool champ!" he called loudly.

A general cheer rose. Kate and Jessica grinned at each other and said at the same time, "He won't."

Lyndsay gave a helpless laugh. "You're support-ive friends, that's for sure. And you don't even need to warn me about what I'm getting into, how he's never serious about relationships. I'm not expect-ing any dramatic reversals of his usual dating pat-tern."

"Why not?" Kate demanded. "You might be just the woman he's looking for."

Lyndsay laughed aloud, causing Will to glance with interest at their table. She felt the sizzle of awareness, like she'd gotten too close to a campfire. She definitely had to explore this attraction she felt for him—the attraction that she'd put down in a book, she reminded herself. That sobered her up a bit. Even if they went out on a few dates, it didn't mean she had to tell him how she'd immortalized him in fiction.

"I'm glad you're giving this a shot, Lynds," Kate said. "Maybe you've been stuck in some kind of rut, doing things the same way and not being happy about it."

Lyndsay thought of her job but put it out of her mind—there was nothing she could do about that right now.

"You really haven't seemed all that happy since I got back," Kate continued gently.

For so many reasons, Lyndsay thought in frustration, *but lately because I haven't been able to tell you my good news.* Yet a public tavern wasn't the right place—especially not with Will so close. "You don't think Tony would have a problem with this, do you?"

"He did mention once that he'd told his friends not to date you in high school because it would be weird for him if you broke up."

Jessica's eyes widened, and she glanced at Lyndsay expectantly.

Lyndsay shrugged. "He said the same to me. I didn't necessarily agree, but after he and you—" She broke off.

Kate gave a rueful grin. "I'm not happy that in some ways he was right. Our divorce *did* hurt the friendship between you and me. But we're all adults now."

Lyndsay wondered for only the briefest moment if Will had taken such a warning from Tony to heart—but he'd hardly wanted her from afar since high school.

"I don't know if I should take dating advice from you," Lyndsay teased.

Will appeared at her side and straddled the chair next to her. "What dating advice did you take?" he asked.

Lyndsay gave Kate a lopsided smile. "The last guy she wanted me to date—he and I were friends before that—ended up breaking it off with me the night I thought he would propose."

"That sucks," Will said, reaching for a handful

of the popcorn. "Is that the guy you dated for years in college?"

Lyndsay eyed him with surprise. "Yeah. I can't believe you remember that."

He shrugged. "I remember. And Tony told me he got his just rewards—didn't he date a prostitute?"

Jessica giggled. "Oh, I heard about that story. He was named in the paper, wasn't he?"

Lyndsay bit her lip, knowing it was funny now, but at the time she'd felt like the heroine of a tragedy. "To be fair, I'm not sure he realized she wasn't just a Zumba instructor."

"He paid money at some point," Will said, "enough to get himself arrested. Got what he deserved."

"Why . . . thank you, Will," Lyndsay said.

Tony came through the door with a tray. "Hey, Lynds, brought you something. I thought you looked tired, so here's a pick-me-up."

She gasped at the perfectly displayed plate. "Ooh, the beer-braised bunny nachos? Love those. Thanks, Tony." She took the plate, along with the beer he'd also brought. Her third—but who was counting?

"Bunny," Jessica said with a shudder, then gave Lyndsay a meaningful gaze of encouragement. "See you guys later."

After a brief wave, Lyndsay focused on her treat.

Kate sighed. "She's eaten like this her whole life and never gains an ounce. Never." She shook her head. "Makes me ill."

When Tony rolled his eyes and walked away, Kate stole a nacho, then followed him into his office, leaving Lyndsay alone with her nachos—and Will. She'd decided to ask him out but hadn't given any thought as to when or how. But right here, where her brother could overhear? No.

"So is Tony right about you being tired?" Will asked, stealing his own nacho.

Lyndsay pushed the plate into the center of the table. "It's Friday, and I've had a crappy day at school—heck, a crappy week."

"I don't remember the last time you had something good to say about teaching."

So he'd been paying attention. She chewed and swallowed a sinful nacho. "I used to love it with all my heart. The kids made it special from the beginning, and that hasn't changed. I love watching the light of discovery in their eyes, or seeing their growing pride in their accomplishments. But other things about the profession have changed. Maybe it's all the testing, leaving no time for us to be creative. Maybe it's the brand-new way we have to learn to teach. Plus, it's the end of the year, and the kids are restless, knowing how much is at stake with these tests—I don't know. Sorry for going on and on. We all have our bad days."

"Not me. I'm lucky—I love my job."

"You *are* lucky. And it's a hard one, too. Do you still love your job when you can't find a cow in a blizzard?"

His white teeth gleamed as those hazel eyes focused just on her. "I'm not saying there isn't the occasional bad day. Like when we lose a calf before it even has a chance at life—that's terrible."

She nodded solemnly.

"I'm not saying my work has life-and-death consequences compared to yours," he added.

As if he didn't want to hurt her feelings. She was touched, and it made her feel mellow and happy as she ate another nacho. Maybe this should be her last beer . . .

"I know what you meant," she said softly. "Both of our jobs matter. You feed people. I teach them. It's just a shame that lately I can't take the same kind of joy in it that I used to." She scooped another nacho off the plate and enjoyed that, at least. "You know, I like something else about your job. I like the family aspect of it. You Sweets and Thalbergs—you share a bond with your families that many people envy."

"Oh, come on, I see how you are with Tony and your dad—it's no different."

"Sure it is. I don't have any grandparents left. You have your grandma Sweet."

"I do. And I'll admit she's one of a kind." He leaned closer. "She shared some secrets with our family the other day—want to hear?"

"Family secrets?"

"No. And she didn't say it in private. There were even people not related to us there. I say it's fair game."

Lyndsay folded her arms on the table and propped her chin in her hand. "Then go ahead."

Will smiled in a way that made her insides do a little dance. He was obviously still amused by the Captain Kirk discussion. Imagine how he'd laugh if he knew what else they'd talked about behind his back.

"Apparently, the feud between the widows and my grandma goes back to high school. Grandma let me in on the name the widows used to go by when they were young." He paused dramatically. "The Purple Poodles."

Lyndsay laughed with delight. "Well, it was the fifties, after all. I think it fits them perfectly."

"But she also told me more. Seems the Purple Poodles were the bad girls of high school, the outcasts."

"Those three sweet little old ladies? It would be difficult to choose which one I'd want for my own grandma. I don't know if I believe this," she scoffed.

"Scout's honor," he said.

"You were in Future Farmers of America, not Boy Scouts."

"You know too much about me."

And I'm determined to know more, she thought.

"Really, the feud started even before that," Will continued. "It seems my great-great-grandma had the first car in Valentine Valley and accidentally ran into a Thalberg cow."

"I heard that one," she said. "Brooke told me it wasn't an accident."

He shrugged good-naturedly. "I wasn't there. All I know is that my grandma and the widows didn't get along. Mrs. Palmer was the leader of the Purple Poodles, a rebel who smoked cigarettes and dated a biker."

Lyndsay choked on her beer and took the napkin Will handed her. Mrs. Palmer was a feisty fast-talker who made her own wild clothes and considered herself an expert at reading tarot cards.

"Maybe I can believe this of Mrs. Palmer," she said. "And Mrs. Thalberg has always been a strong ranching woman who didn't care what people thought of her. But Mrs. Ludlow, proper school-teacher—a bad girl?"

Will shrugged. "All I know is what I was told. Maybe her heart was broken. Maybe college changed her, veered her away from the other Purple Poodles. Maybe that's the reason she and my grandma get along. There's more, but I'll have to tell you another time. We have to dance."

She laughed, knowing he wasn't serious. "I've got my beer and my food. I'm happy, really. And I think you have more gossip but you just don't want to tell me."

But he took her hand, pulled her up from the table, and into the back room. He brought her near the pool table, where there was a little room next to Dom Shaw and Will's cousin Theresa, who moved their bodies in time to the fast music, shaking their hips, doing a couple moves that inspired scattered applause. Oh, great, she and Will would soon be known as the "Do not ever dance in public again" duo.

"Will, I'm not really a dancer," she began, then blinked as he started to shake his shoulders out of time with the music. She covered her mouth against a snicker of amusement.

He leaned toward her ear and said loudly, "I didn't say I could dance, but I know how to have fun and cheer you up."

"And distract me."

She felt the warm tickle of his breath, could have sworn his lips just grazed the shell of her ear.

And then the beer did its job. She loosened up and started dancing with him, dropping her arms on his shoulders, hopping back and forth on each foot.

He laughed aloud and tried to match her, and they were both terrible together. In a wild twist of her body, she ended up bumping into Dom, who caught her by the shoulders with strong hands and steered her back toward Will. She forgot her school troubles, her insecurity about asking him out, even the lingering terror and excitement over her book publication. She just danced until she was breathless.

And stared into Will's face, with that chin dimple that only emphasized his charisma. She probably didn't write enough about that dimple in her book, she thought, then laughed aloud at herself.

"Glad you're having a good time!" Will practically shouted.

She took his hand and spun beneath his arm, but neither of them was good enough to know what to do next. The fast music died away, and before she could retreat, it turned to a country song, slow and moody.

"At last, something I know how to do," Will said.

And then he pulled her up against him, put one arm around her waist, and took her other hand in his. She stared into his t-shirt, too stunned to even look into his eyes. She could feel his hips brush hers, then the long length of his thigh. His hand was warm and callused where it gripped hers, and his other hand might as well have been leaving an imprint on her back, she noticed it so much. Her right hand hung awkwardly for a moment in the air, until at last she set it hesitantly on his broad shoulder, covered only by a t-shirt. She could feel well-toned muscle and bone . . .

And then he grinned down at her, those hazel eyes alight with mischief. "Wow, I didn't realize you couldn't even slow dance."

"Sorry," she murmured, "distracted by thoughts." She let him begin to move them from foot to foot, swaying.

"I must be losing my touch. Surely Captain Kirk would be able to make a woman focus on him while they danced."

A smile quirked her lips.

"There, that's better. Relax. School has to be pretty bad if you're this tense."

She let him think what he wanted. She wasn't about to say, *I'm thinking about how to ask you out . . .*

Chapter 5

Will swayed, but he kept his eyes open. He was worried that if he didn't, he'd start to concentrate too much on the feel of Lyndsay in his arms. It was taking everything in him not to pull her right up against his body, to bury his face in her hair just so he could figure out her elusive scent, something flowery or citrusy or—hell, he didn't know. Like he'd ever cared all that much about a woman's scent before. He liked the feel of her small hand in his, the curve of her back against his other hand. He could feel lithe muscle and—

Okay, enough of that. He was going to have to hold her deliberately away from his hips if he wasn't careful, like he was still a horny high school kid.

"I don't think we've ever danced," he said to distract himself.

Then she tipped her head up to look at him. Talking had been a mistake. Her eyes were luminous in the low light, and he found himself searching their chocolate depths for the glimmers of gold again.

"Sure we danced. At Tony and Kate's first wedding."

"When we were teenagers? I don't remember at all."

She gave a low laugh that sounded far too throaty for his peace of mind.

"I'm not surprised. They had the reception right in the Rose Garden, threw up those tents that ended up leaking, remember?"

"Well, yeah, I remember that, but—"

"They had beer in tubs in the corner, and you guys figured out pretty quickly that if you approached from outside, you could stick your hand under the flap and grab a beer without anyone being the wiser."

He chuckled. "I might have a vague memory of that."

"And little else, I bet. You boys got pretty drunk, and eventually your parents figured out what was going on and kept an eye on you. From then on you were forced to remain inside."

"So only the boys got drunk? Not you?"

"Of course not!" she said, taking a deep, indignant breath.

And that made her breasts brush his chest. If he inched her closer just a bit at a time, maybe—

"How could I drink? I was the maid of honor. I had important duties, like holding the bouquet and straightening the train of her gown."

"Yet you agreed to dance with a drunk teenager."

"You begged me to."

"I did not." He tried to frown his disbelief, but he couldn't help smiling down into her amused face.

"Oh, yes, you did. Doing your duty and dancing with girls who needed partners was the only way you could get away from your angry parents."

"That's not the only reason I danced with you," he said dismissively.

"Of course it was. You'd been back to your regular dating self again by then, so . . ." She trailed off for a moment and her smile faded. "Sorry . . ."

"Brittany. It was a long time ago," he said softly.

And then there didn't seem to be any more to say. He tried to imagine Brittany at his age, thirty-three. Maybe they'd have gotten married and had kids. Maybe they'd have gone their separate ways. He'd never know. And she'd never gotten the chance to live her life and find out.

The song ended, and Lyndsay moved out of his arms. He thought she seemed a little unsteady, and he took her elbow. "Lynds?"

"I'm okay."

"Speaking of drunk—"

"I'm not drunk," she said, waving a hand. But even that made her stagger. "I might have a slight buzz . . ."

"Okay, time for you to head home. If you drove, you know I'm going to take your keys."

"I didn't drive. I live too close."

"Then I'll walk you home. I'll wait awhile before driving myself."

"That's okay. Kate will give me a ride."

They both looked around and spotted Kate in Tony's arms, dancing the next slow dance so closely that a molecule couldn't have gotten between them.

"Kate's busy," Will said.

"Lyndsay, do you need a ride?"

Will turned to see a guy he didn't recognize, looking with concern at Lyndsay.

"Hi, Sean," Lyndsay said, then blinked up at Will. "Have you met Sean? New guy in town. He's a web guy—designer."

"Will Sweet." Will reached out a hand, and Sean took it.

"Sean Lighton. Nice to meet you."

But he wasn't looking at Will—he was all about Lyndsay, eyes full of concern—and it was annoying.

"Lyndsay, you look like you need a ride," Sean said.

She opened her mouth, but Will interrupted. "And that's why I'm escorting her home."

"Oh. Got it." Sean gave him a lame smile. "Take it easy, Lyndsay."

Will turned Lyndsay about before she could respond, then asked, "Did you bring a purse?"

"It's behind the bar. But really, I can get home myself."

"You're swaying—you do realize that."

Her lips parted, but she said nothing. So he took

her hand and began to lead her through the dancing couples and out into the main bar.

"Don't worry about your reputation," she called, chuckling.

When they reached the bar, he stuck his hand underneath, then handed her her purse, eyeing her. "What's that supposed to mean?"

"The fact that you're holding my hand and leading me out of here. No one will think anything of it, including your current girlfriend. Who is she again?"

He'd always liked this side of Lyndsay, relaxed and funny. He led her toward the front door, grabbed his jacket off the crowded hooks, then escorted her out into the dark night, where the air chilled right down. The lightest snowflakes were falling. He shrugged on the jacket. "I'm not dating anyone right now."

"Oh. Caught you in between, I see. That's kinda rare."

She rummaged in her purse and held up a Windbreaker in triumph. The gesture almost tipped her backward until he caught her arm. She pulled the jacket on and zipped it up.

"Aren't *you* worried about your reputation?" he asked. "That dentist you're dating might get the wrong idea."

She snorted. "You remembered he's a dentist? We broke up. Mutual thing."

But she frowned a moment before shaking it off. Literally shaking it off. He tried not to laugh.

"Should I say I'm sorry you broke up?" he asked.

She leaned her head against his arm and smiled up at him. "We should always tell the truth. *Are* you sorry?"

And then he spoke the truth without thinking. "Nope." Maybe he'd had too much to drink, as well.

She started across the parking lot, and he had to take her hand again. "Wrong way."

This time he didn't let her go; he just steered her through the parking lot, then north on Seventh Street. They passed beneath one of Valentine's old-fashioned lampposts, and it gave her skin a soft glow. There were snowflakes in her hair. He found himself wanting to draw the walk out.

"You said we're telling the truth tonight," he reminded her. "I think there's something you're holding back about your breakup with the dentist."

She wrinkled up her nose endearingly. "Oh, yeah. I didn't tell anybody this, but . . . we're telling the truth, right?"

He nodded solemnly, hoping she didn't change her mind.

"So . . . it wasn't a mutual thing, like I told everybody. I'm the one who broke it off. He thought it was time for me to meet his kids."

Surprised, Will said, "And kids make you run screaming for the hills?"

She burst out with a laugh. " 'Screaming for the hills.' Ha! I used that exact phrase as I worried over everything. But no, it wasn't because of the kids. I've got a nephew, don't I?"

"And you're a teacher."

"Right. Love kids. But *meeting* a guy's kids? That's serious. A real relationship. And I realized—I wasn't ever going to be as serious about him as he seemed to be about me. You know?"

"I know." His words came out softly, and he thought of all the women he'd tried to let down gently, for exactly the same reason. "So why did you tell everybody it was mutual?"

She eyed him as if debating whether he was worthy of an honest answer. "Because . . . I don't really know why. It's hard to tell people you had a guy really falling for you, but you didn't feel the same. I *want* to feel the same," she added softly, sadly. "I really do. It's kind of pathetic."

"It's not pathetic." But he didn't truly understand it. He didn't want to feel that way—about any woman. It was too dangerous.

They walked in silence for a few minutes, leaving behind Main Street, with its brighter lights, and heading into the more residential part of town, where the houses were small and cozy and close together. They turned up Mabel Street, and soon they were at her small ranch house. The front light was on, her car was parked in the driveway. He led her up to the door, where he could smell lilacs in bloom and see their ghostly shadow.

She began to dig through her purse. "Stupid keys," she muttered.

"Want me to look?"

"I got it," she said. "Aha!" She pulled them forth with a jingle.

It took her a couple minutes to get the key in the lock, but he knew better than to offer his help again.

The door swung wide, and she stepped inside to switch on a light.

"Good night, Lynds," he called from the front stoop.

She came back, frowning. "You're not coming in?"

"Better not. Gotta work in the morning."

She sighed. "Me, too."

"Grading papers?"

She opened her mouth, then seemed to change her mind. "Yep, papers, that's right."

He wondered what she'd first intended to say. "Good night, Lynds."

"Night."

But she didn't close the door right away. The longer he hesitated, the harder it seemed to be to turn away. But he finally did it, because he had to.

The next morning, Lyndsay sat bolt upright in bed, staring at the clock, which read 10:00 a.m. She'd meant to get up a couple hours earlier, since Saturday morning was usually a productive writing time for her. She put a hand to her aching head. Why hadn't she set her alarm?

Because she'd had too much to drink. And . . . something else had happened.

And then it hit her. She'd danced with Will—and then she'd let him walk her home. Thankfully, she hadn't been so drunk that she'd burst out an invitation to date.

She covered her face with her hands and fell back dramatically onto her pillow. When she got drunk, she rambled. What had she said? She specifically remembered being in the parking lot when he'd turned her toward home—

By taking her hand. He'd held her hand all the way home.

Because you were too drunk to know the way, she reminded herself.

She remembered opening her door, inviting him in—and that had been a worse invitation than a simple date—but he hadn't come in. He'd been a gentleman, she reminded herself. She wouldn't have wanted him to see her stuff all over the house, right? No. More importantly, she wouldn't have wanted to see him come in, plop down on her couch, and turn on a Colorado Rockies baseball game like she was just one of the guys. She refused to think that's how he thought of her, or otherwise her dating plans would fall flat.

He'd danced with her, she reminded herself optimistically.

Only because she'd had a rough week, a little devil inside replied.

As it was, she'd spilled the real reason she'd broken up with her last guy. It was way too easy to talk to Will, especially when she was drunk.

So she was going to ask him out. It was the only way to stop feeling like this, to bury her renewed crush back with high school memories, where it belonged.

She was going to break other patterns in her life, too. She'd find a project at school to become more involved in. She had to stir things up, rediscover the reasons she'd become a teacher. Surely that would help.

Without bothering to shower, she went to her office to start working. But first, she'd send an e-mail to her family and invite them to dinner. It was time to announce the good news about her book.

Monday after school, Lyndsay sat at her desk, waiting for any students who needed help. She had lots of extra time, because she wasn't planning to attend the softball game that night. She decided it would make her nervous to see Will looking sweaty and gorgeous and posing for his female fans.

A couple kids filed in, and she spent about twenty minutes with the first two. After they left, she glanced up to find Matias Gonzalez watching her with hesitation.

Matias was a quiet kid, his curly hair deep black and shiny. He was a little short and chubby, when a lot of his fellow students had already sprouted up to lanky heights, like her nephew, Ethan. Matias always did his homework, even when he struggled with it. He didn't ask a lot of questions, and it was with the homework that she'd always been best able to help him.

The fact that he'd actually come for extra help intrigued her.

She smiled at him. "Hey, Matias, did you have a problem with today's math?"

He shook his head, got to his feet, and approached almost reluctantly. "No, Ms. De Luca, I think I understood it."

"Then what can I help you with?"

He nodded. "The science fair."

"The science fair is in a few weeks," she said, frowning. "You don't have your project started already?"

He slumped into the chair next to her desk. "I keep starting one and stopping. I've tried three so far, and I don't like any of them."

"Have you talked to Mrs. Jorgansen? Being your science teacher, she might have more ideas."

"She's the one who gave me the ideas I don't like. I think she's getting sick of me. Or sick of teaching. She's pretty old."

Amused, Lyndsay leaned back in her chair. "No one can get sick of you, Matias." And people could get sick of teaching at any age.

He hung his head. "That's nice, Ms. De Luca, but . . . I don't get science, I never have. And it's just getting worse and worse. Next year in high school . . ."

He trailed off, obviously miserable months before he had to be. He'd told her earlier in the school year that he didn't get math either, but she'd proven him wrong over time. Somehow in his young life, the kid had gotten the idea to just assume he wouldn't be good at learning every new thing that came along.

"Okay, you've got to stop anticipating the worst. You'll have new teachers at Basalt, and I bet you'll find some part of science interesting. We'll start with the science project. Why don't you tell me some of the ideas Mrs. Jorgansen helped you find, and then what you did on each project."

After about ten minutes, Lyndsay realized that Matias was waiting for something to really strike him, something he could put his whole heart into. She empathized with him. Weren't they all waiting for just the right thing to come along?

"Problem is, Matias," she said as she leaned away from her computer, "you just can't hope for the perfect thing. You've got to give one of these a chance. Doesn't anything look interesting?"

"I don't know. I do like stuff about food. I probably like to eat too much," he said, his blush obvious.

"Okay, food. Didn't we see a project about the sense of taste? That has to do with food."

His dark eyes brightened. "Yeah, that's right. It said people taste things differently if they're smelling something else at the same time. So I could get people to taste food?"

"And record the results in a chart. You could see if different smells inhibit taste more than others, you know?"

"Oh, yeah, cool. Okay, I'll start making food lists. Can I come back for more help if I need?"

"Of course you can," she said. Assuming they were done, she pulled out homework to begin grading.

"Oh, Ms. De Luca, did you know that my uncle broke his leg? He won't be able to be the project leader for the 4-H horse unit."

Lyndsay frowned. "No, I hadn't heard."

Matias ducked his head. "I know he meant to call, since you're our school advisor and all. But they had to operate and everything."

"Wow, sounds very complicated. Did everything go well?"

"Yeah, they had to put pins in to hold it together, and it'll be a while before he's on a horse again, but his boss promises to find other things he can do on the Circle F until he's well."

"That's kind of Mr. Osborne."

"But now we need a new leader. Our parents are askin' around. Do you know anyone who might help?"

"I know several cowboys. I'll put the word out. But remember, right now, your science project is more important."

"Yes, ma'am!"

Chapter 6

Tuesday night, Lyndsay was in her kitchen preparing a big salad when she heard her front door open.

"It's us!" Kate called. "Something smells good!"

"Spaghetti and meatballs," Lyndsay said, drying off her hands as she went into the living room. "Mom's meatballs." She had her mom's recipe box, and she loved looking at all the handwritten notes.

"Of course!" Kate carried flowers, and Lyndsay sniffed appreciatively.

Tony followed her in and handed Lyndsay a bottle of wine. "Red. You'll like it."

"You always know what I'll like."

They grinned at each other.

"I'll just put these in water," Kate called, making herself at home in the kitchen.

Lyndsay couldn't keep the smile from her face. It was so good to have her best friend back after all these years, and to know that at last her brother was truly happy again. "Where's Dad?"

"He went to get Mrs. Thalberg. They should be here any minute."

She sighed. "When he asked if she could come, I couldn't say no."

His eyebrows rose. "You didn't want to invite Dad's lady friend?"

She chuckled at the old-fashioned term. "Oh, it's not that. I just have something important to tell you guys, and I didn't want it spread all over town."

"She can keep a secret."

"I hope so." She'd certainly kept the Purple Poodles secret. But Lyndsay wasn't about to ask for more details on *that* secret, not tonight.

Kate ducked her head into the room. "Is that why you didn't want Ethan to come? I told my parents it was just adults relaxing tonight, and they agreed to pick him up after lacrosse."

"Yeah, I especially don't want this spread around the middle school. So thank you. I hope I didn't offend you."

"Nope, you just made us real curious," Tony said, taking the wine bottle back and following his fiancée into the kitchen.

Lyndsay finished the salad while Tony decanted the wine. By the time Mario and his date arrived, they were all happily dissecting the many flavors in the wine.

Lyndsay took Mrs. Thalberg's sweater and kissed her on the cheek. "I'm so glad you could join us."

"I was delighted by the invitation, my dear."

"I hope the other widows weren't offended."

"Not at all. They don't expect to go on *all* my dates with your father."

The two older people shared a smile of deep understanding. Lyndsay let them have their moment and turned to pour more wine. Soon they all sat for dinner. Her ranch didn't have a dining room, but the table in the kitchen had plenty of room for the five of them.

While everyone was eating their salads, Lyndsay turned to Mrs. Thalberg. "So, about the historical society presidency . . ."

Several forks dropped to plates. Lyndsay eyed the rest of her family in surprise. Why not get it out in the open?

"I saw that you put posters up around town," Lyndsay continued.

"Well, I had to, dear, in anticipation of what Eileen might do. And then last night she started handing out lapel pins at the softball game. Quite clever, actually. They're shaped like a little elegant hat, the kind she's never seen without—I barely remember what her hairstyle looks like—and on the hat band is spelled out 'Sweet.' So happy to see that none of you are sporting them."

"They *are* adorable," Kate admitted.

"Will dropped some off at the tavern today," Tony said, after chewing a cucumber slice. "They're cute, but not many people picked them up."

Mrs. Thalberg's eyes brightened. "How good to hear. Thank you. And you plan to keep them?"

Tony stopped eating as everyone regarded him expectantly. "I don't take sides, Mrs. Thalberg—not until I vote, anyway, and my vote is private. I have a poster of yours up in the window, don't I?"

Mario nodded. "You're a good boy. Thank you."

"What made you decide to run?" Lyndsay asked Mrs. Thalberg.

"Just like I said at the softball game. My concerns weren't being met. I know you all heard about the display we wanted to do for Eileen's mother, the silent film star. Eileen refused to cooperate and stole the idea for the inn. There were several instances where our museum staff—all educated specifically in museum work—had ideas about new exhibits and they were denied or watered down, out of concern someone might be offended. History can't be watered down!" she added forcefully.

Everyone hastily nodded.

"Most recently, I went to the board with my concerns that we shouldn't be expanding the museum by buying the building next door—we'll have to raise entrance prices to afford the loan, and I'm convinced that will drive customers away. But I was ignored. That was the last straw. It was time for this citizen to step forward and take a stand."

Mario looked at her fondly, proudly. "I don't blame you one bit, Rosemary. Young people should see this kind of example of bravery."

Well, it wasn't exactly a ruthless political dictatorship she was standing up against, but . . . it was still important to be heard, and Lyndsay thought it was cute of her dad to think Mrs. Thalberg brave.

"I'm sure you'll make a great president," Lyndsay said.

"I haven't won yet, dear. I do believe Eileen will not give up without a fight. I'll be interested to see what she comes up with for the next softball night. I have ideas of my own . . ."

Lyndsay and her brother exchanged a wary glance.

Kate turned her bright lavender eyes on Lyndsay. "Okay, sorry for the subject change, but you brought us here to make an announcement. I can't wait another moment. What is it?"

At the head of the table, Lyndsay felt all their expectant gazes on her, and she took a deep breath, surprised to feel so excited and nervous and brimming with sheer joy. "I don't talk about it much, but I like to write."

Mario gave a confused smile. "You used to do it all the time as a girl. I remember you setting up the computer in my workshop just to get away from everybody. But I thought you gave that up after high school."

"I did for a while in college, but the writing bug never went away. I kept at it, finished a book, got rejections, wrote something else, got rejections—"

"You sent it out to publishers?" Tony asked, eyes wide. "You wrote this much and you never said anything?"

"I know it's strange, but it was the thing I did

for myself. I didn't want the pressure of people constantly asking me how it was going, or if I'd submitted. I can't even talk about it much with fellow writers online, I'm that private about it."

"And?" Kate urged, hands clasped together as if she could no longer eat.

"What kind of stories do you write?" Mrs. Thalberg asked at the same time.

Kate looked disappointed, but she nodded toward the elderly lady as if her questions should come first.

"I write romances, modern-day cowboys in small Western towns. Kind of what I know," she admitted sheepishly.

"I love to read those," Mrs. Thalberg said. "I have such a big collection, my grandchildren finally talked me into an e-reader. Now I can take loads of books everywhere I go."

Lyndsay smiled into all their expectant faces. "Well, you're going to get your chance to add mine to your collection. I sold a book."

Kate screamed so loud that Tony had to plug the ear closest to her. But his grin was wide and excited, and Lyndsay loved seeing her dad gasp out loud.

"A book!" Kate cried, jumping up from the table to hug her. "I knew there was a reason you mentioned your writing last fall."

"I'm sorry, but I'd newly sold the book then. I just—just couldn't talk about it, like I'd jinx it or something. I was in such a fog. And then you two were getting back together—I didn't want to interrupt that, either."

Tony groaned. "You are an idiot."

Her dad took her hand across the table. "I'm so proud of you, babes."

Mrs. Thalberg just beamed at her, hands clasped to her chest.

Lyndsay felt tears prick her eyes, and she sniffed. "Thanks. Would you like to see it?"

"You have a copy?" Kate demanded.

"An advance copy. It's not out yet." She reached into the towel drawer conveniently nearby, pulled out the book, and held it up.

Kate looked at it in awe. "Your name is so big on the cover." Her voice trailed off in a squeak, and she had to wipe her eyes.

"Damn, I'm trying to control myself here!" Lyndsay said, her voice shaking.

"Give it here," Tony said. "That's a nice mountain scene. Is it set here?"

"No, Montana. I didn't want to seem too . . . oh, I don't know, like I was stealing stories from the people I know." No, she was just stealing a man's personality and body—not that she was going to tell anyone that.

"Your name is so big," Kate breathed in awe.

"And that's my problem."

Tony handed the book to Mrs. Thalberg, who turned it over to read the back. "I don't get it, Lynds."

She sighed. "The thing is, I need to keep this

a secret a while longer. I wasn't thinking when I first got the contract—maybe I should have used a pseudonym, I don't know."

"But why?" Mario asked. "You're not proud of your name?"

"Oh, Dad, it's nothing like that! A lot of people use pseudonyms for privacy. And it's a romance—there are a few sexy scenes in there."

"Ooh," Kate said, taking the book from Mario, who was still looking at Lyndsay expectantly.

"Online, I heard from other teachers who used their real names, and it wasn't a problem," she explained. "But now that it's real . . . I'm more worried. There are stories of teachers getting fired for 'moral turpitude' issues because of their books. Not that I think that would happen here. The principal is a good guy. It's too late to worry about a pseudonym, of course, so I'm not second-guessing, but I've made a decision on how I want to handle it. I'd like to keep this quiet, just between the five of us, until school lets out."

"That's another month," Mario said. "I can't brag about you to my friends?"

"I'm sorry, Dad, but I think it's for the best. That way, if the kids and their parents find out after school is over, all the questions and interest should die down by September."

"Unless you're a *New York Times* best seller," Mrs. Thalberg said.

"Thank you, but they're not printing enough for that to happen," Lyndsay said dryly, then chuckled. "But oh, your belief in me is very welcome. I'll be in the big bricks-and-mortar bookstores and online, but as for grocery stores and Walmart? Don't hold your breath. They bought copies, I'm told, but it doesn't mean they put them in every store."

"So Ethan shouldn't know?" Tony asked, frowning.

Lyndsay hesitated. "I'm going to leave that up to you. If you guys think he can keep my secret for the last few weeks of school, then okay."

Kate and Tony exchanged a long glance.

"I don't know, Tony," Kate said at last. "It might be a lot of pressure on him."

"Or he'd be so relaxed, he'd just start talking about it." Tony sighed. "Okay, we'll keep it to ourselves. He'll want to hear it from Lyndsay anyway."

"You think?" she said hesitantly. "Will a fourteen-year-old boy care about what his aunt does?"

"This humble attitude is getting out of control," Tony said. "Don't make me come over there . . ."

Kate's expression was morphing from understanding to skeptical curiosity. Lyndsay held her breath, praying she wouldn't ask anything she'd have to lie about.

But Kate only said, "So can I borrow this?"

"Well . . . it's my only copy, and I'm still kind of . . . basking. Can I give you a digital version for your tablet?"

"Sure, that's fine. As long as I can read it right away!"

"I'll wait until I can buy it in the store," Mario said. "I'll make sure everyone in the Open Book knows you wrote a book."

Lyndsay gave him a grateful smile and tried to keep tears at bay.

At last they all settled down to eat, asking questions about Lyndsay's process, when she found time to write, how she found her ideas, if she belonged to any writers' groups. It wasn't until she was serving dessert—brownie sundaes—that she remembered her other dilemma.

"Tony, I have another favor to ask. I need you to spread word about something among your cowboy friends."

"Like you don't have any cowboy friends?" he shot back.

"Just wait and hear me out. The middle school 4-H club is doing a special unit on horses. They had a ranch hand from the Circle F lined up to give them help and demonstrations once a week for the next month. They're going to exhibit posters on it at the Silver Creek Rodeo. But anyway, Mr. Gonzalez broke his leg, requiring major surgery. So he's out. Can you ask any of your customers if they'd be interested in working with my students a couple hours a week for a month?"

"You didn't want to just make some calls?"

"I know, but . . . I didn't want to put pressure on anyone to say yes because they know me. Aren't they all anticipating cutting hay in less than a month? I know this is a busy time of year."

"Yeah, you're right," Tony said. "I'll see what I can do."

After dessert, Mario took Mrs. Thalberg home, and Kate and Tony insisted on helping with the cleanup. Lyndsay was telling them about the rejections she'd received over the years, when suddenly Kate put down her towel and faced Tony.

"I can't keep things from you anymore."

Lyndsay's jaw dropped open, and she stared from one to the other. What was going on? Her brother just waited patiently.

"Lyndsay's going to ask Will out."

Lyndsay rolled her eyes.

Kate went on with enthusiasm. "Did you see them together Friday night, sparring adorably?"

Tony grimaced. "I'm not sure Will knows how to spar adorably."

"Lyndsay was adorable. Will was charming."

"I did see you dancing," Tony said, frowning.

"I was drunk." Lyndsay couldn't meet his eyes.

"And you left with him."

"He walked me home, we said good night, and he did not come in."

"Yeah, well, it's probably for the best," Tony agreed.

"Says the person who forbid her from dating his friends," Kate pointed out.

"When did I do that?" he asked Lyndsay.

"High school. You said it would be 'awkward' for you should we break up. The reverse didn't exactly work, though, did it?"

"So, okay, I didn't follow my own rule. Our situation is the *exception* to the rule."

"Double standard," Lyndsay pointed out.

"I don't know if this is a good idea," he said, as if he hadn't heard. "He's a serial dater. You'll only get hurt."

"Hey!" Kate said. "We don't know that at all. You should have seen them flirting together."

"Will flirts with everybody," Lyndsay and Tony said at the same time.

They all laughed.

Tony sobered first. "But honestly, Lynds, I know you're looking for a long-term relationship, and I don't think Will has that in him."

"You don't think he'll ever get married?" Kate asked curiously.

He hesitated. "He never talks about it at all, and he's thirty-three."

"That's just because he hasn't met the right girl," Kate insisted.

"I don't think so. Even guys sometimes talk about eventually settling down or 'when I have kids,' but not Will. He's pretty happy the way he is."

"It's about having a little fun," Lyndsay said.

Kate nodded. "Tasting the forbidden fruit."

Tony frowned.

Laughing, Lyndsay gave his shoulder a push. "I just need to know what's there—and what isn't. Then we'll all move on."

He opened his mouth as if he had more to say.

"Time to change the subject," Lyndsay said cheerfully. "Want to see the author website I learned how to build?"

Kate threw an arm around her shoulder. "Of course! I'm so proud of you!"

They spent a fun half hour looking at her website. She showed them her preorder ranking at online bookstores, and the first early—and good!—review her publisher had gotten for her. As she was discussing the blogs she'd written for reviewer websites, she remembered the interview question she'd received, asking if she'd based the hero on someone. And she couldn't imagine telling Kate and Tony what had happened.

On Thursday, at Sugar and Spice, the Main Street bakery owned by Emily Thalberg, Lyndsay dropped in to meet Kate for a quick dessert after lunch. She'd been able to sneak a few extra minutes away from school so she could indulge her sweet tooth with a fellow devotee.

Kate was already there, sipping coffee at one of the little tables in the corner, when Lyndsay arrived. On the opposite wall was a long glass display case with all the goodies that so lured Lyndsay. In the back, next to the kitchen door, was a refrigerated cooler with cheesecakes and other temperature-sensitive desserts. There were flowerpots on every table, and vases of them heaped in the display windows out front, surrounding the cakes and cookies, reminding a visitor that it was spring. With only a wave toward her friend, Lyndsay went to the counter to browse and salivate.

Kate joined her. "Well hello to you, too."

"I knew you'd come over," Lyndsay said.

Steph Sweet leaned her arms on the counter. Her blond hair was pulled back in a ponytail, and she looked younger than her college age. "I swear, you two are our best customers."

"And we run a lot to make up for it," Kate said. "I ate a healthy salad before I got here, I promise."

"I had a peanut butter and jelly sandwich," Lyndsay said, distracted by all the deliciousness.

Kate threw her hands wide. "How do you do it? It makes me just sick, what you can eat while the rest of us suffer."

"You don't have to suffer," Lyndsay said, not taking her eyes off the chocolate ganache cake.

"I know, I know, I measure my portions. It's just unfair."

"You don't want to meet here anymore?" Lyndsay asked, her smile fading.

"I didn't say that . . . Steph, I'll take a piece of carrot cake and iced tea unsweetened."

Lyndsay relaxed. "I'll take a red velvet cupcake. And coffee. By the way, where's your sister?" she asked Steph.

"Em's in back, getting a couple pies ready for Tony's."

"You want me to drop them off?"

"Naw, Will is due any moment to pick them up."

Lyndsay inwardly winced. She pretended not to notice Kate perk up like she had bunny ears.

Steph grinned. "It's nice to have brothers for the occasional errand. Mom was supposed to do it, but something came up."

They paid and carried their goodies to a table, where Kate said in a low voice, "Isn't that a lucky coincidence."

"Uh-huh," Lyndsay answered, then took her cup to the coffee station for sugar and creamer. Back at the table, she removed the foil lining of her cupcake.

"So, have you asked Will out yet?" Kate asked, then took a bite of her carrot cake.

"Keep your voice down." Lyndsay moaned as the first bite of velvety chocolate hit her tongue. "Can't a girl enjoy her dessert in peace?"

Kate crossed her arms over her chest. "Not if the girl is being cowardly."

Lyndsay leaned over the table and said in a low voice, "We shouldn't be discussing this in his sister's bakery." She glanced at Steph, who was thankfully distracted by an elderly gentleman.

"I just think you should go for it."

"I will, I promise. But I haven't found the right moment yet."

"Do you think he'll turn you down?"

"I don't know, and I'm not exactly worried about it. But asking over the phone seems . . . impersonal, and I won't be able to see his expression."

"I'm glad you're not worried. And when you do

date, if it doesn't work out, it'll be okay. The girls he dates always seem to remain friends with him. They might as well start a little Facebook group of Will's exes, they all get along so well. I don't remember you getting all that depressed when you broke up with a guy. You don't seem depressed over the dentist. But then, you weren't in love with him."

"No. I honestly haven't been in love since John broke up with me just when I thought he was going to propose. Maybe I have that in common with Will, that I've always been wary since then."

Will entered, magically summoned by his name, and the door jingled as if angels had announced his presence. Two middle-aged women at the counter smiled and waved. Everybody loved him, Lyndsay thought, shaking her head with fond exasperation.

Using her finger to pick up a crumb on her napkin and eat it, she eyed Will. He met her gaze, and she felt a charge of awareness, as if a lightning storm had just passed. Was it her imagination, or did his smile fade a bit into intensity before he tugged his Stetson with his thumb, nodded, and turned toward the counter? Lyndsay shook herself and refocused on her friend, who thankfully hadn't seemed to notice anything unusual.

"Okay, now that we can't talk about him," Kate said in a reasonable tone, "let's discuss your writing."

"Shh!" Lyndsay hissed a little more forcefully than she should have.

The ladies at the counter looked right at her, but luckily Will was saying something to his little sister.

Kate's mouth briefly fell open. "What has gotten into you? I said nothing in a loud voice, and I just mentioned writing, not—something specific." She looked suspiciously from Lyndsay to Will, then whispered, "Why would you care if he heard that word?"

"I don't want anyone to hear that word, not right now. I'm not ready, and my students' parents need time to digest it before fall. I've explained all this."

"Yes, and those excuses made sense. But I think there's something else going on."

"Kate—"

"Just tell me now, because you know I'll figure it out."

Lyndsay took a sip of coffee and ignored her.

Chapter 7

Will kept his back to Lyndsay and Kate, trying to ignore his feeling of confusion. His awareness of Lyndsay was undergoing some kind of shift, and he didn't know what to make of it. She'd seemed to stiffen when he'd walked in the door. Maybe she was still embarrassed about being drunk the other night, but he didn't think that was it. Too many times this week, he'd thought back to standing outside her door Friday evening, reliving the moment when she'd asked him in, all warm and sweet and hesitant. He'd turned her down. Idiot. But if he'd gone in, what did he think would have happened?

Emily came out of the kitchen, carrying three pie boxes neatly stacked, turning his thoughts away from things he couldn't change. She was cuter than normal, wearing her BEST BUNS IN TOWN apron, so clean it was as if she never baked. It was still strange to think that just three years ago, he hadn't known he had an older sister, but now he couldn't imagine it otherwise. Emily had been through a bad divorce; her husband had left her partly because she couldn't give him a biological child. Any man who wasn't a fool could realize that kind, gentle Emily would make a wonderful mother, regardless of how they had children. And Nate was no fool.

Emily stepped behind the counter and came to the far end where the cash register was, placing the boxes in front of Will. He started to pull out his wallet.

"Tony has an account with us," Steph said, then glanced at her sister with amusement. "A hefty account we bill monthly."

Will put away his wallet. "Far be it from me to interfere between bakery and client."

Since meeting Emily, Steph had done some growing up. She'd been a much-loved—and spoiled—only daughter, and at sixteen, she'd found it tough to discover she had a sister. After a slow and rocky start, they now planned to go into the bakery together when Steph graduated from college.

"So, when's the move-in date to the new apartment?" Will asked her. "I assume you'll need your brothers to help carry stuff."

Steph gave a little squeal, and Em rolled her eyes good-naturedly.

"I just signed the papers," Steph confided. "Mom kept trying to talk me out of it—said I should save my money—but Monica is giving me a really good deal. No security deposit or last month's rent or anything. She and Travis have been moving stuff out already. I'll need some help this weekend."

"You got it."

Steph looked past him, gestured subtly with her chin toward Lyndsay and Kate, then spoke in a low voice. "I hear you guys danced a couple songs last Friday."

"With Kate or Lyndsay?"

Steph spoke with exasperation. "The available one."

Will exhaled slowly and arched an eyebrow at his other sister.

"Word gets around," Emily whispered innocently.

"And why should word get around?" he asked with disbelief.

Emily spoke with calm patience, as if he were dense. "Because you never dance with her."

"I don't?" He glanced at Lyndsay, who was eating one of his sister's sinful desserts. He admired the little dress she wore, which came to her knees in a teacherly fashion but bared her toned arms and dipped toward her breasts, as if teasing him.

Teasing him? Where had that come from? She wouldn't dress to affect him.

He'd noticed her looks and her intelligence and how funny she could be, but he'd kept his distance, figuring that, regardless of Tony's rules, she was just out of his league.

He left the counter and approached the two

women. "Ladies, how are you this rainy afternoon?"

Lyndsay's bangs were haphazard across her forehead, but they couldn't hide the touch of chagrin in her brown eyes.

"Will, I have to apologize for getting drunk Friday night," she said. "I hope I didn't embarrass you or myself too much."

He pulled up a chair and straddled it. "Don't worry about it. You were hardly drunk, just talkative."

Lyndsay ran a hand down her face. "I think I remember letting you get a word in edgewise."

"You know I don't have a problem speaking up."

He glanced at Kate, who was pointedly eating the last of her carrot cake as if she didn't want to disturb them. That was unusual. One dance with a woman seemed to be giving the whole town ideas—him, too.

Lyndsay abruptly rose to her feet. "Thanks for accepting my apology. I've got to get back to school. See you later, Kate, Will."

He watched her nod to his sisters and leave, walking quickly. Then he glanced at Kate. "Does my breath smell bad?"

She smiled. "Nope. She really does have to get back to school." And with only the slightest pause, she added, "And I have to get back to the office. See you later!"

When she'd gone, he returned to the counter, ignoring the grins Emily and Steph exchanged.

"Guess I'll take this to Tony before heading back to the ranch."

"You do that!" Steph called cheerfully as he walked away.

Because of the pies and the rain, Will drove the half mile to Tony's Tavern. The lunch rush had passed, and the bar was settling down to its usual few guys and their sports on TV.

Tony was behind the bar, hanging up the last of the clean wineglasses. When he saw Will and the pies, he gestured with his head to the kitchen, and Will delivered them. Chef Baranski glanced up with a scowl on his unshaven face, tattooed arms bare above his sanitary gloves. His dark ponytail was shot through with gray beneath a faded ball cap. When he saw Will, he only grumbled, then nodded to the stainless steel counter.

"Put 'em there," he said in a gruff voice, then "Thanks," as if it were torn from his flesh.

Will went back to the bar and took a seat on a stool. "I don't know if I'd want to accidentally run into Chef out back at two a.m."

Tony nodded. "He'd kick your ass."

"But he makes a mean shepherd's pie."

"Is that what you want for lunch?"

"You bet."

Tony punched the order into the computer, then went back to refilling beer in the reach-in coolers beneath the bar.

Will thought about Lyndsay, and how apparently he'd caused gossip by dancing with her and walking her home. Should he apologize to Tony? He'd probably be apologizing more for his recent thoughts than his actions . . .

"Oh, I meant to tell you." Tony straightened up and leaned forward on the bar. "I hear the middle school 4-H project leader had to drop out because of a badly broken leg."

"You mean Gonzalez?"

"Yeah."

"Works for the Circle F. Nasty break. He'll be out for a while."

"Yeah, well, now Lyndsay tells me they need another cowboy. She's the school advisor for the club. It's a monthlong unit, once a week, about caring for horses, riding them, whatever." Tony eyed him, wearing the faintest smile. "Know someone who'd be interested?"

Will didn't say anything for a moment, trying to decide if the gossip had gotten to Tony or not. And then Tony's daytime server, Rhonda, brought him his salad. He forked it around a bit and made his decision. If it was selfish, tough. "Yeah, if she needs help, I can do it."

Tony arched a dark brow and said nothing.

"What's that expression for?" Will asked.

"You're defensive."

"Do I need to be?"

"No."

"Okay, then. I'll help the 4-H." But he'd be helping Lyndsay, and he knew that was the main reason he was going to do it.

"You're good with Ethan," Tony said. "Guess you can handle a group his age."

"No problem."

"It's almost time for the hay harvest. Lynds was concerned she'd be interfering with a cowboy's work."

"It's just a couple hours once a week. I can handle it."

"Okay, then. Want me to tell her I found a volunteer?"

"I gotta stop at the feed store on my way home. I'll swing around to the school and let her know, find out details."

His expression neutral, Tony said, "Okay, thanks."

Will glanced at SportsCenter on the nearest TV. They were showing baseball highlights, but he didn't really pay attention. He was thinking about how he'd just seen Lyndsay, yet was still eager to see her again.

Lyndsay stood in the doorway of her classroom, turning off the lights, when she happened to look up—and see Will Sweet. He was walking slowly down the hall, glancing from room to room, his cream-colored Stetson shadowing his eyes, emphasizing the cleft deep in his square jaw. His sandy blond hair curled a bit behind his ears. Her mouth went dry, and she saw other women doing a double take as he strode past. His long arms swung loosely, veins from hard work meandering up them, the same faded rodeo t-shirt tight over his biceps. His jeans were faded, too, low on his hips, tight across his thighs. He controlled a horse with those thighs, she thought with a shiver. His cowboy boots made a distinct, clipped sound on the wood floor.

When he saw her, his smile widened, his dimple deepened, and his eyes twinkled at her from beneath the shadow of his brim. "Just who I'm looking for," he called, raising a hand.

What was *he doing here?* she thought, pulling herself together. "Hi, Will," she said, a bit more weakly than she'd hoped. "What can I help you with?"

He stopped right in front of her, and she had to angle her head back to see his face. She was too close to the tanned hollow at the base of his throat, and she could see the raindrops moistening the shoulders of his t-shirt.

"Can we talk?" he asked, glancing past her to nod pleasantly at someone.

"Sure." She turned the lights back on in her room and led the way to her desk. She seated herself behind it as if for protection—from herself, of course—and gestured to the chair beside it.

Instead, he sat on the edge of the nearest desk. "Tony told me about the 4-H club needing a project leader. Will I do?"

She wasn't sure what she'd expected him to say, but it hadn't been that. "Sure. That's really generous of you to offer."

He leaned back on both hands and grinned, his head cocked. "You don't sound all that enthused."

"No, no, really, I am," she said, wishing she could kick herself. "I guess I was thinking it would be someone's dad or uncle or—"

"Nate and Em are doing their best to make me an uncle," he answered.

She briefly closed her eyes. "I'm sorry, I'm not making any sense. You'll do a great job with the 4-H. I really appreciate your help."

She'd been waiting for some time alone to ask him out, but hadn't imagined it being at school. She stared at him, and he was studying her just as intently.

She took a deep breath. "Will, would you like to get a drink with me some evening? And I don't mean to talk about 4-H."

His smile faded, then something changed in his eyes. All that heavy-lidded smolder she'd seen directed at other girls switched on. His gaze moved down her body, leisurely, intently, and she felt it like a physical caress, her nipples hardening, her belly clenching, her thighs tightening, and between them—no, she wasn't letting herself go there, not now.

"I've found myself thinking the same thing lately," he said in a husky voice.

The sound alone made her trembling increase. My God, she was in her middle school classroom, and she was worried about losing control.

"I think we could have some fun," she said. "I

know we usually orbit around Tony, you and me, as friends."

"What's changed?" He straightened then, leaning forward, forearms braced on his thighs. His hands were loosely clasped together, and she studied them, wondering how it would feel to be touched intimately by him.

She shivered. "I—I don't know." That was a lie. But how could she tell him that her recent realization that she'd based Cody on him made her want to bring her feelings out in the open and put it behind her? "Maybe I just need to start taking chances, have some fun, even if I risk being hurt."

"You think I'd hurt you?"

"Not deliberately. Maybe I'd hurt *you*," she teased. "Not deliberately, of course."

His faint smile deepened again. "I'm only hesitating because of your brother."

"We're not in high school anymore."

Suddenly he rose to his feet and came toward her almost nonchalantly, removing his hat and setting it on her desk. Her mouth went dry, her neck arched and arched, and then she couldn't take it anymore and had to stand up, too, though she felt as if her legs would buckle.

"I'm not sure we have any chemistry at all," he said softly. "We should check."

He kept coming, and she would have fallen over the chair if she'd backed up that way. The door was wide open; anyone passing could see them, but she didn't make that protest. Instead she found her back up against the whiteboard.

His body didn't touch hers at all, although it was a bare inch away. The heat of him was almost more than she could take, from her breasts to her hips down her legs. And then he touched her chin with his fingers, tilting her head until her wide eyes met his heavy-lidded ones.

"I think . . . this will do the trick," he whispered.

And then his mouth covered hers in a hot, passionate kiss. He explored her lips with his, and she met that exploration gladly with her own. He braced both hands on the board on either side of her head, yet still didn't let their bodies touch. She slanted her head and boldly thrust her tongue between his lips, lost in the taste of Will. His kiss was everything she'd imagined, forceful, knowledgeable, yet restrained, as if he had even more to give but couldn't show her unless they were naked.

And then he lifted his head and looked down at her with eyes that betrayed passion, yes, but . . . something else, something he was keeping hidden. It gave her a moment of uneasiness, but she pushed it away. She let her hand cup his face, felt the faint coarseness of stubble, the lean hollows of his cheeks. For just a moment, she let her thumb dip to the corner of his damp mouth.

"So do we have chemistry?" she whispered.

He let his forehead rest against hers, and their noses brushed. "Tell me what you think, darlin'."

"That's not fair. I asked you out. You know what I think."

His chuckle rumbled deep in his chest, and she wished she dared put her hands there—but not yet. He paused a long time, so long that that hidden . . . something in his eyes played tricks on her mind.

"I think we need to have a drink some evening," he finally said.

The relief and elation she thought she'd feel was tempered by this awareness of faint reluctance in him. But who could blame him? He'd been honest about the complications.

"You should probably hold back your wild emotions," she said dryly, "or it could turn a girl's head."

He laughed in an easier manner, then stepped away from her. She missed his touch already.

"Sorry," he said, picking up his hat and settling it on his head. "This still feels a little . . . strange to me."

"Me, too. Let's just think of it as having fun."

"So after dating different kinds of guys, you've finally decided to try a cowboy on for size."

She eyed him with amusement. "Guess so."

"And Tony won't show up at my door with a shotgun?"

It was her turn to laugh. "I can't guarantee my dad won't take offense."

"Guess we'll have to take a chance. How about tomorrow? I have to work through the early evening, but then I'm free." He looked right at her mouth, as if he was already anticipating repeating the kiss.

And she was all for that. "Okay. How about if I come pick you up? I did ask you out, after all."

That good-old-boy grin came back. "All right. See you around seven?"

"Sure."

He started to turn, but he paused, and for a moment, she ached to be kissed again.

Instead he simply nodded. "Have a good evenin', darlin'."

And then he walked away, and she was treated to the sight of his ass in those tight jeans, and his broad, broad shoulders beneath the Stetson.

When he was gone, she sank slowly back into her chair, almost tempted to touch her mouth, as if the kiss hadn't been real.

And then reality intruded and she thought about her book, and how embarrassed she'd feel if he knew the truth. She had to keep it away from him. She had a few weeks until it was common knowledge, and then . . . she'd find a way to dissuade him from reading it. She'd make sure he thought the book was purple prose, hearts, and flowers. Not a guy thing at all.

Would they even last a month, anyway? Women seldom did with him. Or maybe she'd be the first one to see that they had no future. That made her smile.

Will sat in the school parking lot in his pickup truck, both hands gripping the wheel, even though he hadn't started the engine yet. He wasn't quite sure what had happened. He'd gone there to help her out by volunteering, then he'd seen her in her sexy teacher clothes, imagined what was underneath, and lost his rational self. When she'd asked him out on a date, he'd been relieved more than surprised. He was a red-blooded man, after all.

She'd taken the reins in her own hands and boldly asked him out. She'd started to talk about those complications they were both so aware of, and suddenly, he'd wanted to know what was really there—he'd wanted to kiss her.

It had been an irresistible longing, and at the time he hadn't questioned it—couldn't question it. He'd been so focused on needing to taste her that he'd barely kept himself from drawing her hard against him, desperate for the feel of her arms around his body, even her legs around his waist. Afterward, the enormity of those sensations had made him feel a little rattled. He wasn't used to feeling so out of control, so desperate. He never let a woman do this to him, and it had seriously made him consider turning her down.

And that's when he'd realized he would have been treating her differently from all the other women he'd dated, as if she had some kind of power over him. He wasn't going to let that happen. No, they'd go on a few dates and he'd make sure they both had fun, but in the end, it would be time to move on to the next woman.

It's how things had to be for him.

Chapter 8

All the next day, time seemed to drag. When the last bell finally rang, Lyndsay called the 4-H organizational leader, one of the parents, and said she had a replacement for Mr. Gonzalez—because she hadn't remembered to call them yesterday.

Not that she'd called Kate either. Before she said anything, she would see what happened on the date with Will.

But after that kiss . . . how could there not be a great date? Maybe a series of dates, but that's all they'd be—dates, just to get him out of her system.

But that kiss . . . the memory had lingered on through the evening and into today, which was a little unusual. It certainly made her look forward to the evening with him.

After work, she went home to change, settling on flats, skinny jeans, and a lace top over a blue tank. She grabbed a sweater for the cool mountain air, then drove out to the Sweetheart Ranch. She'd forgotten the beauty of the place, stretched along the base of the Elk Mountains. She used to come in high school for the big barbecue the Sweets threw every year.

There were acres and acres of hay rippling in the breeze, and near the cluster of barns, she could see horses in their corral, grazing. No cattle, though. They were all up on their grazing allotment in the White River National Forest. The house itself was no old farmhouse; it had been built in the '60s when the family had renovated their old house in town into the Sweetheart Inn. This was a two-story expanse of glass, dark wood siding, and elegant landscaping.

Now that she thought about it, she hadn't asked where she was supposed to meet him on this vast ranch. She drove around the circle that led past the front door and parked, but the place felt kind of deserted, with no other vehicles. They probably parked around back.

Just when she was about to head up the front steps, she heard the distant sound of a helicopter approaching. She looked up, shielding her eyes, to see it coming fast from the direction of the mountains, heading right toward her—but that was ridiculous.

The trees seemed to bow and shake when it passed overhead, and the wind began to kick up dead leaves and dirt. Then the helicopter slowed and seemed to hover a hundred yards away, and that's when she saw the two occupants, both wearing headsets. One was giving a wave, and by the dark hair, she thought it was Daniel. And at the controls—Will, dark sunglasses hiding his eyes. She'd totally forgotten the "hobby" he'd acquired a few years back. Or that's how her brother teasingly referred to it. Will always swore that he flew for the ranch, even when other cowboys, including the Thalbergs, snickered.

Will rotated the helicopter so he was the one nearest her, then gestured somewhere back beyond the house. She waved, deciding to drive there, because who knew how far he wanted her to go.

They seemed to be waiting for her, because as she drove the gravel road that went around back, they flew ahead of her like a queen bee leading a lowly beetle. And then she saw where they were headed. Beyond the barns was a newer metal building, obviously a hangar for the helicopter. After parking what she thought was a safe distance away, she got out, then leaned against the car to watch Will slowly bring the helicopter to earth. Grass waved and flattened, dirt kicked up, and no sooner were they on the ground than Daniel hopped out, a shotgun slung over his shoulder. He bent low as he ran beneath the spinning blades toward her.

"Hey, Lyndsay," he said loudly, to be heard above the engine.

He didn't smirk or make a comment about Will and her getting together. She hoped it was going to be that easy with everyone else.

"Hi, Daniel." She eyed the gun.

"Coyote. He'll tell you about it. It takes a few minutes to cool down before he can shut it off. He won't mind if you join him while he waits."

"Okay, thanks."

She headed toward the helicopter, feeling the wind rush over her, forcing her to hunch the closer she got. Will was focused on the controls, oblivious to her approach. She couldn't have shouted his name, so she settled for waving an arm in his line of vision. Startled, he looked at her, and with the headset, sunglasses—and impassive expression—he didn't seem like himself.

Then he gave her a crooked grin, opened the clear door, and shouted, "Sorry this takes so long. Can't shut the engine down cold."

"Can I get in?"

He surprised her by hesitating before saying, "Hop in and put on the headset. Easier to talk."

Still hunched, she hurried around the front to the far side, opened the door, and hopped onto the bucket seat. Will handed her the headset. After she donned it, she was surprised how much the noise of the engine faded.

His voice seemed almost scratchy in her ears as he said, "Hi, Lyndsay."

They smiled at each other.

He kept glancing at his watch. "Gotta time things," he said, and flipped a switch.

"Flying would make an interesting first date," she said.

To her surprise, he didn't offer to take her up

sometime. But he was focused on what he was doing, a laminated checklist in his hand, and she didn't want to disturb him. At last the blades began to slow, and soon they were sitting in a perfectly quiet machine.

Will took his headset off, waited for her to do the same, then said, "Sorry. I didn't mean to be up in the air when you arrived. I haven't even showered."

"Take your time, we're not on a schedule. Daniel said you were dealing with coyotes?"

"Up near our grazing allotment."

Her eyes widened. "So Daniel shot them from the air?"

"He prides himself on his shooting accuracy. It comes in handy. I hope that doesn't make you too squeamish."

She shook her head. "Nope, you have to protect the cattle, I get that."

"Follow me. I'm a fast changer."

They both got out of the helicopter and walked side by side across the dirt path that linked the hangar and the other outbuildings. He led her to a low ranch-style building, utilitarian looking, with no landscaping but a couple of chairs and a picnic table.

"My brothers and I live in the old bunkhouse," he said, opening the main door for her.

Once inside, she couldn't help smiling as she said, "Old?"

The place had obviously been remodeled, for there was a modern, open layout, with a kitchen at the rear, only an island separating it from the rest of the room. A dining table and chairs were positioned to the left, and a sectional sofa was grouped around a big flat-screen TV on the right. On either side, a couple of short hallways had closed doors leading off them.

"Our bedrooms," he said, acknowledging where she looked. "Bathrooms, linen closets, laundry room, that kind of stuff."

"For some reason, I thought you still lived in the main house."

He shrugged out of his tan Carhartt jacket. "That worked for a while, but by the time I was twenty-seven or twenty-eight, I began to feel kinda weird still living at home. But the ranch needs us twenty-four hours a day, so I didn't really want to live in town. This was the perfect solution. Daniel and I are here the most. Technically, Chris still lives here, but since Heather has that big old Victorian for her catering company, she's made the second floor into an apartment. He's there a lot, needless to say." He gestured to the sofa. "Make yourself at home. I'll be quick."

She could tell guys lived in the place, for there was nothing hanging on the walls except a single rodeo poster. She remembered his parents' home, with all the medieval and mystical paintings on the walls: magical forests, waterfalls, and castle ruins were abundant. Guess the brothers didn't take after their bohemian parents. Ranching and cowboy magazines were scattered on end tables, and gaming controls covered the coffee table. She was just heading to the big bookshelf with interest, when the screen door opened and Daniel strode in.

He didn't look anything like what someone would think of as a typical cowboy, not with his tattoos and piercings, his t-shirt with the arms cut out. She didn't even remember the last time she'd seen him wearing a cowboy hat.

He gave her a smile as he went to grab a water from the fridge. "Can you give Will a message for me? Tell him I called that supplier we discussed. Mom didn't get around to it in time, so I took care of it."

"Okay, sure."

After Daniel left, she spent most of the fifteen minutes Will was gone at the big bookshelf.

She had her face in a Danielle Steel book when he returned, dressed in his usual jeans and cowboy boots, but this time paired with a cream-colored, long-sleeve Henley. His light hair was still dark with moisture, and she liked the hint of curls. And he'd shaved, she thought, imagining holding his face in her hands. But not where his brothers could walk back in any moment.

She held up the book. "Danielle Steel?"

"It was my mom's. I was bored one night. It was good."

"I know." She shook her head with amusement. "The rest is pretty typical guy stuff, including Tom Clancy, who I happen to love."

"You read Clancy?" he asked in surprise, coming to stand beside her.

"Yep. I really enjoy his ability to take a lot of apparently random plot threads at the beginning, and weave them together until you're just blown away by how it all connects."

"You sound like a teacher," he said, smiling.

Author, she thought, still feeling proud and giddy over her new status.

"I just like the military stuff," he said.

She nodded. "The helicopters."

"Yeah, that, too."

They shared a grin, and she felt a little shock of surprise that they'd found something they had in common. She'd been telling herself that there couldn't possibly be anything they shared, but she'd discovered it was books. And that was a really good thing to an author.

As they continued to look at each other, their smiles slowly died as the memory of their hot kiss rose between them, as if a visible thing. She couldn't take a deep enough breath, and she almost asked if he wanted to show her his bedroom.

Okay, enough of that. She'd never slept with a guy on the first date, though he was tempting.

"Oh, Daniel was just here," she said, chagrined at how breathless she sounded. "He said to tell you that he called the supplier you wanted called."

Will frowned. "I thought Mom was taking care of that."

"He said she didn't get around to it, so he took care of it."

"Okay."

But a line still lingered between his eyes. She wondered if there were problems on the ranch, but it wasn't something she'd expect him to confide in her.

To lighten the subject, she asked, "Where should we have our drink? I'm tempted to drive us to Aspen, just so we can have some peace and quiet."

"I'll do whatever you want me to do," he offered. "But I don't plan to keep you hidden away."

That touched her. "Thanks. But I say we skip Tony's. We both hang out there enough anyway."

He nodded. "Talk about no peace. What about the Halftime Sports Bar? I was flying through dinner," he admitted.

"Okay, and I'm always up for food."

He glanced down her body, eyes gleaming, and when he spoke, his voice was almost a low growl. "You wouldn't know it."

Her heart seemed to slam against her ribs, and she had to lick her dry lips before saying weakly, "Thanks." She turned toward the door on unsteady legs.

As they drove through the ranch toward town, Lyndsay kept a firm grip on the wheel and said, "It's gotta be pretty exciting to use a helicopter for work."

He shrugged. "Sure, but I'll be honest—we don't have a lot of reason to use one around here. I first saw them being used on hundred-thousand-acre spreads in Texas, where there's four thousand head to round up. They use five or six helicopters all at once, hovering around like cow dogs. With just cowboys on the ground, moving that size herd could take weeks rather than days."

"Sounds really fascinating."

"It is, but I worry my dad regrets the purchase sometimes. Helicopters have a tough time at altitudes above ten thousand feet, depending on the engine and the make. Since we're already at almost seven thousand, that doesn't leave us much room to play with."

"You can use it for other things, right?"

"Wildfires. A couple years ago, they had a dangerous one at the Silver Creek Ranch, and we came in with our bucket swinging from a cable attached beneath. I dipped it in ponds and flew over the fire, making my drop."

"Wow, I remember hearing about that."

"It was a little scary for a while. In this desert climate, you know how we all fear fire. If it starts to spread, we're all in danger."

"Do you do search and rescue stuff?"

She thought his expression betrayed tiredness as he answered.

"Only in an emergency. Chris keeps trying to talk me into renting it out more. He's all gung-ho on exciting helicopter stuff—not that he wants to learn himself. But I like what I do on the ranch. He's starting to make me feel backed into a corner about it, you know? I don't want to be pulled several different ways. I'm a rancher, and that's all I want to be."

He looked out the window rather than at her, and she wondered if there was more to the story.

"I understand about being pulled in different directions against your will," she said softly, even as she cruised Main Street looking for a parking spot. "Teaching's sometimes like that. More kids in the class, not enough help so you can meet the needs of a lot of different kinds of kids and still fill out all the paperwork. It's hard to see an end to the problems."

She found a parking spot on a side street, and they walked in easy silence to the Halftime Sports Bar. Though the sun had set behind the mountains, it wasn't fully dark yet. The old-fashioned lampposts had begun to flicker on. There were couples and groups of people here and there, but May was still off season, and the crowds wouldn't pick up until July. The nineteenth-century buildings alternated between brick and colorful clapboard, one and two stories. There were lots of US flags and planters that would soon be overflowing with geraniums and petunias. Valentine was a beautiful place to live.

The Halftime Sports Bar was different from Tony's—it had obviously been a saloon in the nineteenth century. Beneath an embossed tin ceiling, there was a carved mahogany bar. All the paneling was in dark, expensive woods, making the sports memorabilia stand out. Denver athletes who'd passed through over the decades had signed the displayed jerseys.

As they were led to a table, she saw Sean with another guy at the bar. He raised a hand when he saw her—and his expression openly fell when he glimpsed Will behind her. She waved and held back a wince. He was obviously a guy who wore his emotions openly. He seemed nice, but she'd never really been attracted to him. Yet she hated making someone feel bad.

She glanced over her shoulder at Will and said, "I really like this place, but I tend to hang out at my brother's."

"Me, too. I almost feel like I'm betraying him just by being here. I'm used to knowing all the waitstaff by name."

Their hostess, a redheaded college-aged girl, smiled as she handed them their menus. "Then in that case, I'm Julie Jacoby. I know who you are, Will Sweet. You dated my sister last year."

He faced her, eyes narrowed above a smile, as if trying to place her.

She raised a hand. "Don't worry, we didn't meet. I was finishing up my senior year at Colorado State. I just saw pictures of you."

"Whew," he said. "I like to think I have a good memory for faces, and I thought you were going to prove me wrong."

Julie grinned. "I'll send your server over."

He held out Lyndsay's chair, and she sat down. "Thanks. I think it's better to be here for a date than feel my brother's eagle eye on us all evening. Not that he'd care that we're having a drink, honestly."

"He's protective of you. I get it. I have a little sister. When she started dating Tyler Brissette in high school, after he was getting into trouble and I heard that his brother just got out of prison, well, I had my doubts. But I didn't interfere; I trusted Steph, just like Tony trusts you. And Tyler's turned out to be a good kid, going to CMC, too. Heck, he's doing better than me; I dropped out."

Their waitress brought ice water to the table and introduced herself as Linda, before taking their drink order.

"Why did you drop out?" Lyndsay asked Will after the waitress had gone.

Folding his hands, he leaned his forearms on the table. "Because I was the oldest—at the time I'd been doing a lot of the work on the ranch alongside my dad. When you grow up on a ranch, you start at a young age, caring for baby chicks, calves, and of course for your horse. I'd learned to run cattle into chutes or cut a cow from the herd before I was ten. Now so did my brothers, of course, and Steph's no slouch, although it's obvious where her interest lies. But I was still the oldest, and I loved what I do here, even then. Being away just made me miserable. My parents kept encouraging me to enjoy school, and I learned a lot about animal science, of course, but eventually, I just didn't want to be there anymore. I'd dated all the women I wanted to."

Lyndsay's mouth briefly dropped open until she saw his laughing eyes, and she joined his chuckle with her own. "Nice. I fell for that for a second."

"More like a minute. Your eyes bugged out."

Linda came back with their beer, and they placed their orders. They each wanted the Half-time's famous BLTs.

"And I thought you had dinner already," he pointed out.

"No, I never said that—I was just supposed to. But I ran out of time, or I was too nervous or—" Oh, why had she admitted that?

His eyebrows rose. "Nervous? For a drink with me?"

He caught her hand across the table. It was pleasant to talk to him and feel so connected. His hands were big and strong, callused from the hard, physical work he did.

"It's silly, I know," she said softly.

"It was that kiss," he said in a husky voice, which had gone deep as he leaned toward her. "It . . . changed things."

Her gaze dropped to his lips and lingered. "Yeah, I think so, too."

He straightened up slowly, then took a sip of his beer, never breaking eye contact. "Then we need to put ourselves at ease. Tell me more about college. You lasted the whole four years, so you must have loved it."

"I did. I loved college dances, I played trumpet in a little jazz band, I was a member of a great sorority, I even liked classes. I was president of SHAG—"

He coughed on a swig of beer, and his eyes watered, making Lyndsay laugh as he had to let go of her hand for a napkin.

"SHAG?" he finally gasped.

"Bet you can't guess what it stands for."

"I'm afraid to guess."

"Scaredy cat. Sexual Health Awareness Group. We made students aware of the consequences of their decisions, and we had a booth at any campus fairs going on—we gave away a lot of condoms to promote safe sex. Now aren't you sorry you dropped out?"

One corner of his mouth curled upward. "You've almost convinced me."

"Anyway, I left college filled with starry-eyed optimism. I'm certified in both math and science, and although I didn't get the first job I applied for, I got the second—teaching math in my own hometown. I didn't think it could be better than that. And for a while, it truly was great, and the kids themselves never disappoint me. But you know," she added, eyeing him, "I bet you liked the wilder aspects of college."

"We're not going to talk about dating exploits, are we?"

"Nope. I think we both know enough about each other on that score. You'd have liked fraternity life—or at least the pranks."

"Me, pranks?" he said, his hazel eyes utter innocence.

Linda returned with their BLTs, and when she would have brought Lyndsay another beer, she declined. "I'm driving."

Will toasted her with his second beer. "I could get used to having a designated driver."

"Don't think you can distract me from your pranks. I know all about what you did on one of your annual ski trips with the boys. What were the details when you skinny-dipped in a hot tub and raced across the hotel grounds to the fountain and back, getting yourself in a tabloid paper?"

"Hey, Josh dared me, not the other way around. When he did it, I had to save face and do it, too. I was just plain lucky he ended up in the paper bucknaked instead of me."

"Maybe being young and reckless runs in the family. From what you implied a couple days ago, your grandma and the Purple Poodles had their high school hopping. And I think you know even more than you said."

He swallowed a bite of his sandwich. "Well, it wasn't always pretty. According to my grandma, there was a misunderstanding that she regrets."

"Now isn't that rare," Lyndsay teased, "your grandma admitting a mistake."

"She was too proud, she told me, and it led to problems. Her father allowed her to host a cotillion at their ranch. Mrs. Thalberg's name was left off the invitation list, and the Purple Poodles believed it was because her family didn't think the Thalbergs were . . . of the right social circle."

He used air quotes for emphasis. "My grandma was furious that people thought this, and didn't dignify it by defending herself. Now I know why she was such a stickler for the truth when I was growing up."

"Then what *was* the truth?"

"Mrs. Thalberg had apparently lured away a boy who'd been courting Grandma Sweet."

Lyndsay eyed him in disbelief.

"I know, I know, it seems pretty minor for their big feud to be about a boy," Will continued.

"Well, obviously it wasn't about a boy but the perception that Mrs. Thalberg wasn't good enough. Sheesh, you'd think they'd have talked about it after all these years."

"Telling the truth now is Grandma's attempt at an olive branch. When I was a boy, she always went on and on about telling the truth, and I probably tuned her out a lot. She warned me that pride can be taken too far. It seemed to me like she wanted the truth to come out."

"Her truth," Lyndsay heard herself say before she'd even given it thought.

Will eyed her, his eyes alight with interest. "You think she's lying?"

"No, I wasn't implying that," she quickly said. "It's just . . . over fifty years have passed. Sometimes our memories aren't quite the way we imagine. Or . . . maybe we just see what we want to see. I think there might be more to the story of Mrs. Sweet and the Purple Poodles."

"Sounds like a kid's book." But he regarded Lyndsay thoughtfully. "I kinda think the same thing myself."

They focused on their food again, and Lyndsay bit deep into her BLT, moaning her enjoyment. When she opened her eyes, Will was watching her, his heavy-lidded gaze intent, his smile gone.

"If you enjoy food this much, I have to wonder what other sounds you make when . . ." He trailed off.

She was briefly caught up in the possibilities of "what if." "You enjoy teasing too much," she said ruefully.

"Well, it's fun." And that grin came back, bright as the sun first peeking out from beneath clouds in the morning.

She "enjoyed" another bite of her BLT before changing the subject to something safer. "I called the organizational leaders of the 4-H to say you'd volunteered. You'll have to fill out some forms, be screened, all the stuff adult volunteers have to do to work with kids."

"Makes sense. So what exactly will I be doing?"

"I'll send you some links with ideas for what to do each of the four weekly sessions. The group focused on life on a ranch this past year, with different topics every month—they don't have meetings this summer, so the horse is the final activity for the year. We'll meet at the ranch, and you'll talk us through a different part of raising, caring for, and riding a horse each week. They'll ask lots of questions, of course—you won't have to prepare much in advance."

"Sounds easy enough. And did I hear you say 'we'?"

"Well . . . I am the school advisor to the club. I got you involved—it only seems right that I help if I can."

His gaze drifted leisurely to her lips. "You mean you want to keep an eye on me."

"Now that's not true." Her mouth had gone dry, and she had to resist wetting her lips. Of course she wanted to keep looking at him—it was the perfect pastime. "But kids can be a handful, and I know how to keep things under control."

"Then you think they'll run roughshod over me."

"Not necessarily."

He put down the second half of his sandwich and leaned toward her. "Then what are you thinkin', darlin'?"

"I don't really know," she said helplessly.

"I like to think I rattle you a bit," he murmured, just above the noise of the crowd. "You certainly rattle me."

"I do not! You're never rattled."

"Well, I'm glad to see that that's my reputation. Makes me realize I hide things better than I thought."

"I don't believe you, Will Sweet."

"Then you don't know me as well as you think. Guess that's what dating is all about."

She took a sip of her ice water and thought about all the women he'd gotten to know—and then left behind. Maybe a little mystery would be good between them. Certainly, she had a secret she didn't plan to share anytime soon. . . .

Chapter 9

Will wasn't sure what he'd expected of the evening with Lyndsay, but he was certainly enjoying himself. Oh, there were always women who were easy to talk to, women who were good at the give and take of teasing, women who were honest, even when it made them look silly.

But it was rare to find a woman who was all of this and more—the more being infinitely kissable. It was proving difficult not to stare at her mouth the whole evening—thank goodness it was a natural thing to do when conversing, because otherwise she would have thought he only had one thing on his mind.

He didn't, but wanting another kiss—and more—was certainly right up there.

It was a little disconcerting to be so fascinated with her, but he didn't question it. He didn't need to. At some point he'd learn everything he needed to know, and then he could make the decision about when best to break things off. He was pretty good at that, after all this time.

But no need to think about that so soon. He was simply enjoying Lyndsay. He liked that she wasn't squeamish about his job—a lot of women would have been appalled that coyotes had to be eliminated for the safety of the herd.

And one of the best things about her was that even though she wasn't enjoying teaching right now, she never let that interfere with her love of the kids themselves. Just the fact that she volunteered her time beyond school with the 4-H really impressed him.

And on a lighter note, there was her enjoyment of food, he thought, watching her smack her lips approvingly as she finished the last piece of crust. He'd dated a lot of women who were so focused on having the perfect figure that it made dinners out awkward, as if he should be embarrassed by his appetite. He worked hard all day—he was going to enjoy food.

"So what dessert are you going to order?" he asked.

"I'm pretty full."

"No! I didn't think that was possible where dessert and you are concerned."

She kicked his shin under the table, but amusement still shone in her eyes. Damn, she was cute.

When the check came, Lyndsay put up a pretty good fight about paying at least her share of the bill.

"Hey, I asked you out," she said, her fingers on one side of the check, his on the other.

"You drove, using your gas money."

She snorted adorably. "Yeah, what was that in Valentine Valley, a couple bucks?"

"Regardless, my momma would tan my hide if I let you pay."

Not that he usually told his mom who he was dating. And lately, she'd seemed too stressed to be interested. He put that dilemma out of his mind and gave his credit card to Linda, who smirked knowingly.

He leaned over the table and murmured to Lyndsay, "She thinks I'm getting laid because of this."

"You're not," she murmured back, those flecks of gold in her eyes practically dancing. "I hold myself to a higher standard, surf and turf at the minimum."

"Why didn't you tell me?"

"Because a girl has to have her little mysteries. And I hope you noticed—no mystery tonight about my behavior. One beer doesn't make me drunk. So you won't have to practically carry me home."

"*I'm* the one who might be drunk, and you're taking me home, remember?"

"*Are* you drunk?"

He studied her mouth. "I can be if you want to take advantage."

Her grin was sly and merry all at once. After he signed the check, she retrieved her sweater and purse from the back of the chair and led him toward the door. This time he noticed people staring at them, and an occasional whisper. On the way in, he'd been too focused on watching her ass in those tight jeans.

He wasn't clueless; he knew he sometimes caused talk, although he tried not to do anything too notorious—fountain skinny-dipping notwithstanding.

But he found he didn't want to cause too much speculation for Lyndsay's sake. Out on the street, she came to an abrupt halt, as the rain had begun to come down again, making everything seem darker, except for the little pockets of light around the lampposts.

"Give me your keys and let me go get the car," he said, keeping her beneath the awning.

"Oh, it's not worth it. And besides, I'm the designated driver. Let's run!"

And off she went before he could even answer, surprising him. Most women didn't want to get their hair and makeup wet, but she just glanced at him over her shoulder, laughing with such joy it made his chest ache a little. Brittany used to look at him like that.

Shit, where had that come from? He'd never compared a dead woman to his dates. It gave him a moment of shock, and before he knew it, Lyndsay was at the corner, doing a twirl in the rain and beckoning to him.

He ran after her. It wasn't raining all that hard, but by the time they reached her car, parked beneath another lamppost, he could see mascara running down her cheeks and the variegated strands of her hair turning a deeper brown. With a click of her key fob, she had the doors opened, and they piled in from each side, laughing.

After tossing her purse and sweater into the backseat, Lyndsay yanked the mirror toward her and flipped on the ceiling light. "Oh, my face. I can barely see, yet I know it's bad."

He saw a box of tissues on the backseat and reached over for one. When she tried to take it from him, he held the back of her head with one hand and used the other to wipe at the faint black smudges on her cheeks.

Her smile faded. He could hear the heavy sound of her breathing, knew it was because they'd run— or was it? Was her heart pounding like his from their nearness to each other, not that little exertion back there? Her breath on his face was arousing, and he wanted to pull her into his arms, to really feel her whole body against his this time. But the steering wheel was near her hip, and damn these bucket seats. Where was a good bench seat when you needed one?

In the back.

But he couldn't ask her to hop in back, right on Second Street.

He leaned in to kiss her, slanting his mouth across hers, desperate to taste her, to think of Lyndsay and no one else, certainly not the past. Her lips were damp with cool rain, but her mouth was so warm and inviting. He tasted every part he could reach, danced with her tongue. He wanted to drag her across the bucket seat, but that wouldn't work, so he wrapped his arms around her and held her as tightly as he could. Her breasts were pressed flat against his chest, he let his hand dip down her back to her hip, feeling the curve—until his elbow hit the steering wheel with a thunk.

She giggled against his mouth.

"I feel like a teenager," he said, "making out in the car."

She lifted her head, her gaze glued to his mouth. She shut off the overhead light even as she breathlessly said, "We shouldn't be doing this. I saw parents of some of my students back there—oh, what the hell, the windows are fogged."

And to his surprise, she cupped his face in her hands to pull him back for another long kiss, slower this time. They licked and nipped, and he followed the curve of her jaw with little kisses, loving the low sounds she made deep in her throat.

"Okay, okay," she finally said, putting a hand on his chest when he would have licked his way down her neck. She palmed his chest briefly, eyes closed. "Oh, that feels good, but no, we have to stop now." She sank back in her seat and just looked at him.

He leaned against his own window and looked back, smiling, until at last she started the car. They drove home through the light rain, not speaking, but it was a comfortable silence, and the sound of the rain was lulling. The road through the ranch was dark but for the distant lights of the main house, and they circled past it to the bunkhouse, where only the porch light was on. No one was home.

"I had a great time, Will," Lyndsay said as she put the car in park. She didn't shut it off.

"I did, too. Can we do this again?"

Her sweet smile deepened. "I'd enjoy that. But next Wednesday I'll see you again because of 4-H meeting at the ranch."

"Good, but that's not soon enough. Will I see you tomorrow night at Tony's? We missed our usual Friday there."

"That'll be a big 'we're seeing each other' announcement. You up for that?"

He took her hand and brought it to his mouth, kissing the palm, letting her hand cup his face. Then he lifted his head and grinned at her. "You bet."

They leaned forward and kissed once again, softly this time, just a brush of lips once, twice. He asked, "Do you want to come in?"

"I better not," she said, reluctance obvious in her voice. "We don't want to take things too fast. We're still not certain we have all that much chemistry," she added, chuckling.

"Oh, there's chemistry. I think I've got a Bunsen burner lit beneath me."

She laughed, and the soft tenderness in her eyes was like a splash of cold water in the face.

He straightened away. "Good night, Lyndsay."

"Good night, Will."

He stood on the porch and watched her drive away. He was of two minds about the date. That tenderness had him thinking that dating her was a mistake, that he was going to hurt her when he inevitably pulled away—and he always pulled away.

But she knew that about him; she had gone into this date with her eyes wide open. She wanted to have fun—he'd give her some fun. But that was all.

Still, as he got ready for bed, he found himself remembering how he'd felt when Lyndsay had wanted to hop into the helicopter. He'd been eager even though he considered it his private, peaceful place alone with his thoughts and the occasional memory of Brittany. It was the first time he'd wanted to share it with someone outside his family, and that felt . . . strange.

Lyndsay arrived home and changed into dry clothes, humming with happiness. She'd had such a good time. It was wonderful to finally know that she and Will had *lots* of chemistry.

She thought to check her phone and noticed a bunch of texts from Kate: *Where are you?*

She texted back: *Just got back from a date.*

Kate answered: *WITH WILL! I heard from a friend of a friend.*

And then her cell rang.

Lyndsay pressed the call button. "And who could this be?"

"You went out with Will and didn't tell me?"

Lyndsay laughed. "I asked him out yesterday and the date happened so fast, I didn't have time to call."

"You asked him out and didn't tell me? I have to admit, I never thought you had the balls."

"Hey, I have the balls! Okay, so I don't really have balls, but—"

"Tell me everything about how you asked him out."

And Lyndsay did, adding, "He said he was curious if we had chemistry, and so he kissed me right there in my classroom."

Kate gasped dramatically, making Lyndsay's night.

"Was it a great kiss?"

"Oh, it was a great kiss, and tonight's was even better."

"Tell me all the details."

Lyndsay collapsed on the couch, and they spent a half hour dissecting the date until Kate was satisfied.

"I'm practically an old married lady again," Kate said. "I have to live vicariously through you. Tony and I never even went on dates this last time around."

"That's because you were sneaking around behind all our backs."

"Well, yeah, it was pretty exciting."

"I'm dating right out in the open—as is obvious, since word got back to you so fast."

"So you're going out again?"

"We're meeting up tomorrow night at Tony's—you know that's not normally my night there, but I'm breaking out of a rut, remember."

Kate laughed. "I remember."

"And then we're going to see each other at the 4-H club meeting at his ranch. But besides that, we don't have anything planned yet. We're just going to have fun until we don't anymore."

"Well, aren't you the little optimist."

"I'm a realist, remember? Will only lasts a month or two with a woman. I'm going to enjoy it for what it is." But inside, she was already fighting the sadness of knowing it would all be over soon. "Heck, maybe I'm the one who'll get tired of him first. I'm not going to worry about that in advance though. And another thing I don't have to worry about is that Mrs. Thalberg—or even, accidentally, my dad—might have let something slip about my book being published. I haven't heard a thing from anyone."

"I didn't think she would."

"Me neither, but I'm paranoid over this, okay? Especially now that I'm dating Will."

"Why?"

Lyndsay let out a deep sigh. The secret was just too much for her. "Well . . . there might have been something else about my book I didn't tell anyone—and you cannot breathe a word, pinky swear!"

"I swear, I swear. Tell me!"

Lyndsay took a deep breath. "I created my characters first, spending a lot of time figuring them out, what they look like, how they behave, the way they talk. It wasn't until a couple weeks ago that I realized . . . my hero Cody is an awful lot like Will."

There was silence on the other end of the phone. "Kate?"

"You made Will your hero?" she breathed at last, her voice full of both amazement and laughter.

"Hey, this isn't funny—it could be downright terrible if it got out. When I realized the truth, memories of my old high school crush on Will came back, and I wondered if my subconscious was trying to tell me something. Hence, the dating." She covered her eyes with her forearm. "This is another reason I've been dreading people knowing about my book, another reason I should have used a pseudonym. I don't think his identity is totally obvious—"

"Since you forgot to send me the file, I can't even confirm that for you."

"Oh, right, I'll do that when we hang up. But yeah, I don't think everyone will get it, but . . . some might."

"Including Will. Who you're now dating."

Lyndsay sighed. "I know, I know. If he figures it out . . . he'll think it's funny, right?"

"I don't know. I have to read it first. We're getting off the phone so you can send it. I can sleep in tomorrow, so I'll start reading tonight—oh, Lynds, I'm still so excited for you!"

Lyndsay smiled. "Even with my Will homage?"

"Even then. You've made your dreams come true. You sold a book, you asked Will out. You should be so happy with yourself. Good night!"

"Night."

Another text came through: *Send me the file!*

Lyndsay stared at the phone for a long moment, her amusement slowly fading, before heading for her laptop to send the file. Yes, she'd sold a book, and that was a high that would be hard to top. Asking Will out had meant exploring her crush and putting it back in the past, where it belonged. But since she didn't know how it would turn out, she'd reserve the right to regret it in the end . . .

Chapter 10

After a long day of grading papers and working on her next book, Lyndsay was really looking forward to getting out of the house—even if it meant their friends got the first glimpse of Will and Lyndsay as a couple. She could only hope that since Kate had already heard, word had gotten around, saving her from the expressions of shock.

She got a text from Will at dinnertime: *Can I pick you up around 8?*

Smiling, she responded: *Oh, this is a formal date?*

I think we should arrive together and shock them all.

Then it's a date. See you then.

Promptly at eight, her doorbell rang. She opened it, enjoying the intent way Will studied the length of her body before whistling. She was wearing a white jean skirt with her cowboy boots, and an orange halter-necked top that left her shoulders bare.

"Darlin', you look great," he said.

She blushed with pleasure at the huskiness in his voice. "Thanks. So do you. I love a Western shirt on a man." And tight jeans and cowboy boots, and that certain way he tipped his Stetson . . .

"It's the pearl snaps," he drawled. "Does it to a woman every time."

She laughed. "Let me get my purse."

"Aren't you going to invite me in? I've never seen your house."

"Oh . . . okay, don't mind the mess." But all she could think was, *Where did I put that copy of my book?*

As he perused her small living room and then the kitchen, she remembered she'd left the book in her office. When they entered her little hallway, she quickly closed the door.

"Storage room," she said nonchalantly. "It's a disaster. I've been going through teaching files, trying to decide what's out of date and what's not." God, she was rambling.

He just smiled at her, that dimple in his chin so deep and masculine. And then he saw her bedroom—at least she'd made the bed. But there were shoes all over the floor.

She shrugged. "I couldn't decide if I should wear sandals or flats, and ended up settling on the cowboy boots."

"You made the right choice."

He actually started to step into her room.

"You don't need to go in there." She slid in front

of him, trying to be playful, when she was really starting to forget *why* he shouldn't go in there.

He braced both arms on the doorjamb over her head and leaned closer. "It's a nice, big bed," he murmured, then pressed a kiss just below her ear, beneath the fall of her hair.

Her eyelids fluttered closed and she swayed toward him. God, he smelled so good, like warm soap and fresh rain. But she stopped herself. "Okay, this is dangerous. Let's go to Tony's."

And she ducked beneath his arm to the sound of his chuckle.

At the front door of Tony's Tavern, Lyndsay took a deep breath.

Will pressed close behind her and whispered, "Should we hold hands? Or should I carry you across the threshold?"

"Stop it," she said, laughing. "Let's just try to be normal."

He cupped her face and kissed her quickly. "Whatever you want."

She blew out a breath. "You need to stop doing that. It's hard to think."

"You're good for my ego. I never knew I had such power over women."

"Liar. You've always known." She turned to push open the door. She wouldn't have taken his hand—it's not like she had to show him off by saying, *See, I can date him, too.* But Will took *her* hand.

The place was crowded, as usual, and lots of

people called a hello or gave them a second glance as they worked their way toward the bar. Tony was there with the other bartender, Lamar Cochrane. Lyndsay didn't bother trying to find a spot; she only worked her way to the far end and stood waiting. Will remained behind her, his hands on her hips. She felt like they were already dancing.

Tony approached them when he had a chance, bringing a couple beers. Then he just eyed them impassively.

Lyndsay smiled. "We're dating. You okay with that?"

"Sure." Then he glanced at Will.

Neither man said a thing, but something passed right over her shoulder between them.

"Okay then," she said brightly. "Let's go try to find a table in the back room."

"Good luck with that," Tony said and turned back to work.

This time Will led, holding her hand again, using his broad shoulders to clear a path. She felt downright feminine, and it was sweet.

It was actually easier than she'd thought to sit down, although they ended up with two stools at the counter that ran along one wall behind the pool table. They had friends there, but people were having their own good time and didn't pay much attention to them.

Will sipped his beer and looked around, then had to lean toward her to be heard. "Telling your brother was pretty easy."

"Kate told him I was going to ask you out. But there's that eyeball-laser thing that shot between you."

He shrugged. "It's a guy thing."

"Then let's talk about what you said at the front door, that you never knew you had power over women. Come on, you've practically been dating since middle school. You had to know you exerted influence of some kind."

"Middle school? Wow, you give me a lot of credit."

"It may have been the age of group dates, but you went on a lot of them, if memory serves me."

He grinned and crossed his arms over his chest. "I did."

"And you were often 'going out' with girls"—she used air quotes—"which meant you were dating even though you technically couldn't go anywhere without your parents driving you."

"True. Ah, the difficult years, when I just wanted to find out what it was like to feel a girl up."

She laughed, then had to wipe her mouth. "Don't make me snort my beer."

"You're so cute when you do it. I'm fond of your snorts already."

God, he was good. Who wouldn't want to go out with him? But why did most women seem to give him up so easily, ruefully but not angrily? Guess she'd find out. And it gave her a pang, but one she forced herself to put away. She was getting him out of her system—*not* keeping him.

"So you must have felt up a girl by eighth grade."

"I did, but don't ask me to kiss and tell. It was a magical experience that still lives in my mind. Who knew girls were so soft and felt so good?"

He looked down at her breasts with some anticipation, and she figured he had a reason to feel that way. She was probably going to be a little easy where he was concerned.

"But how did you know you could have your way when you wanted it? It's such an insecure time, especially for girls."

"I was insecure at first, too."

"I don't believe it!"

"I was. Even after the first girl let me touch the fun parts of her, I thought I'd just been lucky. I always felt like I had to work hard to make girls like me."

"You can't tell me you work hard at that now," she said skeptically.

"Maybe 'work hard' is the wrong way to phrase it, but I don't take women for granted."

"No assuming we'll all fall at your feet?"

He dropped his hand to her bare knee, revealed by her skirt. His thumb made little circles.

"Nope. I think in high school I could have started gettin' a big head about it, but Brittany put me right in my place."

The startled, dismayed expression that came over his face made Lyndsay hold her breath.

He glanced away, then gave her a rueful smile. "Sorry. I didn't mean to bring her up."

"You can tell me anything, Will. She was a part of your life."

"Yeah, but one I don't usually talk about."

He said it with his usual polite friendliness, but she heard the "off limits" warning beneath. She wondered if that "polite friendliness" was a little bit like a mask he always wore. She'd never even seen him lose his temper. And he certainly never talked about Brittany.

She glanced into the open area, where Jess was dancing with Dom. Both were looking her way expectantly, and Lyndsay gave them an exaggerated frown. Will arched a brow at her.

"Jess was there when Kate and I were discussing dating you," Lyndsay said. "Sorry."

"It's okay. I'm glad you asked me out."

"Don't say because you would have gotten around to asking me eventually."

"I never would have said that. Because of Tony, I tried not to think that way about you."

"I know. I did the same thing." But she didn't fool herself into believing he'd once had a crush on her like she'd had on him. "So what have you done in the whole twenty-four hours since I last saw you?"

He took a swig of his beer before answering. "Helped my baby sister move into her summer sublet."

"Really? I'm kind of surprised. She lives in Denver during the school year, so I thought she'd be home."

"So did my mom, who's not taking it all that well. But she's putting up a good front." A frown briefly marred his forehead before fading away. "But it's not like Steph's in a bad part of town—like we have all that many bad parts anyway. She's subletting from Monica, the apartment over her flower shop, since she and Travis just bought a house. Steph'll be practically right above the bakery, living next door to Brooke and Adam. If you can't feel safe next to an ex-Marine and a cowgirl, you can't feel safe anywhere."

Lyndsay smiled. "I know she's been living in a dorm, but she must be pretty excited to have her first place, even if it's only temporary."

"She is. And Monica left most of the furniture for her, so that helped. Now she's in the decorating phase, and I had to leave before that drove me crazy. 'Will, hang this. Will, hold that.'" He shook his head.

"Well, I have news that might distract you. I forgot to mention this last night, but I had an interesting discussion with Mrs. Thalberg the other day about the historical society election. Seems she's been at odds with your grandma over some exhibits—"

"Including the one about my great-grandma's memorabilia. I've heard that over and over."

"Yeah, you have to be sick of this already. But also, the widows were against the expansion of the museum, due to the higher ticket prices. So that's what's going on—and not revenge for a high school slight from the fifties."

"I always knew there must be more to it. But I gotta admit, I don't read the newsletters too closely."

"Shame on you. I won't tell your grandma. And speaking of shame, where's your lapel pin? The one shaped like a pretty hat?" She batted her eyelashes at him.

He patted his shirt pocket. "Oh, darn, I forgot it. And besides, I think everyone knows who I'm voting for."

"I should warn you—I hear something might be coming our way as far as the election goes, and probably during the softball games Monday night. I only hope it won't be too outlandish."

"You mean less outlandish than dressing up an elephant as a mammoth and parading it down Main Street? Less outlandish than leading a protest on behalf of a lingerie store by flinging bras into a tree?"

She laughed. "The widows at their best. I don't *think* we have any more parades in our future, but you never know . . ."

"Enough about other people." He took her hand. "Come on, let's dance."

She followed him out past the pool table, where couples crowded the small area. Sadly, the music remained fast a good long time, reinforcing to each other that they weren't all that great at dancing. Kate's brother Dave Fenelli, a sommelier at their family's restaurant, tried to cut in and steal Lyndsay away, but Will wouldn't have it, to her delight.

And then finally a slow song came on. Last

Friday she'd felt awkward beneath her alcohol buzz, but tonight, she slid easily into his arms, letting him pull her right up against him, his thigh occasionally sliding between hers. For wearing clothes, it was pretty erotic. When he pressed his mouth to her bare shoulder, she could have melted into a puddle of desire. His hand rode low on her back, fingers just touching the curve of her butt. His other hand clasped hers and held it against his chest, and she felt his heart beating fast. With his head near hers, their hair gently touched.

They spent another few hours dancing and talking with friends. Kate arrived, and Lyndsay saw her examining Will when he wasn't looking—then Lyndsay remembered that Kate had been reading her book today. Did Cody really come off as Will? It was the strangest feeling—did Kate like the book? Was she disappointed or impressed? But they couldn't talk about it.

Lyndsay had gotten up early to work, so by midnight, she was struggling to cover her yawns.

Will, holding her hand, leaned near her ear and said, "Let me take you home, darlin'."

She enjoyed the way that endearment rolled off his tongue.

This was the second time they'd left the tavern together, but the first time she'd been drunk and blissfully unaware. Now she couldn't help wondering what he was thinking. Earlier in the evening, he'd made it clear what he was thinking from the moment he'd tried to step into her bedroom. But he was a guy—he was always thinking about that. Sex was about exploring and conquering new territory for them, at least at the beginning. She didn't mind at all being his new passion.

She slid into the pickup, smiling in surprise as Will shut the door for her. "What a gentleman." Then she covered another yawn.

Wearing that adorable crooked smile, he came around the front and got in.

And that was the last thing she remembered—until Will was carrying her up her front walkway. She awoke, drowsy and confused, to find herself snuggled against his chest, his arms behind her back and beneath her knees.

"Will—?" she murmured, lifting her head, feeling dazed, her contacts blurry as she blinked her eyes repeatedly.

"You fell asleep," he murmured against her forehead. "Your purse is on your stomach. Can you reach your keys?"

"Put me down, Will. Honestly, I'm awake." And she yawned again.

"Well, only because I have no choice if we're going to get into the house."

He lowered her legs, and she enjoyed the sensation of briefly sliding along his body.

"Hmm," she said appreciatively, then swayed.

"Hey, you almost dropped your purse," he said, amusement laced through his words.

"What—? Oh, yeah." She felt like she could barely function.

When she came up with the keys, he took them from her and unlocked the door. And then he swung her back up into his arms and headed into the house.

"Will!"

"What? I'm not going to watch you stumble around. I'm going to take you to bed."

Those words should sound erotic, but not like this. "I'm so sorry." She buried her face in his chest and just breathed in the soapy scent of him. "Wait, you can't put me to bed. I've got to take my contacts out."

So he turned away from the bedroom and put her down in the bathroom doorway.

He leaned against the frame to watch her take out her contacts. "So why are you so exhausted? Isn't today a day off for teachers?"

Still feeling bleary and dazed, she opened her contact case and spoke without thinking. "I had to get up early and write all day." And then she held her breath in a little gasp.

He cocked his head and looked at her in the mirror. "Writing? What were you writing?"

She couldn't meet his gaze and was glad she could focus on removing her contacts. "Lots of stuff. Teachers have a lot of paperwork." That wasn't a lie—she didn't want to lie to Will. But if she told him about her book, he'd want to read it, and it was too soon in their relationship for him to know she'd resurrected her long-ago crush on him. She hoped he'd be flattered, but maybe he'd be embarrassed—or even mad.

He cocked his head. "Even after our date last night, you got up early?"

She shrugged and put on her glasses, turning to face him. "Gotta do what we gotta do, right?"

But he was studying her with a bit too much interest, as if he didn't quite believe her but knew it wasn't his place to question her.

"Okay, then I'll let you get some sleep," he said, and leaned forward to give her a quick kiss.

A kiss in her bathroom. Her second date couldn't go any better, she thought with frustration. "I'm sorry, Will. You should stay and have a drink."

"No, it's okay. I got up early, too. Seems we're two people who work too hard."

She followed him to the front door. "I'll see you at the softball game Monday night?"

"Yep. To think you used to forget them, and here you are reminding me."

"I won't forget them anymore, since the widows and your grandma plan to make the next few interesting."

He put a hand to his heart. "I'm hurt. You don't want to watch my athletic brilliance?"

She laughed. "I am looking forward to it immensely. I always do." She caught his sleeve when he would have opened the front door. "Will—" she whispered.

Whatever he heard in her voice made him turn around. She slid her arms around his neck and pulled his head down for a kiss. Drawing her tight against him, he deepened it, taking her mouth hungrily. She could feel the beating of his heart against her ribs, felt his erection against her stomach and rotated her hips against his. His shoulders felt incredible, his neck strong, and his hair, so thick and soft and—

He broke away first, lifting his head. "Go to sleep, darlin'. We have all the time in the world."

But they didn't—she knew that, and she pressed herself harder against him, but only briefly. Then she let him go. She'd have to get used to that.

Chapter 11

At the Silver Creek ball field Monday evening, the sky was deep blue, with not a cloud to mar its perfection. The mountains rose up on either side of the valley as if they were another ring of spectators. But chill evening air had already settled over Valentine Valley, and Lyndsay wore a fleece as she carried a picnic basket across the grass. Rather than sit in the stands, she spread out a blanket where Will would be able to see her from the dugout.

Mrs. Thalberg's banner was still in place, although now there was another one, with Mrs. Sweet's logo of a broad feminine hat and VOTE FOR EILEEN SWEET across the brim. Maybe she thought using her actual photo was vulgar.

"Now this is unexpected."

Lyndsay felt a jolt of pleasure just hearing Will's voice. He was wearing his Tony's Tavern uniform and a ball cap, and he was carrying his mitt. She leaned back on her hands in the grass to gaze up with admiration.

"Hi," she said, feeling almost shy after the abrupt end to their second date.

"Is this all for me?" he asked, squatting down, his forearms resting on his thighs.

"Only if you play well."

"You're a demanding girlfriend."

She felt a little thrill at the term. "You have no idea. And aren't you making an assumption here? I don't think I'd call myself your girlfriend just yet."

She loved the way his eyes seemed to darken and grow heavy when his thoughts turned sensual. He reached out and touched the top of her foot, barely covered by a thin little sandal, and she shivered. He rubbed his fingers along the strap, then up until his hand circled her ankle—like he was going to pull her legs apart.

It shot a trembling heat deep within her belly, and her lips parted as she met his gaze again.

"Hey, none of this in front of kids—my kid in particular."

Lyndsay jerked her head up and saw Kate approaching, wearing a teasing smile. She had on jeans and a Tony's Tavern t-shirt beneath an open zip-up sweatshirt.

At her side, Ethan was tossing a ball repetitively into his mitt. He was grinning, but he didn't do more than glance down at Lyndsay on her blanket before tossing his ball at Will as he rose.

Will caught it. "Just wait until you're old enough

to be on the team. I won't be so easy on you." He gave Lyndsay an intimate smile and turned to jog after Ethan.

Kate sat down beside her, cross-legged, and with a blissful sigh, Lyndsay lay back on the blanket, folded her arms beneath her head, and stared up at the swaying trees framing the blue sky.

"Things are going well, I take it," Kate said, laughter threaded through her voice.

"Hmm, yes. We're taking things slow and easy."

"Three dates in four days? That's slow and easy?"

"Well, Tony's on Saturday couldn't be called a date, since we would have gone there separately anyway. And today? I'm here to support my brother."

"You have a brother on this team? I had no idea. What's his number?"

"I don't know anybody's number," Lyndsay said, closing her eyes.

"What's Will's number?"

"Ten."

"Aha!"

Lyndsay opened one eye. "Are you surprised I know that?"

"I'm not aha-ing about you at all. I think the next skirmish in the historical society election has begun."

Lyndsay sat up and eagerly looked around. Near the stands—and beneath Mrs. Sweet's banner—her granddaughters Emily and Steph had set up a table and were now unboxing tiny items individually wrapped.

Kate and Lyndsay exchanged an eager glance, stood up, and walked toward them.

"Hi, Em, Steph," Lyndsay called.

Steph gave a cheerful smile, but Emily appeared more nervous.

"Whatchya doing?" Kate asked.

"A favor," Emily hedged.

Lyndsay bent over the table to see what they were unpacking, then picked up a sugar cookie that had been frosted in bright green. Written across it were the words *Sweets from Mrs. Sweet*.

Emily sighed. "Grandma Sweet asked for our help."

"Don't act so apologetic," Lyndsay said. "She's your grandma—of course you should help with her campaign."

"Em's worried people will be offended." Steph rolled her eyes. "I keep telling her they're getting free cookies—they won't care. You guys can be the first."

But Ethan, chasing a rolling ball, snatched one first and kept running. "Thanks!" he called.

Laughing, Lyndsay unwrapped her cookie and took a big bite. "Oh, these are as good as always. I think your delicious baking will make lots of people consider their vote more carefully."

"You're just being kind," Emily said, smiling at last. "Grandma had to do something. She'd put up a tasteful display in the lobby about the importance of voting for the historical society president, but we had to point out to her that *locals* needed to be reminded to vote, not tourists." Suddenly alert, she called, "Hi, Grandma!"

Lyndsay turned to see Mrs. Sweet gliding toward them gracefully, wearing a summer dress more suitable for a wedding. Her granddaughter Theresa labored beneath two chair bags slung over her shoulders.

"Good evening, ladies," Mrs. Sweet said, smiling at them all. "I do hope you're enjoying the cookies."

"We are, thank you, ma'am," Lyndsay said.

Mrs. Sweet's sharp gaze focused on her. "I understand you're dating my grandson, William."

"Yes, I am."

"A smart decision on his part."

"You're just saying that to influence my vote, Mrs. Sweet," Lyndsay teased.

"Then you'll be surprised to hear, young lady, that just last week, I was pointing out your character strengths to him."

Lyndsay's mouth fell open, and she glanced helplessly at Kate, whose eyes were wide. "Why— that was very kind of you, ma'am."

Mrs. Sweet sniffed. "I certainly won't hold it against you that your father is foolish enough in his old age to trail around after my opponent."

"Grandma!" Emily said, her voice aghast.

Kate was biting her lip hard, and Lyndsay knew she was desperately trying not to laugh. That wasn't helping her own rising amusement.

"I'm just speaking the truth," Mrs. Sweet answered. "Lyndsay knows that, don't you, dear?"

"I know you're speaking your opinion," Lyndsay said pleasantly. "I can't fault you for that. I just disagree with it, of course. If he and Mrs. Thalberg enjoy each other's company, why should it bother you?"

"You're right, it should not. It has nothing to do with our civic duty to keep the historical society and museum thriving. Now please enjoy another cookie, and consider me when it's time to cast your vote."

Kate finally spoke up. "We always consider before we vote."

Mrs. Sweet nodded and moved away, taking several cookies with her as she went to greet people she knew.

"*Please* take another cookie," Emily said regretfully. "Really, we have plenty. And . . . I don't know what has gotten into my grandmother."

"The pressures of the election," Kate said. "And of course, now we all know that Mrs. Thalberg has taken a man away from her, so she must still resent it."

"Well, she didn't take my dad away from anyone," Lyndsay protested. "But yeah, I'll take another cookie, thanks. You guys have fun!"

Steph winked, but Emily only gave a weak smile. Kate and Lyndsay walked back to the blanket together.

"That was interesting," Kate said in a low voice.

"You'd think after over fifty years, she'd leave resentment behind."

"Yeah, but it's not just high school, remember. They've been getting on each other's nerves for years. This election just seems to be the culmination of it. At least they seem to be fighting fair . . ."

Her voice trailed off as she saw a pickup truck slowly coming across the lawn in reverse. In the bed was Mrs. Thalberg's election sign.

"I don't get it," Kate said. "They have a sign here already."

The pickup parked near the cookie stand, and Mrs. Thalberg slid out of the cab unassisted. Her son Doug—father of Nate, Josh, and Brooke—got out of the driver's seat. He had brown hair going gray and a bushy mustache. His glasses glinted beneath his Stetson. He hurried around the pickup, too late to help his mother. But he took the cane for his wife, Sandy, and offered an arm for her slow descent. Sandy had MS, and though she had occasional flareups that put her in the hospital or a wheelchair, she mostly got around just fine with her cane.

Sandy limped toward her mother-in-law, who was waiting at the rear of the truck. Doug touched his cowboy hat in greeting to Kate and Lyndsay but didn't stop. He lowered the rear door of the pickup to reveal two giant plastic tubs, one piled with two-liter bottles of soda, and the other—a keg of beer.

Lyndsay and Kate looked at each other and burst out laughing.

"I know, I know," Sandy began, "but—"

"I thought it was a good idea," Mrs. Thalberg said placidly. "A ball game on a beautiful night makes everybody thirsty, don't you agree?"

And sure enough, people were leaving the cookie table—with a cookie in hand, of course— and heading right for the cups of beer Doug was already pouring. And printed on the cup? *Vote Thalberg.*

The other two widows, Mrs. Palmer and Mrs. Ludlow, strolled up with their various friends and relations in tow. Mrs. Ludlow went to talk to Mrs. Sweet, but Mrs. Sweet never came near the pickup, of course.

Beer and cookies in hand, Lyndsay and Kate headed back to the blanket, surprised that the first inning had already passed. Luckily, there was no score.

"Now that we're alone again," Kate said, "I can tell you what I've been dying to say all day—I loved your book!"

Lyndsay gasped in delight. "Oh, I'd hug you if I didn't want to spill beer down your back."

"What book?"

Some of the beer did spill as Lyndsay whirled around. It was Jessica, carrying her own beer and cookie, catching up with them.

"Tell her," Kate said. "She won't tell anyone else. She's a reporter—she knows how to keep a source quiet."

"She's a reporter! They disseminate news."

"What news?" Jessica asked. "What book?"

Lyndsay hesitated, then happily admitted, "I've written a book."

"Wow, I didn't know you were a writer," Jessica said. "We have even more in common. And you're a lot more private than I thought, to keep that from another writer."

"I know, I know, it just works better for me that way."

Kate piped in, "She's leaving out the good news. Her book was bought by a major publisher and will be in bookstores in just a couple weeks."

Jessica's mouth dropped open before she could help it. "Oh my God, that's wonderful. You must be so excited! I've got to ask—how long did it take you to sell?"

"I've been serious about writing for the last eight years."

"You never gave up—good for you! What do you write?"

"Romance."

"One of my favorite reading habits! Oh, wait, you should have told me earlier so we could plan when to run the best promotional interview. A romance writer from Valentine Valley! There's no better hook than that."

"No, we can't do that yet," Lyndsay said. "I had my publicist hold off contacting the *Gazette* so I could talk to you personally. It's got to be a secret for now." She looked all around, but they were still alone as they stood around her blanket. "Nobody knows but the two of you and my family. It's got to stay that way for a little while."

"But why? Promotion is important so you can get a lot of sales the first week. That's how you make lists!"

"I know, I know, but as I've already told my family, I'm just a newbie romance writer, without the print run to make it big. For now, I just want this kept quiet until school is out. That way, by the time we return in the fall, the worst of the questions and shock will be over. Hopefully any of my squeamish parents will let their outrage go."

"Outrage? Over a romance?"

"It happens."

"Okay, I promise I won't say a thing—until you give me the word."

Lyndsay made herself relax, and the three of them sat down on her blanket. Then she got to have the joy of hearing someone other than her editor wax poetic about why she liked *A Cowboy in Montana*. Although Kate steered clear of mentioning who the hero was based on, Lyndsay knew she'd have to ask her about it another time. Was it obvious? Or could she breathe easily when friends and family eventually read it?

Lyndsay's happiness felt complete, here in this moment, sitting with her girlfriends, who finally knew her secret, and watching with satisfaction as Will ran hard for home plate.

Oh, she hoped he'd be sliding into home plate in the bedroom pretty soon . . .

Will was pleasantly sweaty and tired by the time the game was over. Tony's Tavern had beaten Hal's Hardware and was undefeated so far this season. And Lyndsay waited on a blanket just for him, a picnic feast all on her own.

Of course, before he could get to her, he had to say hello to his grandma, who was taking this vote way too seriously. Preserving the history of Valentine Valley was important to her, so she *should* take it seriously, but Will found it hard to be forced to publicly choose sides in a town as small as Valentine Valley.

Even Mrs. Thalberg wouldn't expect him to vote against his own grandma. He stopped to say hi to the Thalbergs first, although he declined a beer.

"Guess you'd take one if the cup didn't promote my mother," Doug Thalberg said, smiling.

Will grinned. "I might. But that's okay. Lyndsay brought some goodies for me."

"And you can have cookies," Sandy pointed out. "Your sisters did a wonderful job."

"Ah, so you tried one—didn't your tongue burn?"

They all laughed, and Will was glad most people weren't taking the campaigning as seriously as the two ladies running. Then he visited with his sisters and grandma. He had a cookie before Steph spoke.

"Lyndsay was chatting with us before the game. That was cool of her to bring a picnic basket for you."

Will rubbed his hands together. "Yep, I can't wait to see what's inside."

"Probably something sinful," Steph said. "You know she loves her food."

"William, I might have offended your young lady," Grandma Sweet said.

He saw his sisters exchange a glance. "And why would you have done that?" he asked curiously.

Grandma sighed. "I do believe this election brings out my competitive nature. I had no idea."

Will tried to keep a straight face.

"I implied that her father was foolish for seeing Rosemary. It was not my place to pass judgment— even if I do believe it is foolish."

"Okaay, I'll tell her you regret it."

"Thank you." Then she put on a big, unnatural smile and went to see another potential voter.

Emily leaned close and whispered, "She said nice things to Lyndsay, too, don't worry."

"I won't," he whispered back.

After a few more minutes, he joined the three young women at the blanket. Kate and Jessica got up without even coordinating it.

"Gotta run," Kate said. "Ethan has homework. You teachers are such slave drivers, even near the end of school."

Lyndsay shrugged. "Gotta pass those tests. But he will. He's a smart kid."

Kate glowed at the compliment. "We'll talk later," she said to Lyndsay, raising her eyebrow meaningfully.

Jessica waved. "Have a good evening, you guys."

And then it was just the two of them.

With a sigh, Will stretched out in front of Lyndsay, rested his head back in her lap, and closed his eyes. "Aah."

He heard her chuckle even as she pulled his ball cap off and raked her fingers back through his hair.

"You poor baby," she crooned, "working so hard to triumph over the other team. All of your sacrifices were certainly worth it."

"Oh, I know. I have a brush burn on my thigh from sliding into home." She didn't say anything, so he opened one eye. "Want to kiss it better?"

She laughed and briefly covered his eyes with her hands. "Are you hungry?"

He took her hands and held them to his chest. "I did have a cookie, but only one. I'm a hungry ball player. Whadiya have?"

She leaned over the basket and began to rummage through. "A very traditional romantic basket, the kind I'd prepare if you were taking me to see Shakespeare in the Park."

He eyed her skeptically. "Do you like Shakespeare in the Park?"

"I do. So you're saying we won't have that in common?"

"Oh, I'll take you if you'd like to go, and I'll enjoy spending every moment with you. The Shakespeare part? Not so much."

"Shakespeare is an acquired taste, I'll admit. And much of it is not panicking when you don't understand every word. You have to let it wash over you, take in the action, and you'll understand the gist of it."

"If you say so."

She began holding items up. "We have wine—and since I'm assuming you didn't drink a Thalberg beer in front of your grandma—"

"You're correct."

"—then you'll be thirsty. I brought grapes and strawberries, several kinds of cheese and crackers, some veggies and dip, and shrimp cocktail on ice."

He rolled up onto his elbow to look at the spread before him. "Lyndsay, this is pretty amazing. Thanks for taking the time to do all this."

She smiled and blushed, and he liked the way just a simple compliment pleased her. He sat up but still stayed close enough so that his right knee brushed her left, and they kept all the food in front of them. For a while they just chatted about their respective workdays, then his grandma's second-hand attempt at an apology. Lyndsay accepted with better grace than his grandma probably deserved. They grazed on the delicious food, watching the kids play on the playground and the last of the softball players having a beer at the Thalberg pickup, along with their cookies from Sugar and

Spice. His brothers made sure to tell him they'd be just thrilled to finish moving the last of the dams that evening, and he promised he'd do the same for them another day. The sun had gone behind the mountains, but the sky was still a clear, beautiful blue. They pulled on jackets but didn't make any attempt to leave.

Lyndsay asked him about how they irrigated the hay fields, and it launched another discussion about water rights, and how the water commissioner regulated how much spring runoff they could divert across their fields. Hay fields needed to be flooded at least twice before cutting, and it took weeks of moving portable dams around to get the water to flow just where they needed it to be.

Sometimes women were bored listening to the description of his work as a cowboy—they expected it all to be the glamour of riding horseback across vast fields or herding cattle across the beauty of the mountains. He did that, too. But there were a lot of dirty, messy jobs to be done on a ranch. Lyndsay seemed truly interested in all of it.

Gradually, the sky faded toward gray. Grandma Sweet and her cookies, and Mrs. Thalberg and her beer, had gone home, the kids and parents had disappeared on a school/work night, and it was just Lyndsay and Will lying side by side to see the first wink of a star.

Will came up on his elbow and gently feathered her bangs across her forehead, then followed a lock of hair down behind her ear. She regarded him with such gentle trust that it gave him a moment's pause. But he let his faint concern go, leaning down to give her the softest kiss, and then another, enjoying the sweetness of her parted lips. His hand had come to rest on her stomach, and without realizing it, he began to slide it up her rib cage. He felt her take a deep breath, which lifted her rib cage even harder into his hand, but he stopped just at the soft lower curve of her breast and she let out her breath.

With a sigh, he kissed her forehead. "The park officially closed at dusk. I guess we don't want Sheriff Buchanan kicking us out for making out like teenagers."

He sat up, taking her hand and drawing her up, too. He put his hands in her hair to brush it back from her face but ended up bringing her mouth to his again. He permitted himself just one kiss. It was difficult to stop when he gazed into her flushed face and dreamy eyes. He helped her to her feet, and together they folded the blanket and put it back inside the basket with their leftovers. Taking her hand, he led her toward the parking lot. Their two cars were the last ones there.

"Will you be okay driving home?" he asked.

"I didn't have too much to drink, and you only had the glass of wine."

"Then we're okay. I can't talk you into pretending otherwise so I can be forced to take you home?"

She smiled. "It's a school night."

"Teachers," he said, shaking his head. When

they reached her car, he said, "So I'll see you at the ranch after school on Wednesday?"

"I'll be there, and I'll try to arrive before the kids in case you have any questions."

"I looked over all the information and guidelines you sent. I think the only trouble I'll have is stopping. I like talking about what I do."

"So you've talked to a group of kids before?"

"Well, no, but it can't be that difficult, right?"

She bit her lip to keep from laughing, and he wondered if he should be more worried.

Chapter 12

Lyndsay sat down on her couch and called Kate when she got home. "Now this isn't what you think," she said when Kate answered. "I don't want to sigh dreamily over my picnic date with Will—even though I could."

"Of course you could," Kate answered, amused.

"But since Jessica interrupted us when we were talking about my book, I couldn't ask, but now I can. What did you think about my hero?"

"Cody was very sexy and funny and intense. You certainly got the cowboy details down right."

"Kate, you know what I mean! Did he come off totally like Will?"

Kate paused. "I'll be honest. I already knew the truth, so yeah, I could see the resemblance."

Lyndsay closed her eyes and sighed.

"But—and this is a big but—you'd already told me. I honestly don't think I'd have realized it otherwise."

"Really? You're not just saying that?"

"A lot of guys have sandy blond hair and hazel eyes. A lot of cowboys must have great bodies. And yeah, he's friendly and funny and a flirt—but again, I've read a lot of romances. There are a lot of heroes like that."

"Okay, but you know that scene where he takes his girlfriend's grandma's earrings and has them made into a necklace—"

"That was so romantic!" Kate interrupted.

"I know! Well, that one scene is sort of like something Will did once. For Brittany."

"Oh," Kate said in a quieter voice.

"I didn't realize what I was doing at the time. It was during revisions, and my editor suggested I needed a romantic 'grand gesture'—her words—and the idea just came to me. This was before I even realized that Cody was a lot like Will. The details are a little different—it was her grandmother's ring rather than earrings—but still. It just worked so perfectly in the book. As a writer, I take bits and pieces of my life or the things I've experienced and use them all the time, after altering them, of course. A funny line someone said, a favorite board game of my family, stuff like that. I guess Will's romantic thoughtfulness stuck with me longer than I thought. But now . . . I don't know, Will's a little more . . . sensitive about Brittany than I thought he'd be."

"How do you mean? She died a long time ago."

"I know, sixteen years this spring. But he accidentally brought up her name himself, and he was shocked and upset by it. He said he didn't like to talk about her. I knew he'd taken her death hard for a couple months, but by the fall, he was dating again and seemed himself. I never thought it would still be so painful for him. It's a side of him I never imagined, you know?"

"Well, this is why we date, to learn stuff about each other."

Lyndsay sighed. "I guess I'll just have to hope that by the time he gets around to reading the book—*if* he gets around to reading it, because it is a romance, after all—he won't see himself in the pages, since he'll already have moved on to date someone else."

"Wait, wait—what did you say? That was really convoluted. Do you already assume you two are finished in a month or two?"

Lyndsay stared at the phone in surprise. "Of course I do. I'm not stupid. That's his pattern. And I'm just dating him to finally put my high school crush to rest."

"We're all about breaking patterns, are we not?"

"*I* am, but not him. This is *Will* we're talking about. The only woman he dated longer than two months was Brittany, and they were probably each other's 'first love.'"

"He said that?"

"Well, no, I'm just assuming by his behavior when the subject of her came up." She hesitated, frowning. "You know, I never thought of it that way, that she was the only one he dated a long time. It was a year and a half or two years, wasn't it?"

"I don't remember. You two were a grade behind me, after all."

"Hmm. Well, anyway, I can't change the scene in the book. Thanks for making me feel better about the hero. As long as people aren't pointing at me on the street and laughing, guess I'll be okay."

"They won't do that. You'll get lots of compliments, trust me. And I'll have Tony read it, especially that one scene you're talking about. I'm sure he'll be able to reassure you, too. It's a really good book, Lynds, very romantic and happily-ever-after."

"That's what we like." Quietly, she added, "Thanks, Kate. That means a lot to me. I'm so glad you've come home for good."

Kate cleared her throat, but her voice broke a bit as she said, "Me, too. Talk to you later."

Wednesday afternoon, Lyndsay arrived at the Sweetheart Ranch before her students did. Rain had passed by in the morning, but now the sky was overcast. Though she'd changed into jeans, hiking boots, and a t-shirt back at school, she was glad she'd brought a fleece. She parked her car and got out, only to find Will's parents standing at the corral, watching Will riding in the distance.

Faith smiled at her. "Hi, Lyndsay. I've promised Will I won't embarrass him by hanging around, but I had to see him with a group of kids."

"It's gonna be interesting," Lyndsay said. "I really appreciate you all allowing the kids to come here. Some of them are from ranches themselves, of course, but others are townies like me. I'm sure I'll be learning something, too."

Joe said, "Will's good with the horses, so you've got the best."

Will's horse trotted toward them, its brown coat gleaming with patches of gold hair near his rib cage. Lyndsay felt a little light-headed at the beautiful image Will made, perfect control and harmony with the horse, masculine, with a flannel shirt over his t-shirt, his hat shadowing his face but for the square shape of his jaw with the sexy cleft in the chin.

And then she remembered his parents standing right next to her, and she felt a little flustered and foolish.

Will lifted a hand as he reined in and the horse danced near the fence. "Hey, Lynds, your kids here yet?"

"Not yet. Do you want them here, near the horse pasture?"

"Naw, I thought we'd start in the barn for to-day's lesson. I'll bring Silver here in with me. Meet you over there."

Lyndsay walked with his parents along the corral to approach the barn, a huge, two-story wooden building that might have had old beginnings but had been renovated sometime in the recent past. Inside were a dozen horse stalls, all with their doors open. There were several "people" doors ajar, and she could see into the tack room and what seemed to be an office.

Two dogs bounded out to greet her, both white collie mixes, one with black patches and the other with brown. Lyndsay bent down to pet them as one tried to lean against her legs and the other circled excitedly.

"The black mottled is Boomer, and the brown is Patton," Joe said. "They're as good with kids as they are with animals."

"Good to know, thanks."

"I'll be interested in meeting your group," he continued. "I do a lot of work at the high school with an organic garden. Be good to get them interested."

"Then now's your chance. I think the first are arriving."

It took two SUVs and a pickup to bring all ten kids. After putting several horses in their stalls, Will moved among the newcomers easily, meeting the parents before they left, introducing himself to each of the kids individually. Joe Sweet did the same thing, and Lyndsay found herself standing back, watching with Faith.

"He's a special young man," Faith murmured.

Lyndsay knew the woman's concerned-mom eyes were focused on Will.

"Sometimes I worry about him—but what mother doesn't, right?" Faith added.

She brightened her voice at the end, but Lyndsay wasn't fooled. She wondered why Faith should be worried, when it seemed Will was a confident man who loved his work and had lots of friends. Okay, he wasn't the settling-down type, but Lyndsay wasn't sure that was something to waste your time worrying over. You couldn't change a man—not even his mom could.

Lyndsay knew better than to even say hi to Ethan unless he initiated the conversation. He was a good kid, but at fourteen, he got embarrassed easily.

Matias, the young man she was helping with his science fair project, greeted her shyly. He seemed a little in awe of Will, which she understood. Sometimes Will just seemed larger than life. Ethan was Matias's mentor, the eighth grade "big brother" to seventh-grader Matias. She liked watching Ethan include the younger boy with his friends, and though Matias didn't talk that much, he glowed with the feeling of being included.

Then at last Will raised his arms and his voice to gather everyone's attention. His parents left, his mother obviously reluctant. Lyndsay hung back, there for moral support and guidance only. Will brought his horse Silver forward, holding him by the halter as he began to talk, starting with the fact that they didn't have a breeding program at the Sweetheart; they bought their horses saddle-broke already. He talked about the breeds, focusing on the American Quarter Horse, which so many ranchers used as cow ponies. To her surprise, he betrayed some nervousness by talking a little too fast and even rambling a bit, going off topic. He'd figure it out eventually.

While he talked, Lyndsay enjoyed the sound of his voice and learning about horses, but at the back of the crowd, she could see when trouble was beginning to brew. The ranch kids, who you'd think might be bored, were far more respectful and attentive. But she had a couple of townies in her group, whose parents had moved from larger communities to Valentine for its small-town flavor and morals. They'd put their boys in 4-H to learn about ranching—and the boys weren't happy about it.

Alex's black hair was swept back off his forehead and hung to his shoulders. He was wearing sunglasses, even in the shade of the barn. Logan's brown hair was buzzed on the sides but left longish on top, and he'd adopted a perpetual scowl of boredom. They stood at the back of the group, occasionally whispering something to each other, and Will was simply ignoring them.

Alex got out his cell phone, and his fingers started flying. He said something to Logan, the two grinned, then Alex lowered his phone to his side. Logan pulled his out, too, but didn't glance at it.

Silver suddenly flattened his ears and bared his teeth. Will glanced at him in surprise, then put a hand on his neck and said something softly, but Silver proceeded to stamp his hoofs and swish his tail back and forth.

"Why don't you kids step back," Will said. "I'm not sure why he's so agitated, but let's give him some space."

Silver was breathing heavily by this point, and Will talked gently to him, rubbing his neck and remaining so calm that Lyndsay could hardly tell he was concerned. But she thought his face reddened as whispers and giggles spread among the kids.

Lyndsay looked at those two cell phones, still clutched in the hands of the triumphant boys. She was standing in the back and couldn't use The Glare, which teachers had long mastered from the beginning of time. So she approached the two boys and spoke quietly.

"Are you using the Mosquito ringtone?" she asked.

Alex jumped, obviously so involved in his prank that he hadn't heard her approach. "Uh, Ms. De Luca, I don't know what you're—"

"Stow it. Being a bully toward a poor horse isn't cool. Turn off the phones. And isn't the end-of-the-year dance coming up? Logan, I heard you asked Melissa. What a shame you might not be able to go. Alex, I understand your mom signed up to be a chaperone."

They quickly turned off their phones and shoved them in their pockets. Arms folded across their chests, they sullenly kept their gazes on Will.

Silver had gone docile again, and Will went on with his talk. Soon he opened it up for questions, and that seemed to visibly relax him.

Until Matias asked about the helicopter.

Will kept smiling, but Lyndsay could have sworn he'd tensed up a bit. Just as he'd done with her, he explained the various uses of a helicopter on a ranch, then ended with, "But we're doing a unit on horses, not helicopters. Next week we'll do some horseback riding after we talk about how to saddle and care for a horse."

"Why can't we ride the helicopter?" Alex asked.

The kids waited silently, expectantly.

"Sorry, we don't give rides. We just use it for work."

"Okay, guys," Lyndsay called, "I hear your parents approaching. See you tomorrow at school."

As the last car left in a carpooling line from the barn, kicking up dirt and gravel, Will stood watching them, thumbs in his jean pockets, his expression pensive.

She was smiling, pleasantly surprised at how patient he'd been, how genial in the face of unexpected problems. She'd never thought of him as great dad material, but he was.

She held back a little sigh. If he couldn't last longer than two months with a woman, it was pretty apparent he didn't plan to be a dad. And it was such a shame. Much as she dealt with other people's kids all day, she wanted her own desperately. A woman heading toward thirty-four had to know that about herself, and she knew.

She tucked her arm through his and rested her head on his shoulder. "I think you did a great job."

"For my first time, you mean. I don't know how you do it. What was going on with Alex and—what's-his-name?"

"Logan. You'll get their names eventually."

"Yeah. After Silver got agitated, I saw you talking to them, and then like magic, he settled right down."

"Have you ever heard of a Mosquito ringtone? Most people over thirty can't hear it, but kids can."

"A ringtone? I read that they developed it to play over loudspeakers to keep teenagers from loitering by stores."

"Then they turned it into a ringtone. The boys were calling each other quite deliberately to see what would happen, and Silver could hear it. Not me. Guess I'm too old."

"Me neither. I didn't even see what was going on," he said, shaking his head in disgust.

"You were focused on Silver—as you had to be."

"But you focused on the kids, too. I don't know how you teachers keep track of everything. If you hadn't been here . . ."

"You'd have been fine," she said with a chuckle. "I think you taught the newbies a lot—Matias was certainly impressed!—and the old hands learned some tricks."

"The old hands?" he said, looking down at her, a smile turning up one corner of his mouth. "You make them sound ancient instead of thirteen."

"And fourteen, don't forget. So, can you do this again next week?"

"Sure, and I promise to keep a better eye on the boys. Guess I wasn't above a prank or two at their age."

"But I bet not a prank that would bother an innocent animal."

He rocked back on his heels and glanced at Silver. "You're probably right about that. Maybe you can give me more pointers before then. I was only thinking I had to be prepared about horses, and that was the *easy* part."

"You were very prepared about the horses. I can see the kids are really excited to ride."

"Are you? I've never even asked if you've ridden."

"I've been on a horse a time or two. But I'm certainly no expert."

"Then one of these days, you'll have to show me what you got. But maybe not at this moment."

With his body, he walked her backward until she came up against the barn, pinned in place by his hips pressed hard to hers. She forgot about where they were, forgot about taking things slowly and drawing it out. She simply clung to him, letting his strong arms hold her up. His hands slid down her back and cupped her butt, pulling her even harder against him. She let her head drop back. He swept moist kisses down her neck, and she sighed and burrowed into him.

He murmured into her hair, "Perhaps there's something you can help me with. We could sort the equipment up in the hayloft."

"Sort the equipment?" she echoed, dazed.

"Don't you want to see what's up there? It's not hay."

"Now that's tempting." She gasped as he lightly bit where her neck met her shoulder. His day-old beard scraped her sensitive skin. "What's even more tempting is I've never been in a hayloft."

"Ever?"

"Ever."

"Well, it's an experience every young woman should have. Now go climb the ladder and I'll make very certain you don't fall down."

But he kissed her again, and before she knew it, she was like a languid rag doll in his arms as he guided her toward the ladder. Dizzy, she turned and began to climb, knowing he was watching her from just below. The hayloft had shelves along the sides, and in the center—heaps of fabric, different colors and thicknesses, with various buckles and Velcro straps protruding.

When Will was standing at her side, she gave him a curious glance.

"Horse blankets," he explained. "Some are for warming, some for cooling, some for flies. These are newly washed, and I haven't folded them away in their bins yet . . . what a perfect opportunity."

And then he gave her a gentle push backward, and she grabbed hold of him and pulled him down with her. He landed partially sprawled atop her, but he'd caught himself so she didn't have the impact of his weight. She wrapped her arms around him and pulled him tighter, and he settled on top of her.

He covered her mouth with his, slanting his head, tasting deep within her. She moaned, arching into him, then gasping when she felt his hand at her waistline, beneath her t-shirt.

He kissed her cheek, murmuring, "Was that a yes or no gasp?"

"Yes. Oh, please, yes."

But he was so slow, as if his aim was counting her ribs individually. His mouth was moving down her neck, his hand up her torso, and when at last he cupped her breast through her bra, she clenched his leg tight between her own. But it wasn't enough. As he teased her nipple through the thin, lacy fabric, she spread her legs wide so that he could settle deeper against her. She wanted to moan at the tantalizing pressure against her most sensitive place, but it was still broad daylight outside—anyone could come into the barn and hear them. She muffled her cries against his shoulder, shuddering when he rolled his hips against hers.

She dug her heels into the wool blankets and pushed back against him. It wasn't enough. She needed to feel his skin against hers, so she reached down his back and pulled both his shirts up as far as she could. He braced himself on one hand so she could pull them off his head and one arm, then he tossed them aside.

And she was able to see that gorgeous chest up close, the chest she'd seen on display in "The Men of Valentine Valley" calendar or on hot summer days when they'd all been hanging out. He had the pecs and abs of an athlete—of a cowboy. She spent a moment just running her hands across his skin, feeling the scattering of dark blond hair, then lightly touched his nipples.

He trembled. "Lyndsay—"

She lifted her head and licked him, feeling the pebble-hardness. When he moaned, she put her hand against his lips and met his half-closed eyes.

"Shh," she whispered.

"Let's see how quiet you can be, then."

And he pulled her shirt up. She lifted her upper body, and the shirt came off easily. But he didn't pause to admire, just held her up with one hand while he quickly unclasped her bra.

She arched a brow at his expertise, but he only shrugged, too intent as he lifted the white lace away from her skin. She wanted to hold him again, to feel his hot skin against hers, but he kept himself propped on one elbow, staring down at her with such admiration and need that she didn't have a moment to wonder how she compared to all the other women he'd been with. Of course, she'd been with several men, but no one had ever been able to compare with Will.

And maybe that was one of the reasons she'd never found the right man to marry. Was she always subconsciously comparing them to him? But surely that was only physical.

And then he bent his head to her breast and paused just above it, glancing up at her beneath light brown eyelashes, as if waiting for permission.

She pulled his head down and bit her lip to keep from crying out when he took her nipple deep into his mouth and sucked. She shuddered beneath him, hips grinding into his as he licked and nipped and then sucked her deep again. She arched up against him, feeling mindless as she descended into a heightened sense of desire, her nerve endings fairly zapping as they came to life. He moved to her other breast, and with this one he became as light as a butterfly alighting just on the tip with a flick of his tongue, over and over. And then his hand clasped her other breast and caressed it.

She lifted her head and put her mouth into his hair, whispering, "I know we're practically out in the open, that any of your family could come in. But I need you, Will. I need you."

He pulled her up onto her knees, and they kissed passionately, naked skin to naked skin. Then his hands dropped to her jeans and unbuttoned and unzipped.

Forehead to forehead, he met her eyes with urgency. "Are you on the pill?"

"You bet I am," she said with a grin.

He briefly closed his eyes as if in thanksgiving. "And I have a condom. We're good to go."

While he still kissed her, he tormented her with his fingers down inside her jeans, touching her lace underwear, just dipping beneath, until she had to clutch his hot shoulders or sink right into a puddle.

With strong hands, he slid her jeans right over her hips, taking her underwear, too. He paused the briefest moment, while her clothing hung just beneath the fullness of her hips, just covering what she most wanted him to take, as if he were torturing himself.

She pushed them down to her knees herself, then sank onto her elbows, lifting both legs high. He unlaced her boots, then pulled everything off until she was naked, but he kept her legs together with one big hand, as if silently telling her what he needed. Slowly, he tipped her legs toward her, and she felt the fingers of his other hand slide gently between her thighs, teasing, tickling, as she trembled and writhed. His gaze darted repeatedly between her breasts and her thighs, as slowly, slowly, his finger moved ever closer to what she so desperately needed him to touch.

At last he just touched the moist center of her. She held her breath, afraid she'd scream, her back arched with the tension of hovering on the edge of such perfect pleasure.

And then he slid his finger inside her, and she clasped both hands over her mouth to cover her moan. He released her ankles and spread her knees, his chest rising and falling rapidly with his heavy breathing. His wet finger traced her, dipping inside and back out, circling, touching her clitoris softly, then circling harder. He came down at her side, leaning over to take her breast into his mouth again, and it wasn't long before she lost her mind completely, fading into the whirlwind of pleasure until it crashed over her and receded, leaving her shuddering.

At last she opened her eyes to see him up on his elbow leaning over her, a sweet, sexy smile of awareness on his face—he damn well knew what he could do to a woman.

"What are you waiting for?" she whispered as demandingly as she could.

He jumped to his feet and began to unbuckle and unzip. Lyndsay came to her knees and pushed his hands out of the way, her head tilted so she could meet his eyes. Without looking away, she tugged at the waistband of his jeans, bringing them slowly down over his hips, catching his briefs with her fingers to bring them along, too. When they dropped around his feet, she put her hands on his thighs and leaned forward to pleasure him. He arched and threw his head back, and by his ragged breathing, she knew what it cost him to keep silent. At last he pushed her away, and when she would have helped him with the condom, he did it himself.

"Come on and ride me, cowboy," she said, then gave a deep chuckle.

He came down on top of her and she welcomed him against her. Hands braced on either side of her shoulders, he teased her with his erection, sliding against her, dipping briefly then moving away, until she began that slow climb to bliss again. She did her own teasing, cupping his chest, lifting her head to lick his nipples, until at last, with a moan buried against her mouth, he sank deep inside her. He held still for one exquisite moment so that she could feel the fullness of him. And then he started to move, thrusting strongly, then gently, altering his pace and his hips, so that her body never knew what he would do next. She felt fractured and desperate, clutched him to her, lifted her hips to meet his as if she could silently show him what he did to her.

When he came to a complete stop to lavish attention on her breasts, she clutched his ass tight with her hands to urge him on.

"Impatient," he said lightly, before concentrating again on her nipple.

When she was quivering with anticipation and need, whispering his name over and over, he started to move again, deepening his rhythm. They were slick with heated perspiration from being in the loft, and from being locked together. They moved as one, finding the pleasure, taking it higher, until at last Lyndsay found her climax and shuddered down through it, leaving her a sated, exhausted heap of contentment. After a few more thrusts, Will joined her over the edge, burying his face in her neck as he slowly sank against her, into her.

The silent moment seemed to stretch out, and she let herself touch his warm, moist back and slide her hands into his damp hair. The weight of him felt . . . right and good. Being with him so intimately touched a place inside her she hadn't imagined, a sweet place that made her ache to feel even closer to him.

"Where's Will?" called a man down below.

Wide-eyed, Lyndsay covered her mouth so that

not a sound would escape. Will lifted his shoulders and stared down at her, his reckless grin almost infuriating her.

He mouthed, "Chris."

"I don't know. Lyndsay's car is still here. They're probably off somewhere."

"Daniel," Will mouthed.

She closed her eyes as if she could shut out the world. At least it wasn't his parents.

As if on some kind of psychic wave, Chris said, "Mom said dinner'll be ready soon. Should we call Will?"

"Naw, leave 'em alone. It's not like he makes it to dinner regularly."

And then their voices began to fade as they left the barn, still chatting.

Lyndsay's tense body went boneless beneath him. "I can't breathe," she whispered against his ear.

He lifted himself off and to the side, gathering her against him.

She started to push away. "We need to get dressed."

"Just stay still. Let's wait for the bell before we start making a racket."

"Bell?"

"Dinner bell. My mom's old-fashioned that way. Then we'll know we won't be interrupted again. So just stay here, all hot and sweaty, up against me."

She *was* hot and sweaty—they were both perspiring in the humid warmth of the hayloft. But she enjoyed being flush against him, feeling the mellow thud of his heart as it slowed down, enjoying his erection still hard against her hip.

"So, have you ever done this up here before?" she asked in a soft voice.

He eyed her speculatively, as if trying to decide if she meant it. "I live on a ranch—every teenage boy tries to get a girl alone in the hayloft."

"I'm so easy that way."

He laughed softly. "I do like that about you."

She turned her head to look into his warm hazel eyes. He rested his head on his extended arm, and his other hand seemed to want to span her diaphragm, fingers curled on her rib cage, thumb riding between her breasts.

"So . . ." she began, trying not to think arousing thoughts when his brothers were so close at hand, "what should we talk about? Because if I lay still, I'll fall blissfully asleep."

"And your snoring would bring my brothers running?"

She elbowed him in the stomach, satisfied at his playful grunt. "I don't snore."

"I'll have to find that out for myself," he said, kissing her cheek, then gently biting her earlobe.

She felt him remove the condom. Closing her eyes, she whispered huskily, "Come on, we need something to distract us. Anything exciting happen today?"

"Well, you heard about the anonymous flyer that mysteriously appeared at every store all over town, didn't you?"

She eyed him curiously, almost nose to nose. "I was in school all day and then came directly here. What flyer?"

"This you'll want to hear, since you love books. Someone wanted the whole town to know that we have an anonymous author in our midst."

Lyndsay was positive that all the color must have leached out of her face. Thank God for the humid heat up there in the barn rafters. She kept still, concentrating on her even, if shallow, breathing, then said very casually, "Anonymous author? What do you mean? I thought you meant the flyer was anonymous."

"It was. Hell, maybe the anonymous author thought up this marketing strategy. Regardless, the flyer said that everyone should keep an eye out for the upcoming debut of a local author, and there'll be more hints to follow. You know how we love a good mystery around here."

All she could do was nod.

Who'd decided to play around with her secret?

Chapter 13

Will didn't blame Lyndsay for being all stiff and nervous lying naked up in the hayloft when his brothers had been right below them. But she'd been a good sport and hadn't thrown on her clothes, as if their relationship was a dirty secret. But although he'd tried to soothe her with town gossip, she still seemed unsettled.

But at least she was still naked. Her skin glowed in the gloom. Her nipples were dark, the line of hair between her thighs as dark brown as her highlighted hair used to be. He wanted to pet every part of her, but he sensed she was no longer in the mood.

But she was still naked.

She'd been incredible, daringly agreeing to their tryst in the hayloft, accepting whatever he'd wanted to do—initiating incredible pleasure on her own. No wonder his hard-on lingered—he couldn't stop thinking about what they'd done together.

To keep himself from sliding inside her again, he thought about his first experience teaching. He felt like he'd rushed and stuttered at first, but the kids had been pretty patient—except for Alex and Logan, who'd thought it funny to hurt a horse's ears.

And Will had been clueless. He'd been surprised by Silver's behavior, but he'd thought he would eventually figure out the reason. Then he'd seen Lyndsay approach the kids at the back and speak quietly to the two teenage boys. Though the boys had looked sullen, they'd obeyed her instantly, and Silver had calmed right down. She had that authoritative vibe of a teacher, and he'd liked seeing her use it.

The sound of the dinner bell ringing in the distance brought him out of his reverie.

Lyndsay stared up at him. "So . . . your brothers are definitely heading to dinner?"

"I haven't heard them by the barn in a while. There's no reason for them to come back here."

To his delighted surprise, she rolled him onto his back and straddled his thighs.

"Do you have another condom?"

His body stirred to life under her deliberate, hungry stare. "You bet I do."

This time it was her turn to ride the cowboy, and he loved the way her breasts bounced and her hair fell down around her shoulders. It was erotic to watch himself disappear inside her. And when at last she collapsed on his chest, he held her close, stroking down the sleek bumps of her spine.

He'd spent a lot of years deliberately not thinking about Lyndsay as someone to date, had closed his mind away from sexual thoughts about her. Now he wondered what the hell he'd been thinking. She made him laugh; she made him horny. And she enjoyed sex as much as he did, even sex in risky places.

She propped herself up on her elbows and looked into his eyes, hair a mess all around her shoulders. "So . . . will anyone notice me sneaking out of here?"

He threaded his fingers through her hair. "Naw, they're all busy eating. You sure you gotta go?"

Her expression sobered as she studied him. "Yeah, it's a school night. And it sounds like once again I've been keeping you from your work and making your brothers bear the burden."

He shrugged. "They owe me." But he patted her ass and felt a stab of regret as she got to her feet. Then he consoled himself by putting his hands behind his head and watching her dress.

She eyed him when she was in her underwear and bra—they matched, all white and lacy and feminine.

"So . . . you're not going to dinner?" she said.

"And answer questions about how we disappeared?"

She winced.

"I'll grab something to eat in the bunkhouse."

"I'd suggest we get something, but . . ." She glanced at her watch. "I have an errand to run."

"No problem."

Still in her undies, she pulled her phone out of her jeans pocket and frowned at it as she read. Then she sent a text off and gave him a distracted smile as she donned her jeans and t-shirt. She was retreating from him, back to her own life, her own concerns. She didn't explain anything to him, and he didn't expect it.

And for the first time, he felt like he wanted to know. He backed away quickly from that thought. It was none of his business.

When Lyndsay was at last dressed, she teased, "Now don't lounge around naked so long that you fall asleep. How will you explain that to your brothers?"

He sat up. "Could be ugly. I'll come down with you, like we just came in from a ride or something."

He pulled on his clothes, then followed her down the ladder. He had her pause in the shadows while he checked out the yard between the barn and the house.

"All clear," he said.

When she would have walked swiftly past him, he caught her in a hug and gave her a thorough kiss. "I had a great time today."

She smiled. "I did, too. We should do this again sometime."

"I'll call you."

She nodded, and with a wave, she hurried toward her car. Will watched her move in the twilight, liking her athleticism, remembering how well she'd put it to use.

Reluctantly, he turned and jogged toward the bunkhouse.

Driving away from the ranch, Lyndsay allowed her thoughts to linger on Will. She felt a warm glow of happiness and the knowledge that their intimacy had been even deeper than she'd imagined. He'd been thoughtful and sweet—*and thorough,* she added to herself, knowing she had a Cheshire cat grin. She wanted to bask in the memories, but new problems intruded no matter how she tried to put them off.

Thoughts of the anonymous flyer made her grit her teeth. Someone was taunting her with the secret of her book debut. She couldn't believe it was the owner of the Open Book. She'd already talked to the woman a couple months ago, confiding her secret, since the owner would soon see the publisher's sales catalogue anyway. In return for the owner's not putting the book on the shelves until after school let out, Lyndsay had agreed to tell all her friends and family to buy their copies there and to allow the store to host a book signing in June. No, she couldn't believe the bookstore would want to lose her business by putting out a flyer like this.

The only other people who knew were her family and Mrs. Thalberg. Kate, Tony, and her dad wouldn't distribute a flyer against her wishes—it could only be the widows, who always thought they knew better than everyone else. She didn't care that it was eight at night; she headed for the boardinghouse.

But on the way, she stopped at the grocery store, and there, amidst the newspapers lining shelves near the front entrance, was a colorful flyer with the words LOCAL AUTHOR MAKES GOOD blaring across the top. There was even a picture of her book cover, with the title and author's name blurred. But you could see that it was a cowboy romance. Just like Will had said, the flyer promised to provide more hints to her secret identity.

She groaned and rolled the paper into a ball in her hand without realizing what she'd done, then glanced around guiltily. She'd thought she had everything under control, had convinced her family to wait, had even let Kate persuade her that Will probably wouldn't recognize himself.

And then—this flyer.

Kate and Tony had texted her about it several times during the day, but she hadn't had a moment to glance at her phone. At the ranch, she'd texted back that she'd heard about the flyer and was going to do something about it. She got back in her car and drove to the Widows' Boardinghouse, on the southern side of the creek at the edge of Silver Creek Ranch land.

The house was a beautiful old Victorian with wraparound porches and gingerbread trim. She drove past the front entrance, with its big WIDOWS' BOARDINGHOUSE sign, and around to the kitchen, where her dad's car was parked next to the widows'. Well, he should know what was going on. She marched up the steps and rang the buzzer.

When the door opened, the smell of something spicy wafted out at her, and for a moment she felt faint—she hadn't eaten since lunch, and she'd certainly exerted herself enough.

"Lyndsay," Mrs. Palmer said, her Western twang drawing out her name, "what an expected surprise."

Expected? Yeah, they'd expected her, all right. Lyndsay knew they weren't stupid. She held up the wrinkled flyer.

Mrs. Palmer's grin didn't fade, although her eyes twinkled mischievously within the deep lines of her face. "Come on in so we can—"

Lyndsay walked right in past her.

"—talk?" Mrs. Palmer finished.

The other two widows and her dad were seated in the cow-themed breakfast nook, enjoying a pan of lasagna. Sliced fresh bread was heaped in a cloth-lined basket, and a bottle of red wine stood nearly empty in the center of the table.

Mario stood up. "Hi, babes."

"Dad," she said, nodding but not smiling. She held up the flyer again. "Did you know about this?"

"I didn't. But if you'll let them explain—"

"Explain?" Lyndsay interrupted in disbelief. She rounded on Mrs. Thalberg, who gave her a calm look. "I trusted you with a secret. I feel betrayed."

Mrs. Thalberg's forehead wrinkled in a frown. "I was worried you'd consider it that way. I admit

I hatched a plan without telling you, but I thought in the long run you'd thank me."

"Thank you?" Lyndsay echoed, throwing her arms wide. "I specifically told you I wanted no one else to know until school was out. I trusted you at a family dinner—"

"Lyndsay," her father interrupted, his expression and voice going cool. "Be careful what you say next. You haven't heard their explanation. I accepted *your* explanation of why you wanted to keep the book publication a secret—even though I didn't agree with it. And you'll notice that Rosemary and her friends have kept it secret, too."

"But they're dropping hints about revealing it!" Lyndsay shot back in frustration.

"They don't plan to announce your name until you're ready," Mario continued. "If you'd have let Rosemary speak, they would have reassured you. What I don't understand is why you are this upset. The ladies want to help boost the revelation of your book debut. They won't go public until you're ready."

Lyndsay opened her mouth but realized belatedly that she was still thinking about Will, and what he'd think if he read her book. Was she panicking more about that than anything else?

Mrs. Ludlow briskly pulled out the chair next to her, and Lyndsay sank into it.

"I'm sorry," she said, gazing with wide eyes at Mrs. Thalberg. "I—I panicked. I shouldn't have gotten angry."

But her father was still frowning at her.

Mrs. Thalberg sat down beside her and touched her hand. "I owe you an apology, too. I should have told you I'd be telling my housemates your news. I . . . tell them everything," she admitted helplessly.

"I know. And if I'm honest with myself, I knew you'd tell them. And I trust you all," she added, looking at each of them in turn. "But hearing about this flyer and then seeing it in person . . ." She trailed off, still finding it difficult to unclench her gut.

"It was a shock," Mrs. Palmer said matter-of-factly. "It was my idea not to tell you. I thought you'd like the surprise of knowin' you had help with your big debut."

Lyndsay covered her face with both hands. "I'm so sorry," she whispered from behind them.

"We all are," Mrs. Thalberg said. "Let's agree we all should have talked more. Now, would you like some lasagna?"

Lyndsay's stomach chose that moment to give a very loud gurgle.

Everyone laughed, easing the tension, and even her father seemed to let go of his unhappiness with her.

Soon Lyndsay was digging into the gooey-cheese goodness of pasta, meat sauce, and mushrooms.

"You know," Mrs. Ludlow said casually, "we debated using our Facebook pages to hint at your news."

Lyndsay froze with a piece of bread halfway to

her mouth. "But then people could question you and maybe you'd get sick of keeping the secret."

"Our thoughts exactly," Mrs. Ludlow agreed. "We preferred to remain anonymous, right along with you. We've had a lot of practice writing anonymously, starting way back."

Lyndsay noticed that her dad deliberately focused on his plate, as if he didn't plan to speak. "Can you tell me about it?"

The widows all exchanged a look, and a conversation seemed to silently pass between them.

"Okay, we'll trust you with our secret," Mrs. Thalberg said cheerfully.

Which made Lyndsay feel even worse for barging in and throwing accusations around instead of calmly asking for an explanation.

"Don't be so dejected, my dear," Mrs. Ludlow said.

Lyndsay gave the old woman a chagrined smile, then took another delicious bite of lasagna.

"We used to write a secret gossip newspaper back in high school," Mrs. Thalberg said. "We called it *Daisy Won't Tell*. We found out who was dating who, things like that."

"I do believe we did a good deed by unmasking that teacher who preyed on his students," Mrs. Ludlow said with conviction.

"Was this when you called yourselves the Purple Poodles?" Lyndsay asked.

"Ah, you've heard of us," said Mrs. Palmer with glee.

"Let me guess," Mrs. Thalberg said dryly. "Eileen Sweet."

"She told Will the name, and he told me," she admitted.

Mrs. Ludlow arched a white eyebrow. "It does not matter who knows—infamy can be satisfying in itself. What else is now common knowledge?"

It felt a little strange to talk about something secret in the widows' lives—when she'd just been railing about her own secrets. "It seems . . . Mrs. Sweet quite regrets the problems that started between you all in high school."

Again, there was another silent zap of widow communication.

Mario ate a piece of buttered bread, looking from one lady to the next with interest.

"Oh, really," Mrs. Thalberg said.

"She regretted that it seemed as if she didn't invite you to the cotillion because of your social standing, but she said that wasn't it. It was about a boy, right?" Lyndsay asked, hoping for more information.

Mrs. Ludlow waved a hand. "We knew the truth about that. Others believed what they wished, of course."

Mrs. Thalberg crossed her arms over her chest and regarded Lyndsay impassively. "So she's sorry for that now? Amazing how she hasn't said that directly to me."

"And very interestin' how she brings it up now," Mrs. Palmer said, "during an election. She's scared of losin', of course."

"Did anyone ever find out you were behind *Daisy Won't Tell*?"

"Nope," said Mrs. Thalberg. "And that's why it's so fun to resurrect our secret writing on your behalf."

"That's very sweet of you, thanks. But next time, would you mind telling me about it so I don't have a heart attack?"

"Welll," Mrs. Palmer drew the word out, "we promise to try. But sometimes, inspiration just strikes at the craziest moment!"

Lyndsay prayed to the literary gods that her personal cheerleaders could keep themselves under control for a few more weeks.

When she got home, she stayed up for an hour, grading papers. She was so tired that the equations seemed to run together, but she found herself excited again remembering that tomorrow she'd be meeting with Matias to oversee his science project. It was becoming the bright spot in her school week.

At last she went to bed, but instead of sleeping, she lay awake in the dark and relived the magical hour in the hayloft with Will.

And it had been everything she'd dreamed. He'd made her feel so desired, so needed. He'd known just what to do to make her shake with urgency— and she'd been able to do the same to him. Some deep part of her had assumed that sex with Will would be . . . just sex. But the exact opposite had happened. It had been both mind-blowing and far too intimate and special. She felt connected to him now in a way she hadn't imagined, an invisible tether that silently mocked her earlier belief that dating Will would be as easy as "getting him out of her system." She was beginning to suspect it might not be that easy . . .

And then he sent her a "Sweet dreams" text and her insides seemed to melt.

Chapter 14

Late Thursday afternoon, Will showed up at Tony's house after Tony's shift at the tavern. Dom and Matt Sweet, Will's cousin, were coming, too, for a guys' pizza and video games night. They'd been rare lately, and Will was still rather amazed they'd all been able to arrange their schedules. He'd put in a long morning moving dams in place of Chris and Daniel, so they'd promised to take his turn tonight.

"Where's Kate?" Will asked, dropping a couple boxes of pizza on the kitchen table before putting a six-pack of beer in the fridge—a five-pack now, since he had one in his hand.

"At her parents' for dinner, then a movie," Tony called from the living room, where he was pulling out the game controllers.

"And Ethan?" Will asked, leaning in the door-way between both rooms.

Tony's face went a little impassive. "His new job at Carmina's Cucina."

"Aah," Will said. "At the competition."

"At his grandparents'. I know it's a better atmosphere than a tavern for a fourteen-year-old kid, but . . . I wish he could hang out with me."

"Most parents want to get rid of their kid for a night."

Tony shrugged. "Guess all those years of not seeing him on the weekends when Kate and I used to share custody, well, they make a man feel like he missed too much. Speaking of kids," he said as Will came in and sank onto the couch, "how did the 4-H meeting go?"

"What'd Ethan say?"

"You were fine, according to him. But what did *you* think?"

Will shrugged. "Lyndsay caught a problem I totally missed with a couple kids. It's sure harder than it seems to deal with a group rather than just one or two. Or maybe Ethan is just way too easy to deal with."

Tony glowed with quiet pride. "Thanks. So he didn't bug you about the helicopter?"

Will rolled his eyes. "Not him. But I don't give rides. It's a ranch tool, not for joyriding." And it was his brief time of peace and reconnecting to the past—but he'd wanted Lyndsay to share it, he remembered uncomfortably.

"Really, a ranch tool?" Tony asked with skepticism. "I seem to remember you buzzing Deke

Hutcheson's cattle and causing a stampede that tore down a couple fences and stopped traffic for an hour or two."

Will grimaced. "I was still learning how to fly. I didn't mean to go so low. Deke still thinks I'm a reckless fool. He had me repairing fence for days— which was well deserved, I know." He glanced at the clock on his phone. "So where are Dom and Matt?"

"Late. Dom was getting back into town today, and Matt had a long day overseeing the planting of annuals at the inn. Relax while I go warm up the pizza. My tablet's right there, if you're bored."

Will picked up the tablet, opened the cover, and the screen turned on. But instead of a desktop with icons, he was looking at a Word document. He was about to minimize it, thinking it was something for Kate's law firm, when he caught the sentence "She felt her eyes tear up at the thoughtfulness of the gesture."

That wasn't a law brief. Someone was reading—or writing—a story. So he kept reading, drawn into the romantic scene where the sandy-haired hero with hazel eyes surprised his girlfriend by taking her grandmother's earrings and making them into a pendant. He felt an uncomfortable twist deep in his stomach the more he read. Cody was a cowboy, and he was wearing a hat with a tooled band around it made by his friend . . .

The twist became a prickle of unease that chased down his spine. The guy sort of reminded

him of . . . himself. And that scene, where he'd
remade antique jewelry for his girlfriend—Will
had done that long ago for Brittany. He'd made
no secret of it back then; all of his friends and
family had known. But had someone deliberately
incorporated it into a story—okay, instead of a
ring it was earrings—but a story with a hero who
was . . . him?

He closed the tablet and set it carefully onto the
coffee table, as if it were a snake. No guy would
write that—was this Kate's tablet, Kate's story?
And was she writing it about *him*?

He could see Tony through the kitchen doorway.
The poor guy—Will couldn't tell him. He and Kate
were only just getting back together. They seemed
so happy. But if she was writing about Will, how
could she be happy? And why had she used such a
personal part of his life?

None of it made sense. All he knew was that he
should probably find a way to talk to Kate about it.

But what was he supposed to say? *Hey, are you
writing fantasies about me?*

He ran a hand down his face.

"Something wrong?" Tony asked, walking in,
holding a beer.

"Just tired. It's a long hard day, being a cowboy."

"Whine, whine."

Will suddenly remembered the flyers about a
local author—could the author be Kate? Was she
hiding her book because of her profession? He

couldn't believe she'd publish a story about a hero that so closely resembled him, when he was a good friend of her future husband.

When someone knocked at the front door, Tony called, "Come on in!"

Dom and Matt walked through the door, carrying chips and dip and even more beer.

"I've got this Iberico ham you need to try," Dom said. "Convinced one of my stores to import it from Spain."

Dom owned a food brokerage catering to high-end grocery stores. He traveled the world searching for unique and rare food items—and that was a challenge for the jaded Aspen market.

Matt collapsed in a chair, head back, eyes closed.

"You look exhausted," Will told his cousin. "And it's obvious you spent your day outside, because you're almost as dark as Dom."

Dom grinned, white teeth gleaming in black skin. "Not a bad thing to be at all."

Matt let out a sigh. "Grandma is a perfectionist. Do you know I have to have all my people use a ruler and measure how far apart the geraniums have to go?"

Will chuckled. "It looks good when you're done."

"Hmm," Matt said, but he appeared pleased at the compliment.

Soon they were eating pizza, drinking beer, talking about their jobs and their dates, but always, in the back of Will's mind, was his bewilderment over what to do about Kate and her book.

On her brief lunch break Friday, Lyndsay read a text from Will. He said he wanted to see her that evening but couldn't get away from the ranch. Did she want to come spend some time as a cowgirl?

Did she ever. She was touched that he wanted her to see such an important part of his life. And she was dying to see him in his element, of course. She anticipated riding a horse up into the mountains to check on the cattle, or maybe she'd learn how to groom a horse as he tested next week's 4-H lesson on her.

When she arrived, they weren't alone, but she paused a moment just to look at him. She hadn't seen him since they'd slept together, and watching him heft a roll of canvas from his shoulder into the pickup truck gave her a delicious shiver with the memory of what he could do with his very physical, fit body. Sadly, she couldn't burrow into his embrace and kiss him, like she wanted to. Chris and Daniel were hanging around near the storage trailer, smirking, as Will brought forth a set of hip boots and a shovel.

"This is the irrigator's uniform," Will said, smiling at her.

She felt her own smile fade a bit as she regarded the hip boots. "So . . . we're going to get wet?"

"Not with these babies. Muddy, maybe . . ."

She chuckled, shaking her head. "So much for the romance of the old west."

"The romance of the old west always included hard, dirty work. Gotta feed the cattle during the winter, which is the reason we grow hay. Up here in the mountains, we can only harvest one crop a summer, so it's critical we don't have mistakes. And since we're such an arid state, we have to irrigate. Wild hay can be under water a week or so, but not alfalfa—twenty-four hours max. Which is why we move dams every twelve hours or so. There's a real art to being able to find the water's best path through a field. You ready to help?"

She nodded, letting him sling the heavy hip boots over her shoulder. Then she grabbed her shovel and followed him toward the truck. Chris and Daniel waved to her happily.

"And what are you two going to do with all your free time?" Lyndsay called.

"Our turn to have dates," Chris said. "We'll treat our women to some fine dining and dancing."

"*Not* ditchwork," Daniel added. "Didn't think our brother could get more romantic than the time he took a date to watch a calf being born and got blood all over her."

"Okay, okay, let's not scare the poor woman," Will said. "She's about to see the beauty of the ranch."

"Or a lot of mud," Daniel said dryly.

She saw a lot of rolled-up canvas, bright orange

in the bed of the pickup truck, poles sticking out the ends.

"Canvas dams?" she asked, hopping into the truck. "That seems fragile."

"The ditches aren't more than a couple feet deep. And the dams aren't canvas anymore, though they're still called that. They're of a really strong synthetic waterproof material. We have some new ones to put in to replace damaged ones. Otherwise, we move the ones that are already there."

With the windows down and the breeze rearranging their hair, they drove across the ranch, through acres of pastureland full of green plants. Cottonwoods grew in clusters in the distance, and east and west of them, mountains rose in jagged peaks, earthy tops rising above the tree line dusted with the last of winter's snow.

"It's a beautiful ranch," Lyndsay said, lifting her hand to feel the rush of wind.

Will smiled at her. "Thanks. You can see why this is the only life I want."

"I'll reserve my opinion on your sanity until I see what you want me to do."

He laughed.

Ten minutes later, they reached a large field surrounded by fence. Will parked at the far corner, nearer the foothills. She started to open the door, but he caught her shoulder.

"Not so fast," he said.

And then he kissed her, and everything fell away beneath the desire that rushed through her body like a flame to burn her. She caressed his shoulders and back, felt the urgency of his hands on her breasts and hips. They suddenly broke apart and stared at each other, breathing hard.

"Whoa, that was intense." His voice was hoarse with strain.

She gave a shaky smile. "Just the way we like it."

He looked around. "We're alone. Maybe we could—"

"Hold your horses, buddy. We almost got caught the other night. Let's do the job and see what happens later."

He slumped behind the wheel. "I hate when you're the voice of reason."

"Someone has to be." She leaned against him, hand on his thigh, until he froze. Then she gently bit his earlobe, smiled, and got out of the pickup.

A few minutes later, as she put her hip boots on, she watched him struggle with a headgate, where boards were settled into carved grooves. At last he got them up, and water flooded down a long earthen ditch.

Will opened the bed of the pickup and pulled out the first rolled-up dam. "Let's go!"

He was as patient with her as he'd been with the 4-H kids, showing her how to stretch the poles across the water-filled ditch, then gradually lower the dam, holding it in place with large rocks. Eventually, she was able to rest her arms on her shovel, panting, sweaty, and watch the water run through the nearest field. She got mud on her face, and a splotch of it in her hair, while Will looked as pristine as a cowboy model in a magazine, with only a little sexy perspiration dotting his forehead.

And even that made her think of hot, sweaty sex in the hayloft . . .

They spent another hour putting in a couple new dams and moving others. Will even rescued a fox caught in a broken fence wire. He was so gentle and careful. When the fox ran off, she did the "awww" face until Will reddened. She felt, briefly, like a cowgirl, and she was pretty proud of herself—if exhausted.

"We need a rest," Will said. "You did a great job—I had no idea how strong you are."

"You couldn't tell the other day in the hayloft?"

His glance shimmied down her chest, leaving little ripples of desire in its wake.

"Oh believe me, I could tell. And don't start me thinking about it, or I won't be able to feed you. It was my turn to bring a picnic, after all. Want some?"

"I'm ravenous," she said solemnly.

Soon, the damp, clammy hip boots were off her, and she wiped the mud off the rest of her as best she could with help from Will, who pointed out all the flecks she missed. Instead of a basket, he had a square cooler in his pickup. He brought out chicken he'd grilled himself, along with cut-up fruit and a couple bottles of Coke, and they sat on a blanket.

For a while they talked about the other dirty jobs she hadn't known about on a ranch, and then they settled into a peaceful silence, lying side by side, holding hands, looking up at the clouds. At last he came up on his elbow, and her heartbeat got a little faster in anticipation. But instead of kissing her, he traced a finger down her arm and appeared hesitant.

"Is something wrong, Will?"

"I have something I want to ask you, and it'll seem like none of my business, but really, I have a reason."

"Wow, you're rambling, and that's not like you."

"Except when I'm talking to teenagers," he said dryly.

She reached up to cup his face. "You're too hard on yourself. Did you know it takes a teacher a couple years before they really feel in control of a classroom?"

"Did it take you that long?"

"Oh, no, I was an incredible teacher instantaneously."

He leaned over to kiss her lightly, then said, "I'm not surprised."

They gazed into each other's eyes. Then their smiles died, and he leaned even closer.

She put her fingers over his mouth. "If you don't ask me the question you just mentioned, we will totally forget about it."

He sighed and glanced toward the Elk Mountains. "Maybe that's a better idea," he murmured.

"Now I'm really curious." She folded her hands behind her head. "Go on, ask away."

"Kate's your best friend, right?"

She blinked at him. "And . . . Tony's one of your best friends. Of course, you have so many."

"Yeah, I'm a popular guy."

But his forehead was lined with worry, so she didn't tease him again, just waited.

"Though they're planning their wedding for July," he began slowly, "Kate's not having second thoughts, is she?"

"She never got over my brother," Lyndsay insisted, eyes wide. "They're so in love it's kind of sickening to be around them. You've said so yourself. What is it, Will? What's wrong?"

A grimace twisted his lips. "I was at their house yesterday, ready for video games and pizza with the guys. When it was just me in the living room, waiting for Tony, he told me to use his tablet. Then I saw . . . a story, a document someone had obviously typed."

Lyndsay swallowed hard as all her fears bubbled to the surface. She'd tried so hard to keep her secret, knew he'd misinterpret everything—wait a minute . . .

"So you saw a document on their tablet," she said, relieved that her voice didn't squeak. "Why are you this spooked?"

"Because . . . it seemed about me."

He eyed her expectantly, as if she'd laugh—and she'd never felt less like laughing. "About you?"

"I know, I know, it sounds crazy. I only read a

couple pages before feeling guilty, like I was doing something wrong even though Tony had told me to use the tablet. But it was a fictional story, and the guy was a cowboy who looked like me—and I wouldn't have cared about that, except the scene was something that had sort of happened in my past, like Kate had copied it."

Lyndsay knew Kate had promised to have Tony read that scene, to see what he thought. And they must have left it open on the tablet . . .

"It's just so unexpected," he continued when she didn't speak. "Any suggestions about what I should do?"

She opened her mouth, but nothing came out. He was obviously weirded out by the whole thing—if she told him she'd written it, it might be even worse, since they were dating, and she hadn't told him what she'd done.

She hadn't done anything on purpose, including using a scene straight out of his life . . . but how do you tell a guy that? She felt tongue-tied with her uncertainty. She remembered what Matt had once said about coming out, how it was freeing to be yourself, even if not everyone accepted the decision. But she was so worried about how Will would react. Maybe she needed to accept the fact that if she was this worried, their relationship was becoming more than casual dating to her. And that would be such a big mistake.

She sat up, unable to relax anymore.

Will did the same, then studied her. "I guess this must surprise you, too, since you're pretty speech-less right now."

"Yeah, I've been too confident in their relation-ship to even worry about them."

"Then can I ask you a favor? Can you talk to Kate about this, find out what's going on? If I'm totally wrong, I don't want to embarrass her. And I can't go to Tony."

"Yeah, I understand. Sure I'll talk to her."

His smile broadened with relief. "Thanks. You're saving my ass. So let's put that aside. I've shown you some of the stuff I do during my day—how was yours?"

She tried to relax, knowing she didn't have to make a decision to tell Will the truth about his ties to her book right now, but it was difficult. "Well, you remember Matias, right?"

"The shy kid who stood next to Ethan, right?"

"Right. He's the boy I've been helping with his science project. With some brainstorming, we came up with a food-related topic, how one food tastes different when you're holding a dif-ferent food to your nose. He picked some really fascinating samples—tasting something sweet like candy, while smelling something sour, like a lemon. He brought some in to show me—he's so excited making the chart and enlisting the help of his family and friends. It's really adorable. Oh, and he raved about you, too."

"Me?" Surprise widened his eyes.

"He really enjoyed learning about horses. He says you inspired his summer 4-H project. I won't be surprised if he works up the nerve to ask more questions."

"I'd like that."

"Your parents seemed pretty happy you were working with the kids," she said.

Will shrugged and looked away across the hay field. "I was kind of surprised Mom remembered."

"What do you mean?"

"She's been a little forgetful lately. Not a big deal."

A Do Not Discuss sign might as well have been printed on his forehead in bold letters. She couldn't go against that, not when she herself had things she was trying to keep private.

And as he leaned over to kiss her, her last coherent thought was that she was caring too much about what he thought and felt, that maybe she was already aching for a real relationship with him, rather than just dating to put him behind her.

And that wasn't smart.

Chapter 15

On her way home from the ranch, Lyndsay pulled up in front of Kate and Tony's, desperate for some good advice about her dilemma. She knocked on the door, and when Ethan answered it, she gaped at him, clearly forgetting all about him. Nice aunt she was.

"Hey, Aunt Lyndsay, Mom didn't say you were coming," he said, opening the screen door wide.

"Uh, guess I forgot to remind her. Is she here?"

"Sure, she's in the kitchen."

Lyndsay followed Ethan through the living room and into the small kitchen, where Tony and Kate were standing shoulder to shoulder at the kitchen sink, leaning into each other, smiling goofily.

"Get a room," Ethan said genially, as if he said that all the time.

Smiling, Kate glanced at her son, then her eyes widened when she saw their visitor. "Hey, Lyndsay. I—"

"I bet you forgot the walk we planned for tonight," Lyndsay interrupted, glancing at the oblivious Ethan, and then away.

Never slow on the uptake, Kate said, "Yep, I did. Let me change out of my work clothes. Give me five minutes?"

"Of course."

Ethan sat down at the table, a textbook open before him. Tony eyed Lyndsay with that impassive brotherly stare that said he knew something was going on.

"That doesn't look like our math book." Lyndsay peered over the boy's shoulder.

"And it shouldn't. We have an English test tomorrow, remember?"

"Totally forgot."

"Which is why you assigned homework," he grumbled.

She grinned. "Hey, my test is coming up soon. You have to be prepared. Equations don't solve themselves."

"Ha ha. Like you haven't said that before."

She rubbed Ethan's unruly hair, and he ducked away. She glanced at her brother, who was drying a dish, still watching her with barely veiled suspicion. She gave him a bright smile, grabbed Kate's abandoned towel, and started to dry.

"You have mud in your hair, Lynds," Tony said.

Ethan gaped over his shoulder and guffawed.

"I was at the Sweetheart Ranch with Will, moving irrigation dams, if you must know."

"Is that what passes for romance these days?"

"It does," she answered with dignity.

Five minutes later, Kate was back, wearing yoga pants, a zipped lululemon jacket, and Nikes. "Let's go."

Kate's patience lasted a block westward before she said, "What the heck is wrong?"

"Everything," Lyndsay said melodramatically.

"You broke up with Will?"

"No, but this is about him. He was at your house last night and Tony told him to pass the time using your *tablet*." She emphasized the last word meaningfully.

"So?" Kate's light brown eyebrows drew together. "I just use that for reading documents, checking the news and e-mail, stuff like that."

"What *else* have you been reading?"

"Your book? Oh, your *book*!" She gasped. "I'm so sorry! Will read it?"

"He read the scene you guys left open—the one I took from his life. He recognized it right away."

"Oh no, did he confront you about it?"

Lyndsay hesitated, then glanced sideways at her friend. "No, because it was on your tablet, and my name wasn't in the header, so he thought . . . you wrote it."

Kate's mouth fell open for a brief moment, and then she started to laugh. "Oh, man, he thinks—oh, wait until I tell Tony."

"I'm glad you're not upset, but I don't think it's all that funny. Will's worried something's wrong with your relationship with Tony, since you've written down . . . fantasies . . . about him."

Kate coughed as she tried to squelch her laughter. "Oh, okay, I guess that could look bad. He told you all this, did he?"

"Yeah. I didn't tell him the truth—I was too shocked and didn't trust myself to make a rational decision. I didn't openly lie to him either. I didn't say much at all. Then he asked me to talk to you about it, and the safe response seemed to be to agree."

"You don't think he'd be flattered?"

They reached First Street, and in the dusk, the single lights in each window of the Sweetheart Inn glowed warmly against the dark mountains. Will's family owned that building.

Lyndsay resolutely turned down First toward Main Street. "I don't know. The more I get to know Will, the more I have a strange feeling he's not going to be all that flattered. In some ways, he's a more private person than I thought. He's really good at putting on the appearance of the happy-go-lucky Will everyone expects. Kind of like a mask, you know?"

Kate studied her closely. "That's really interesting."

"He was really freaked that someone wrote about him in a heroic, fantasy way."

"No, let's clarify that statement—he was freaked because he thought *I*, his good friend's fiancée, wrote about him. When he finds out it's you, the sexy woman he's lusting after? I think he'll be fine. Men love that sort of thing."

Lyndsay sighed. "I don't know. I have a bad feeling about this."

"Then you don't want to tell him?"

"Oh, it's not a matter of wanting to—I *need* to tell him, I know that. I just . . . need to find the right way, and I don't know what that is. Are you fine with his bewildered looks for a couple days?"

"Sure, if Tony's okay with it. If Will starts giving him sympathetic, sad looks . . ."

Lyndsay grimaced. "Would two guys really do that? Or would they just ignore something so weird?"

"You could be right. Regardless, you have a couple days. As long as he doesn't start talking about me to people."

"He'd never do that. Like I said, he's worried about you guys."

They turned down Main Street, where the old-fashioned lampposts glowed in little patches of light as far as the eye could see.

"Speaking of hidden things about Will," Kate began slowly, "Tony told me something I hadn't realized about Will's high school girlfriend, Brittany."

Lyndsay frowned but remained silent.

"Did you know Will was supposed to meet her the night she died?"

"No, I'd never heard that." She felt a lurch in her stomach for poor Will.

"He didn't show up because of a ranch emergency. He tried to reach her, but neither of them had cell phones back then—not that there'd be great reception. So anyway, instead of waiting the storm out at wherever their 'special place' was, when he didn't show, Brittany tried to go home."

"Oh no," Lyndsay said, coming to a halt in front of the stone columns of the Hotel Colorado, then slumping onto a bench. She stared unseeingly at the pavement. "And he blames himself for it all," she whispered.

Kate sat next to her. "We don't know that."

"Oh, yes we do. I saw him with her parents. It's very obvious he's been doing whatever he can for them for the last sixteen years. Sure, he could be doing that out of friendship, but by the way he reacts when her name comes up—the sadness and dismay, the quick change of subject—he's also doing it out of guilt. That poor man has been blaming himself all these years for her accident."

They sat in silence for a few minutes as a car occasionally drove by and the sound of people chatting rose and fell.

"What are you going to do about it?" Kate asked.

"Nothing, I suppose. He obviously doesn't want to talk about her, and since this won't develop into some long relationship, he'll want to keep things light between us."

"There you go again," Kate said with exasperation, "putting a finite end on a relationship that's just begun."

"That's always been the plan," Lyndsay insisted, but inside she wasn't feeling all that certain anymore.

"I think you're afraid to hope for more, like there's a part of you that doesn't want to get hurt if the worst happens. I know you've been burned before, Lynds, but don't let that stop you from trying to have it all."

"But this is *Will*," Lyndsay said with exasperation. "I could fall in love with him too easily—I think I'm halfway there. I didn't mean to open my heart like this. I had no idea the feelings I'd once had for him would resurrect themselves so strongly." Her voice trailed off in bewilderment, then she sighed. "He doesn't want that from me, Kate. And now I see that he doesn't want that from anyone, and it's not just because he's a player who enjoys lots of women."

"So you're content to know that the man you're almost in love with will never have a great love of his own because of a tragedy when he was a teenager, one he's never gotten over."

Lyndsay turned her head and just blinked at her friend. "That's kind of harsh."

"But it's the truth. Maybe you can help him see what he's doing to himself, how he's only living half a life if he won't let himself love again."

Lyndsay blew out a breath. "I have no idea how to do that. It seems . . . impossible."

"I think you can afford to be patient, to wait for the opportunities to point out the error of his ways. You can't lecture a man out of the grief and recrimination he can't let go of."

"You have a lot of confidence in me," Lyndsay said ruefully.

"I have confidence in love. How can I not, after having thrown away the great love of my life and then being lucky enough to find it again?"

Lyndsay gave a crooked smile. "It's still weird to hear my brother called the great love of your life."

"Hey, maybe you can be the great love of Will's life."

Lyndsay felt a pang of sadness and loss. "I believe he thinks he already had that, and isn't looking to replace her. I don't know if I can compete with her memory."

"You don't have to be in competition. Just be yourself. Wow, that sounded hokey, even to me."

Lyndsay chuckled. "Thanks for the advice. I'll let you know how it goes. And I hope Will doesn't cross the street when he sees you coming."

"I should jump into his arms and *really* freak him out."

"I never thought I'd say this, but he's way too sensitive for that kind of teasing."

They smiled at each other.

Lyndsay's phone beeped, and she glanced at the text before raising wide eyes to Kate. "It's Will. Says he forgot to ask if I wanted to hunt for wild morel mushrooms first thing in the morning. We'll go by horseback."

"Well, well. The dates are coming fast and furious for you two." Kate's amusement faded. "You're going to go, right? Don't worry about the book thing. It'll sort itself out."

Lyndsay sighed. "I hope so. Because I'm going to keep seeing him."

She sent a text accepting, and asked what time she should arrive. When she looked up, Kate was shaking her head.

"Mushroom picking," Kate said. "That Will, such a romantic."

"But if anyone can make it romantic, Will can," Lyndsay said with assurance.

Damn, Lyndsay looked good on a horse, Will thought as he followed her away from the gravel road on Sweetheart Ranch property and toward the cottonwood stand that lined the creek near the foothills of the Elk Mountains. Puffy white clouds floated across the sky, and though the day was still in the fifties, it seemed to promise warmer temperatures. He was watching her hips sway and her long brown hair stir in the breeze. It was early, only eight on a Saturday morning, but there was no sleeping in on a ranch, and Lyndsay had jumped in wholeheartedly. She wore tight jeans tucked into her cowboy boots and a cropped black jacket over a purple V-neck t-shirt.

She could ride a horse with ease, and something inside him just . . . relaxed and mellowed as he watched her.

"Will?"

"Huh?" Startled, he realized she'd looked over her shoulder and said something, but he'd been too busy admiring her ass in the saddle.

Her smile slowly widened, and she might even have blushed. After their time in the hayloft, he didn't think he could make her blush anymore, but he was wrong.

"I asked if I was headed in the right direction."

"Sorry, yeah, right for the cottonwoods and aspens. We'll walk through the trees to look for the morels."

She slowed her mount until Will moved up beside her. She said, "I've never done this before."

"Morel hunts? I grew up doing them with my mom. She knew all the best places." He felt a twinge of worry and put it aside. "And of course, you never share the location with anyone, even your best friends. Consider yourself lucky."

"Oh, I do," she said solemnly. Then she glanced at the basket hanging from a strap on his saddle and said in a teasing voice, "And how lucky I am to be with a man and his Little Red Ridinghood basket."

"Hey, you can't put mushrooms in a plastic bag—the humidity would make them rot. I know all the tricks. I even brought you your own pocket knife. Now come on, let's see what we can find."

He slid off Silver and was right beneath Lyndsay before she could swing a leg over the saddle.

She eyed him. "I've ridden before; I think I can get down."

He lifted his hands. "Let me help you. This is a cowboy's greatest thrill, you know, helping a lady off a horse."

She chuckled, then leaned toward him, bright and fearless against the brilliant blue sky. He caught her about the waist and deliberately let her slide down his body, enjoying all the soft parts.

"Such a cliché," she said, but her voice was a little breathless.

So he kissed her, enjoying the softness of her lips and the boldness of her tongue. It was a long time before her gray quarter horse, Barney, bumped her from behind. She laughed against Will's mouth, and they separated.

Will sighed. "Guess we should get started. My brothers are expecting me in a couple hours. We've got to move cattle up in the mountains this afternoon."

"Then lead the way, oh fearless mushroom hunter."

He hobbled the horses to let them graze, then grabbed his basket and took Lyndsay by the hand. They walked slowly into the woods and began to look for mushrooms at the base of the trees.

"Now, if we were on the south side of the Elks, we'd find tons of morels, but they're harder to find here."

Using a stick, he brushed aside undergrowth around the base of the trees and fallen logs.

"What do they look like?" she asked.

"Frankly, they look like pinecones, very hard to spot. But the head really looks like a sponge."

"Right, I've seen those in the grocery store." Then she pointed. "Is that one?"

And scattered around a cottonwood, near the bank of a stream, were lots of little morels, ripe for the picking. He showed her how to cut them at the base, mentioned how they were different from the more poisonous false morels, which looked more like the folds of a brain rather than ridges and pits, and whose stem wasn't hollow, like true morels. They wandered around for an hour, picking the occasional mushroom and leaving the small ones.

"So what does your mom cook with them?"

"If you have enough of them, you can do a dux-elles, where you sauté them in butter and shallots and herbs, reduce it to paste, and put it over steak."

"You sure sound like you know what you're doing in the kitchen."

He shrugged and attempted a humble attitude. "I experiment a bit."

She gave his shoulder a push. "Does your mom have something special planned for them?"

He let out a deep breath and scanned between the trees, checking on Silver and Barney rather than meet her eyes. "I don't know. She mentioned a couple weeks ago at a party we held for Em and Nate that she wished she'd had them for a special dish."

"Birthday party? Anniversary?"

"An adoption party. They're in the middle of pursuing a private adoption, and we were celebrating their appearance on the adoption agency's website."

Her expression went all soft and sweet. "That is adorably nice of you all. Em's such a part of your family now, it's hard to believe we didn't even know she existed a few years ago." She hesitated. "That had to be tough on your family, finding out you had an adult sister."

"Tough on my dad. When he discovered Em's mom had lied to him, that he'd missed out on her entire life . . . he was pretty wrecked for a while. And her mom hadn't treated her that well, which made us all kind of sick, considering how lucky our family has been. But Em—she's great. How could we not love having her as our sister? And the change she's brought about in Steph—"

"Now, come on, I know kids. Steph was at the most immature stage when she learned she had a sister."

"You mean when she learned the horror of not being the only girl in the family?"

Lyndsay smiled. "Well, okay, it's a self-centered time in a kid's life. But maturity helps, and I'm sure she would have grown out of it all on her own. But I get it, Em has brought out the best in her."

"It was a slow process, I admit. At first, Em was as wary with us as Silver was when he had a tendon injury that kept him in his stall for days on end."

"You're comparing your sister to a horse?" she asked, nose wrinkled in amusement.

"She wouldn't mind the comparison, since Silver is an excellent horse. But we hadn't had Silver long when he was hurt, and he just didn't trust me. It was a slow process of getting him used to me. Trust isn't something you develop in a day, right?"

He saw a fleeting expression of concern cross her face, but it disappeared so quickly that he wondered if he'd imagined it.

And then he had a ridiculous thought—maybe *he* was sort of like a wary horse with Lyndsay. Being with her made him want a closeness that guilt hadn't let him feel in years. Something had broken inside him long ago, leaving him no heart left to give. He didn't deserve a woman like her.

But with Lyndsay, he felt . . . alive in a way he hadn't experienced with anyone since . . . maybe since Brittany. Something feeble but growing seemed to tighten and warm his chest whenever he was with Lyndsay. It was a tenderness that had to be fought, he knew, because he couldn't hurt her—wouldn't risk it. He wasn't a man who normally felt afraid, but he was afraid to cause her pain.

But he couldn't make himself stop seeing her, even though he knew he probably should.

"Look, more morels!" she called, moving ahead of him toward the base of a giant cottonwood tree.

Relieved at the distraction from his thoughts, he squatted down with his pocket knife and sliced through the stem.

"It really does look like a sponge," Lyndsay said, shaking her head.

She laughed up into his face, and it was all he could do not to kiss her again with urgency and desperation—all of which were far too revealing.

Early that same afternoon, Will and his brothers were leading their horses into a trailer, getting ready to head to their summer grazing allotment in order to move the cattle from one pasture to the next, when he received an unexpected visitor. A dark-haired boy hopped off his bike.

Chris and Daniel both glanced at Will with curiosity.

"He's in my 4-H group," Will said quietly. "Give me a sec." He handed Silver's halter to Daniel and approached Matias, who waited by his bike shyly.

"Hi, Mr. Sweet," the boy said with hesitation, not quite meeting his eyes.

"Hi, Matias. You can call me Will, you know."

His eyes widened. "Thanks, Will."

"So . . . what are you doing here today? You know our next meeting isn't until Wednesday, right?"

"Yeah, but . . . you said we could ask you any questions, and I thought of one."

Will smiled, but he held back a laugh. "Okay, shoot."

"So we have to do a project for the 4-H horse unit. I know I could draw or do posters or something, but I'd like to work with real, live animals, you know?" He took a deep breath, then spoke in a rush. "Could I maybe 'borrow' one of yours? Not take it away or anything, but come here to work on it, like maybe . . . learning-to-ride-a-horse?"

The last part was spoken so fast that Will could hardly understand it. He put a hand on the teenager's shoulder. "Slow down, buddy. Why don't you tell me what you have in mind?"

"Well . . . I don't want to distract you from your work. If it wouldn't bother you too much, I could ride over twice a week to learn, just like for an hour. It would only be for a couple weeks. We're going to exhibit our projects at the Silver Creek Rodeo in June. Since I don't have a horse of my own, or an animal to raise—and you said your calves are up in the mountains—I thought learning to ride would be something I could do."

"You've given this a lot of thought, which I like," Will said. "How can I say no?"

Matias grinned, his dark eyes sparkling with happiness. "I'd be like your student, you know. I could pay you for the lessons."

"That's okay, I don't need it. I'm always happy to introduce people to the love of a good horse." He glanced at his brothers, who were leading all three horses inside the trailer. "I can't do it now, though. But I understand you might be in a hurry to get started. Do you have a cell phone?"

Nodding, Matias pulled it out of one of the pockets of his cargo shorts.

Will pulled his own out. "Give me your number and I'll text you when we get back late this afternoon. I'll have to talk to your parents first, of course."

"Sure." Matias rattled off his number.

"Mind coming back out then?"

"Mind? I don't mind at all. Thanks, Will! See ya."

Will stood for a moment, knowing he was smiling as he watched the boy bike back down the road. Then he finished helping his brothers load the trailer, and it wasn't until all three were sitting in the cab of the pickup, with Will driving, that Chris asked about Matias and Will explained.

"I don't know," Daniel said from the back bench, "being with Lyndsay is making you do different things."

"I don't know what seeing Lyndsay has to do with it. I volunteered to help the 4-H before we even got together."

Chris eyed him. "Yeah, but I think you agreed because you knew she was the advisor."

Will shrugged. "Maybe that was part of it."

"Well, you don't normally do much with kids, do you?"

That was uncomfortably true. "Chris will take care of that when he gets married. Look, I have something else I want to talk to you guys about. Have you noticed anything . . . strange with Mom?"

"Strange?" Daniel repeated. "Strange how?"

"Sleeping in when she's supposed to get things

done, being forgetful. One of us tends to fill in for her, but it's happening more and more."

"What are you trying to say?" Chris asked, frowning.

Will hesitated, the pickup angling upward as he took the road into the mountains. "There are a lot of wine bottles in the recycling, and Dad and we don't drink much wine."

"You're kidding," Daniel said forcefully. "Mom's not an alcoholic."

"I didn't say she was," Will answered quickly. "I've never seen her falling down drunk or anything, but . . . she's drinking more than she used to. I finally talked to her about it."

From the backseat, he heard Daniel mumble, "Bullshit."

Chris grimaced. "Bet she was offended."

"She was. She totally denied it. She wasn't angry or anything. She said she understands I love her and was just worried. She promised she'd be more attentive and not let her involvement in the Mystic Connection distract her from the ranch."

"So she had an answer for everything," Chris said.

"She gave you the truth," Daniel said stiffly. "I think you're wrong, and I hope you didn't really hurt her feelings."

Will let out a deep breath. "It's not like I'm going to Dad or anything. I said my piece to Mom. We'll see what happens next."

Chapter 16

Lyndsay went to the softball game Monday night feeling uneasy for a lot of reasons. For one thing, she didn't know if the election animosity had risen to a new level. There were still posters around town, but the two presidential candidates themselves had been strangely quiet. In anticipation of tonight? Hard to tell. There'd been no new flyer promoting an anonymous author, thankfully.

But mostly, Lyndsay was feeling bad about Will. She hadn't seen him since Saturday, though they'd had a couple sweet phone conversations. She'd claimed she had work to do, and she had, but it hadn't been so much end-of-school-year stuff as it had been her second book. And thinking about her second book made her think about her dilemma over the first one. Will hadn't asked her if she'd talked to Kate about being the author. Lyndsay figured he was giving her time.

Oh, he was giving her time all right, she thought,

dropping her blanket on the grass. It was she who was taking cowardly advantage of his generosity.

Will was warming up with the Tony's Tavern team, and when he saw her, he gave the biggest wave and an intimate smile. To be the one he looked at like that forever—she felt her throat close up and her eyes sting. After giving her own wave, she had to glance away, blinking. She'd begun to know him well enough to sense that when she told him the truth, he'd be spooked. That was the cause of her procrastination, her absolute fear that she'd lose him.

She really had made the stupid mistake of falling in love with Will Sweet, Valentine Valley goodtime guy and confirmed bachelor.

Taking a deep breath, she tried to focus on laying out her blanket. She smiled at Jessica, who came toward her wearing a big grin.

"Hey, Lynds, come see what the historical society election has come to. I'm already writing a piece about it—it's a lot more fun than the real news!"

Mrs. Sweet was standing inside a booth, the kind used at carnivals, with a banner across the top sporting her hat logo. She was dressed in her usual daily finery, and in front of her were individual bottles of beer. As Lyndsay approached, she could see the hat logo on the beer label, too.

"It's her own craft beer," Jessica whispered, "which she had the microbrewery create for her. I think she thought she would do Mrs. Thalberg one better, but I don't know. It makes her seem like she doesn't have her own original idea."

Lyndsay smiled at Will's grandma. "Hi, Mrs. Sweet. Love your hat."

It was a blue woven cowboy hat, with a gauzy scarf tied around it, befitting the elderly matriarch of a ranching family.

"Thank you, dear. You're welcome to try the beer, of course. I'm not usually a fan, but this one is rather tasty." Mrs. Sweet actually opened the bottle herself before handing Lyndsay the beer. "How are things with William?"

"Just fine, ma'am, thanks. He had me out to the ranch a couple days ago, showing me all about irrigating hay fields."

Mrs. Sweet's eyes narrowed. "Not very romantic of him."

Lyndsay laughed. "His brothers said the same thing, but I like seeing what he does on the ranch."

"I think the two of you should come to the inn and have dinner with me one of these days."

"I'd like that, thank you."

"I'll speak to William." Mrs. Sweet offered Jessica a beer, then turned to her next customer.

Just a few yards away, Mrs. Thalberg had set up her own booth, complete with brochures and a clipboard for signatures, just like Mrs. Sweet, but this one also had—brooms. Sean Lighton was standing in front, holding a broom and listening to Mrs. Thalberg's stump speech.

"Are those what I think they are?" whispered Jessica, her expression full of confusion.

"Hi, girls!" Mrs. Thalberg called.

Sean looked up and smiled at Lyndsay. He glanced around, and somehow she knew he was looking for Will.

Lyndsay debated putting the beer behind her back, as if it somehow made her a traitor, but instead, she just held it low at her side. "Hi, Sean, Mrs. Thalberg. We just had to come over and see what's going on."

The woman grinned. "Works every time. Here, you can each have one."

She handed over a simple, old-fashioned straw broom, and then they saw the writing down the handle.

"For a clean sweep," Lyndsay read, "vote Thalberg."

Mrs. Thalberg beamed. "Catchy, huh?" Then she leaned forward and whispered, "Any implication that Eileen is a witch is simply not true!"

Lyndsay bit her lip, trying not to laugh. Jessica's snort erupted, and she covered her mouth.

Sean chuckled. "Now, Mrs. Thalberg, I can't believe you said that."

"You all go watch the game," Mrs. Thalberg said. "Take your brooms with you! When enough people have brooms, we can play Quidditch!"

"You read *Harry Potter*?" Lyndsay asked.

"Of course. Makes me feel young again."

Lyndsay and Jessica waved before walking away.

Lyndsay thought Sean was about to follow them, but he only called, "Good night, ladies. My game's over, and I've got work to do at home. You both understand—our jobs aren't over at five o'clock."

"I hear you," Lyndsay said. "Good night."

Jessica eyed her after he left. "Someone has a crush."

"I know. I keep running into him, and I kind of feel like he's biding his time, waiting for me to be free."

"Do you want to be free?"

Lyndsay shrugged, melancholy settling over her again. "No, but it's not all up to me, is it?"

Jessica gave her a sympathetic smile before looking at the broom in her hand. "Guess I should run this back to the car . . ."

"Throw it on my blanket and come back for it later."

They watched the softball game, and this time, Tony's Tavern lost a close one to Vista Gallery of Art.

As Lyndsay approached the team, she heard Brooke grumble, "We lost to a bunch of artists." When Brooke saw Lyndsay, she said, "Nope, no dating, no distractions. The players are going to the tavern. We need to bond as a team and figure out what went wrong."

"Your husband is on the team." Lyndsay pointed to Adam, who tried to appear clueless as he took off his baseball cap and raked a hand through his damp, light brown hair. "In a sense, you'll be on a date."

"Technicalities. When we play, he's a teammate, nothing more."

There were several good-natured groans.

Lyndsay smiled at Will as he approached. "You go ahead. I have stuff to do at home anyway."

"Are you sure?" He slid his arm around her shoulders and kissed her temple. "I haven't seen you since Saturday morning, a whole two days. How about dinner tomorrow night?"

"That would be great. Your grandma says we should come to the inn and eat with her."

His eyes narrowed. "I'm not sure I want my first dinner date with you to be with my grandma."

She grinned. "Whatever you decide." Putting a hand on his chest, she leaned up for a quick kiss. "Have a good night."

As she walked away, she glanced over her shoulder, and she felt a surge of pleasure that Will was still watching, not bothering to hide his disappointment.

And then she hated that her pleasure was followed by a faint feeling of relief. Until she told him the truth, it was going to be a wall between them, even if he didn't know it.

Will didn't stay long at Tony's. Partially it was his worry about his mom, but also, the tavern just wasn't the same without Lyndsay—he never would have believed that to be true, but it was. He slipped out after his second beer and decided to walk to her house. When he got there just after ten, the lights were on, and it looked so cozy and welcoming. When he heard a trumpet playing, he remem-

bered a couple years ago that Lyndsay's jazz band
had had a gig at Tony's.

He stood outside in the shadows by her front
door, just listening. She was playing a song he
didn't recognize, but her talent at manipulating
the valves just couldn't be denied. She was partway
through the second song before it dawned on him
that he probably seemed suspicious hanging out in
her front yard. He rang the bell.

The trumpet playing stopped immediately, and
he sensed her presence on the other side of the
door. When he waved at the peephole, she opened
the door, still wearing the sundress she'd had on
earlier, narrow straps at her shoulders, narrow,
multicolored horizontal stripes all the way down.

"Will!" Her smile was wide and pleased.

"I hope you don't mind me dropping over. Tony's
. . . just wasn't Tony's without you."

Her eyes were soft and tender, and part of him
wanted to deny that tenderness. But tonight . . . tonight he just let it go.

She stepped back, opening the door wider.
"Come on in."

"I heard you playing," he said as he went past
her. "I'd forgotten how good you are."

"You're just saying that because you used to
make fun of us band geeks in high school."

He winced. "Did I? That's terrible."

"Well, you weren't being mean," she said, closing the door. "You were teasing, but I was pretty
sensitive then. All teenage girls are sensitive."

"Good thing you said that rather than me."

She laughed.

"I'd really love to hear your band play. Do you have any upcoming dates?"

"We take the summer off—which doesn't make sense for a teacher, but it does for the rest of the band. I'll let you know if something comes up. Go on and have a seat on the couch. Can I get you something? I have beer."

"That sounds great, thanks."

He wandered farther into the living room, which looked well lived in, but not dirty. Just cluttered and homey. There were books everywhere, stacked underneath the coffee table, and on a shelf in the corner. He studied the titles, lots of romances, but other stuff, too, the Clancy they'd talked about, some photography books about Montana—Montana?—some suspenseful thriller stuff.

Lyndsay came back in, carrying two beers by the necks in one hand and a bowl of pretzels in the other. "Sorry, I don't have a lot to eat in the house."

"I don't believe it. You love to eat."

"But one has to grocery shop to eat, and I just ran out of time this weekend."

They both sank down on the couch, and she tucked her legs up under her, the pretzel bowl between them.

"You didn't last long at the tavern," she said. "Brooke's motivational speech went short?"

"Naw, I just wasn't enjoying myself all that

much." He almost told her he missed her, but he
held back. If he told her too many romantic things,
it would hurt her more in the end when they broke
up. But he was starting to wonder if he'd hurt just
as much.

"I like your grandmother's beer," she said, smiling at him as she took a pretzel.

"It was okay. Isn't it almost time to vote? I'm
starting to dread my own softball games, wondering what she'll be up to next."

Lyndsay chuckled. "It's next week. I thought she
was pretty tame tonight. Mrs. Thalberg, on the
other hand . . ."

"Brooms? Okay, the slogan was catchy, but it all
seems kind of silly."

"She does have brochures about the changes she
wants to make, stuff like that. The brooms are just
a gimmick to get people to come talk to her."

"Well, it must work, because every time I came
to the dugout, I glanced over and both ladies were
chatting away with the voters." He took a swig
of beer, then eyed her. "Speaking of chatting . . .
were you able to talk to Kate?" He was surprised
to notice a blush steal up from her neck and across
her cheeks. "It's all right if you couldn't talk to her
yet. I understand it might be difficult to bring up."

"Especially when Tony's around," she added.

"Oh, right, you can't talk about it in front of
him. There's no rush."

She looked so pretty with pink cheeks, her lips
damp from the beer. He took the pretzel bowl and

put it on the coffee table, then took her beer and his away.

She eyed him, her smile faint and seductive, then leaned toward him, resting her hands on his thighs. Her top gaped a bit, and he saw the swell of her breasts, a hint of peach-colored lace. And then she kissed him, still moving forward now across his body as he sank back into the pillows against the arm of the couch. She practically crawled on top of him on all fours, hands moving across his chest, knees coming up on either side of his hips, one knee sinking down the back of the couch, bringing her hips down on his.

She rose above him, her smile now sultry and knowing, then dipped her head, her mouth above his but not quite touching as she whispered, "I'm not wearing panties under this dress."

His slow arousal turned into an immediate hard-on, and he slid his palms around her ribs and down over her ass. She grinned at him when he found the hem of her dress and began to pull it upward, letting his fingers skim the backs of her thighs. She was breathing heavily now, eyes half closed. She started giving him tiny little kisses, on his lips, his forehead, his cheeks, even the tip of his chin, where she dipped her tongue into the cleft.

"I've been wanting to do that forever," she said huskily.

"It's only been a couple of weeks," he answered, chuckling.

She tilted her head to take his open mouth with

hers. He palmed her ass then, absorbed her gasp and moan with his mouth, feeling her shiver as he massaged and caressed, then dipped his fingers between her thighs. She cried out, and he loved the uncontrolled sound of her passion. He slid one hand around to the front and cupped the heat of her, penetrating her moistness.

"Can you lower the top of that dress?" he asked hoarsely.

"Only if you can unzip your baseball pants. Sexy, by the way."

They laughed against each other's lips. He unzipped and released his erection, and then she lowered her hips to rub her hot wetness along the length of him. His head fell back as he descended into a haze of such pleasure he never wanted to surface again.

Then she sank down more firmly, and he half opened his eyes to see her unzipping the side of her dress, then shrugging the straps off her shoulders. He only got a brief glimpse of the bra before that was gone, too, and he was able to fill his palms with her breasts. He played with her until he had to taste, then he brought her forward and over him again so that he could lick her nipples again and again. He played between her legs, too, and the whole couch shook along with her shivers.

"I have a condom in my wallet," he said, "but it's underneath me."

"And I have one right in the coffee table drawer, just hoping you'd show up."

"God, you're brilliant."

She leaned over to the table, but he didn't make it easier, thrusting his finger inside her, using his thumb against her clitoris. She fumbled the condom and almost dropped it until at last he took it from her.

"Hurry, hurry," she said against his mouth, before suckling his tongue with her own.

When he was suited up, she took him in her hands to guide him, then sank down, taking him deep into the hot depths of her. They held off as long as they could, joined together but not moving, kissing and caressing. He felt himself pulse inside her, listened to her breathing pick up and the little whimper that escaped. God, she turned him on. And her dress bunched around her waist was an erotic sight. At last he cupped her hips with his hands and lifted her. She needed no further urging, just surged against him and up, over and over. He was able to capture her nipple occasionally and suck it deep. When at last she came, he took their pace faster until he found his own pleasure.

She collapsed on top of him, and he cradled her against him.

"Damn, why am I still wearing a shirt?" he murmured against her hair. "I can't feel your skin."

"You felt enough of it, believe me," she said, chuckling.

He slid a strand of hair behind her ear, studying her face. "There are flecks of gold in your eyes," he said softly.

They kissed again, lightly, gently.

"Come to bed with me," she said at last.

He didn't hesitate at all. "Okay."

And when he woke up in her bed at dawn, he realized he'd spent the night, the first time ever. He never slept in a woman's bed—it was too intimate, too promising of a future he wasn't going to give. But he hadn't been able to make himself leave her. And as the first glow of the sun touched her closed eyes, her lips pinkened by his kisses, the brush burn from his stubble across her chin, he thought he'd never seen a more beautiful sight.

And that got him out of bed. He was dressed before she came up on an elbow and sleepily said, "I could drop you off at your car."

"It's only a few blocks away. Go back to sleep until you need to get up."

"I need to get up. The school year's not done yet."

"Then I won't keep you." He gave her another kiss, although even that was dangerous. The sheet only covered her to her hips, and her breasts might as well have been a magnet to his steel. He kissed her mouth, then each nipple. "Gotta go."

And he felt like he was running away.

Though Lyndsay told herself this meant nothing, there was something about a guy spending the night that seemed more . . . serious. She floated through the next day in a happy haze, managing even to forget about having to eventually break the news about her book. It was the easiest buildup to end-of-the-year tests, as it seemed nothing about her job could affect her good humor too much.

Dinner that night at the Sweetheart Inn French restaurant was fun. Mrs. Sweet didn't actually join them until dessert, so Lyndsay was able to spend an enjoyable hour looking at Will in a jacket and buttoned-down shirt over his jeans. He was sort of embarrassed about it, complaining the jacket was too restrictive on the bulging muscles of his arms, which made her giggle.

They talked about everything from politics to world events to the sheep the Sweetheart Ranch planned to invest in next. They even exchanged stories about crazy exes, although never once did he bring up Brittany. But they were too public to talk about "the book." She was both relieved and frustrated.

Wednesday afternoon, she met her 4-H group at the ranch. Now that the kids were hands-on working with the horses, there weren't any discipline problems, since even Alex and Logan wanted to learn to ride. Matias seemed particularly engrossed, and for once he forgot his shyness and asked a lot of questions. Lyndsay rode for a while and enjoyed showing off for Will.

After the kids left, she stayed in the barn and helped him oat the horses and put away all the equipment in the tack room. As he lifted another saddle and made to move past her, she said, "No helicopter questions today?"

He arched a brow. "I was smart enough to have it in the hangar."

"I don't know," she continued when he emerged again. "I still think the big kid in you is eventually leading up to rides."

He didn't even crack a smile. "Nope, won't be happening."

It was her turn to arch a brow, but she didn't argue with him. He did seem pretty serious about his resolve.

She wasn't certain whether to believe him. She hadn't always been good about judging the character of a man—hence the disastrous long relationship with a guy who dumped her just when she thought he was going to propose.

"You know what I'm most surprised about?" she said. "How good you are with kids."

He followed her back outside to the corral, where they leaned their forearms on the fence and watched the horses graze.

"What's so strange about that?" he asked. "Kids are just little people, and I get along with most people."

"Most? I've never met a person you *didn't* get along with. But kids? That takes a special patience, a real interest. It makes me wonder—do you want kids of your own someday?"

The moment the words were out of her mouth, she second-guessed herself. Would he think she was pushing their relationship too far too fast?

He didn't say anything for a long moment.

"I'm sorry," she said. "That's very personal."

He looked down at her, eyes squinting against the sun. "People talk about whether they want kids all the time. 'I want two,' 'I want three.' My answer has always been, nope, I'm not the settling-down type, and kids need that kind of stability."

She tried not to feel sad about it—she knew who he was.

"Kids can drive parents crazy, like I did with my mom. I wasn't the easiest kid."

"No!" she said with exaggerated disbelief.

He grinned. "I forgot rules, like remembering to come home before dark. I didn't really mean to be bad, I just got involved in something and lost track of anything else that should have mattered. My mom always had to worry about me, and I feel bad about that. Guess it's my turn to worry about her."

"You mentioned she was getting forgetful."

"I think I know why." He hesitated. "I'm worried she's starting to drink too much."

"You think she's an alcoholic?" she asked, stunned.

"No, not at all. Not yet," he clarified, and he took a deep breath and let it out. "I've never seen her rip-roarin' drunk, she's not horribly hung over in the morning, she doesn't have blackouts. But . . . she always has a wineglass with her every evening, and I didn't normally pay attention to how often she refilled. But now I'm seeing a lot of wine bottles in the recycling. I told my brothers, and they didn't want to believe me, but . . . Daniel's been doing things around the ranch for her because she's been too 'sick' or sleeping in, or whatever. But it's adding up. I talked to her, and she blamed her overcommitment to her new partnership in the Mystic Connection, but I think she's just making excuses, even to herself. I finally went to my dad about it, since I wasn't getting through to her."

"What did he say?" Lyndsay asked with concern. It had to be horribly difficult to see a problem with your parents, the ones who've always led your family and been the bedrock of stability.

"He goes to bed earlier than she does. He doesn't see her drinking that much. He said he'll start keeping track of the bottles in recycling. But Lynds—I told her I noticed. If she really wants to hide her drinking, she can find another way to get rid of the bottles."

"I'm sorry, Will. You've been worried about this for a while, haven't you?"

"How did you know?"

"You've occasionally seemed far away, a little distracted. I'm glad you finally talked to me about it. I think it helps to get these things out in the open. For what it's worth, I think you made the right decision, trying to talk to your parents about it."

He gave her a crooked smile. "That helps, thanks. I'd told my brothers I wasn't going to 'tattle' to my dad, but . . . I finally felt he had to know the truth."

"And now both parents know your concerns.

Maybe they'll talk to each other. Or maybe your mom will realize she's been sliding into a dependency that's not healthy."

"Makes sense. Hope that happens."

His smile faded as he suddenly stared hard at her. "It's pretty selfish of me to talk to you about my mom, when yours isn't here anymore."

"Never think that. I have good memories of my mom."

"I remember her a little, in a fuzzy kind of way. That must have been tough, losing her so young."

"Cancer is hard to understand when you're nine. And I didn't realize how young my mom really was, only in her late forties. Since they were so much older than the other parents, someone thought she was my grandmother once. The chemo . . . she hadn't looked so good by then."

"That was really thoughtless of that idiot," he said and gave her hand a squeeze.

She shrugged. "The guy didn't know any better. And he was a guy—he didn't notice stuff like that."

"Guys don't notice things?"

"See, you're a guy—and you don't even notice that you don't notice things!"

She met his gaze—and burst out laughing. He had to join her.

When their laughter faded, he said, "You know, back to kids, I'm surprised how much I'm enjoying the 4-H kids."

"If you can take a kid at this age, who's immature but beginning to realize he has his own mind and can be rebellious, you can handle almost anything. And they start out so easy as babies—they just lie there and want to be held—not that I'm advocating having a kid, sorry. It's just . . ." She had to look away, because it was too painful. Her voice came out husky. "You'd be a good dad."

Those words hung there between them, and she felt all the yearning of an impending broken heart. She wanted kids—it was a real deal breaker with her. And then she decided to just be open.

"You know, Will, you'd have to run for your life from me if you actually wanted kids." She briefly put her hand on her forehead. "And I can't believe I'm telling you this."

He eyed her impassively, saying nothing, but his jaw tightened.

She rambled on. "I'm thirty-three years old. I'm sort of getting ready to find the right guy and settle down. But the right guy for me has to want kids. If you wanted kids . . . well, I'll be honest, I could get serious about you." *My heart is already serious about you.*

Her feelings were out in the open. And instead of saying anything, he stared at her, really studying her. She waited for a fake twinkle in his eye, that charming grin he seemed to put on when he wanted to keep his emotions private, but he stayed serious.

She put a hand on his arm. "You don't have to say anything, Will, honest. I wouldn't be with you if I didn't really feel a connection. I may have dated pretty regularly, but it was never just to have a man around. I had to really want to be with him."

"And I'm flattered," he said quietly. "But—"

"No, it's okay, don't say it." *I don't want to know that I'm not the type of girl you can ever love.* "I'm enjoying this just for what it is."

She hadn't intended to be so blunt. And since she was being blunt . . .

She sighed. "If I'm going to make you uncomfortable," she said, turning toward him, "I might as well go the distance. I need to tell you something else that I've been worried about."

He sported a brief, crooked smile. "Gee, Lynds, should I run away now?"

She was glad that he was still able to tease after what she'd just confessed. "It's about Kate and the book."

He looked at her with those piercing hazel eyes. "What did she say? God, it'll destroy Tony if she doesn't really love him. These last few days, I've been watching them at the tavern, and I'm feeling kind of sick about it all."

"Kate and Tony are fine, so don't worry a bit about them." She took a deep breath. "Kate didn't write the book. I did."

Chapter 17

Will's first feeling was of intense relief that his best friend's fiancée wasn't fantasizing about him. "Jesus, that's good to know," he said, letting out his breath in a long, slow exhale.

Lyndsay watched him closely, as if waiting.

And then he really looked at her. "*You* wrote it?"

She nodded, then lifted both hands as if to placate him. "You've got to understand that I've been writing for eight years now, Will, and I'd been rejected for *years* for my first book. I even wrote when I was a kid, but thought teaching was a more practical, safer choice."

"You've been *that* serious about writing, and I never heard about it?" It seemed easier to concentrate on the facts of her secret, rather than truly think about what it meant to him.

"I never told anyone, not even my family. Writing is something I did . . . just for me. By keeping it to myself, no one was pressuring me about whether I was submitting, or how many rejections I'd received, or bugging me to read it. The merest *thought* of that kind of pressure gave me writer's block."

"If you didn't want anyone to read it, why did Kate have the file?"

Lyndsay twisted her hands together. "Because people are going to read it now—a lot of people. I sold it, Will. A publisher bought it."

He couldn't help smiling at her. "That's really great, Lyndsay, congratulations. When does it come out?"

She watched him hopefully. "End of next week."

"Wow, that soon." But inside, his brain was beginning to pound with panic. Why had *Lyndsay* used parts of him and his life in her book? It didn't make sense—he'd never gotten any kind of romantic vibe from her back in the day.

She briefly paced away from him and back. Two horses lifted their heads away from the grass and stared at them.

"I know you're thinking about my hero, Cody," she said. "Kate assures me she wouldn't have had a clue that Cody had a little of your personality unless I'd told her."

"But that scene I read, the one that was a lot like what I did for Brittany—"

"Kate was having Tony read the scene, which is why it was open. Tony didn't even remember what you'd done back then, honestly, and if your best friend doesn't remember, no one will."

He nodded, but he didn't know what to say.

"What you did for Brittany—it was such a romantic gesture, Will," she said quietly, staring at the horses, her gaze unfocused. "You were so young, and to have thought of that—well, I really admired you for it. I remember Brittany showing us the necklace, and she was so happy that you'd done something so special for her. I never forgot it, and apparently neither did my subconscious. I didn't even realize what I'd based the scene on."

It was so strange to talk about Brittany. No one talked of her to him—he'd made sure of that—except her family. He owed them anything they needed from him. It was his fault they only had memories of their daughter, and if it eased them to talk about her, he was always there to listen. But for him, it had always been agony. But . . . not with Lyndsay. She seemed so sympathetic and matter-of-fact, and she didn't act like she had to walk on eggshells about the sensitive subject.

But she was watching him too closely. He hated pity and didn't want to see it in her dark eyes—didn't want that from *her*.

"You know," she said softly, "you made her last years very special. There are women who never find that in their lifetimes, and Brittany had it."

He just stared at her. He couldn't speak, or he'd blurt out all his recriminations, his guilt, the fact that Brittany would never get married or have babies or achieve her dreams.

"As for my book," she went on, "I didn't even realize at first that Cody looked like you, and maybe had some of your . . . charming attitude and way with women."

"But you did realize it at some point."

"Yeah," she admitted, "although not until just a few weeks ago, when a blogger asked me if I based my hero on someone, and the truth just . . . hit me. I'll be honest, Will. Back in high school, I had a crush on you for a while. You'd always been so nice to me."

He blinked at her in confusion. "I thought we were just friends."

"We were! You had Brittany. Tony was so weirded out by the thought of me dating his friends that he made me promise not to. But when I was having a bad Valentine's Day, you bought me a friend carnation. You probably don't remember—"

"I remember."

Her mouth dropped open. "You do?"

"Sure. You looked so upset and I just wanted to cheer you up. But I didn't mean to lead you on."

"You didn't. It was all in my head, and I got over it. Or at least I thought I did. And then . . . somehow . . . parts of you became parts of Cody."

She looked chagrined and embarrassed, leaving him confused.

And terrified. His heart felt all strange and tight that this gorgeous, smart woman saw him as . . . some kind of hero. He wasn't a hero; he felt like a fraud. She was all wrong about him, and in the end, he'd disappoint her.

She took a deep breath. "Just so you know, Cody isn't *really* you. He just has some of your character- istics. . . . and he sort of looks like you . . . and yes, he's a cowboy—but it's Montana!"

"You're right, ranching in Montana is *nothing* like Colorado," he teased. He could feel the genial mask settle back into place like an old friend. The mask that had made his family feel better after Brittany died, the one that kept hidden all his guilt and doubts.

To his surprise, he saw Lyndsay's gaze focused on him as if she saw the difference. But she couldn't, he knew that. No one ever did.

"I promise," she continued, "that I won't ever say a word about my inspiration. Heck, I hate to talk about my writing process anyway."

"Were you keeping the publication a secret from everyone because you didn't want to tell me?"

"No. I'm proud of my work, but . . . I'm a teacher, Will. There are going to be people who might be upset that I wrote it, who won't know how to talk to their kids about it. I just want to delay any kind of announcement until school is over. That's the end of next week. Then the kids and their parents will have the entire summer to get used to it, so hopefully it won't be an issue in the fall." She let out a shaky breath. "I'm sorry, Will. I've been afraid of your reaction—heck, I'm afraid of the whole reading public's reaction, like I'm really a fraud and don't know what I'm doing and my editor made a mistake—sorry, I'm rambling. But, regardless of my recent realization about Cody, I am still so thrilled beyond measure that my dream of being an author has come true."

He tipped his hat back and gave her a genuine smile. "I'm really proud of you, Lynds. There aren't many people in the world who can stick with a dream for years and make it happen."

Her smile trembled a bit, but she didn't say anything. Almost as if in silent understanding that the conversation was over, they turned back to the corral and rested their arms on the fence once more. But they didn't touch.

After about ten minutes, Lyndsay said, "I guess I should go. Work night, and all."

"Okay, I'll walk you to your car."

The air was cooling, the sun had dipped behind the mountains. Behind them, the horses nickered to each other, and magpies called from the trees. It was a peaceful beauty he was used to, but he never took it for granted. Now, tension as murky as a swamp was so thick that he should have been able to see it.

When they reached her car, Lyndsay gave him a searching look, then a quick kiss. "Good night, Will."

As she drove away, he watched her, hands in his jeans pockets, until the cloud of dust in her wake disappeared. He went on with his evening chores like a good cowboy, while his mind swirled with so many contradictory thoughts. But one stood out. He was filled with dread, knowing he could never live up to the man Lyndsay had created "Cody" to be. He couldn't change who he was.

Or had he never wanted to change?

By the time he was lying in bed that night, sleepless, staring at the shadows on the ceiling from the open window, he came to a kind of conclusion, not that he felt good about it. He was going to have to cool things off with Lyndsay. He wasn't the man she seemed to think he was, and he'd only disappoint her and lead her on, when they had no future. But they had another date already planned, the first birthday party for Olivia Thalberg at the Silver Creek Ranch. He'd wait to talk to Lyndsay until after that.

But it didn't give him any peace.

Lyndsay was surprised to find that she dreaded a little girl's first birthday. She couldn't even imagine sitting in a car with Will, knowing she'd have to look at his deliberately pleasant expression, so she said she had to work late and would meet him there.

His face—she'd seen it completely change after he'd heard about Cody; he'd just wiped away the confusion and concern and replaced it with that smiling-cowboy expression. She hadn't realized how much he'd actually trusted her with his emotions until he'd taken that intimacy away again.

Her fears about what he'd do when he learned about her book had been well founded. He was pulling away from her. Now she'd have to consider what should happen next.

And then there was another flyer from the widows. She'd seen it when she'd gone to buy a gift bag for Livvie's present. It had more bold lettering about the soon-to-be-famous local author—and this time, an excerpt of the first page of the book had been included! At least it was about her heroine, rather than the hero . . .

When she got to the Silver Creek Ranch just before dinner, there were cars and pickups parked along the gravel drive heading toward the main barn, and the big log house, and the yard between, which was full of tables and chairs. Colorful lanterns, still dim in daylight, were strung around the border. As she walked closer, she could see tables of food inside the barn and, just inside the entrance, a two-level cake wrapped in pink lace with a big white bow—all icing, she knew—with little puppy dogs on top surrounding the number 1. Lyndsay leaned closer to gape in amazement.

"Didn't Em do a great job?" Monica Shaw asked, linking arms with her.

Monica's black curls sprung out from her head like fireworks in a night sky. She was slender, with hollowed cheeks and dark, almond-shaped eyes.

Heather came to stand on the other side. "Em just gets more brilliant all the time. Pretty soon, she'll be in such demand, she won't be able to find time for my catering business."

Lyndsay nodded. "I'm always so impressed—

and mostly because regardless of the creativity, everything always tastes so good."

"Come on and sit with us," Monica said. "Heather and Chris are with us—I'm sure we've got room for you and Will."

If Will wants to sit with me, Lyndsay couldn't help thinking.

Out in the yard, a tall centerpiece of balloons towered over each table, with Hershey's Kisses scattered about. Monica and Heather showed her to their table, where Chris and Travis were deep in discussion but stood up to offer hugs when she joined the group. Travis was Monica's boyfriend, a tall ex-Secret Service agent with auburn hair in a short military cut.

Lyndsay popped a chocolate Kiss in her mouth and studied the dozens of people, all of whom she knew well, except perhaps for Chasz, Whitney's brother, and her parents, jet-setters Vanessa and Charles Winslow, who kept a condo in Aspen so they could visit often. To Lyndsay's surprise, she saw Will holding the birthday girl. Livvie was in a pink dress the color of her cake, with a big bow in her dark wispy hair and little white shoes on her chubby feet. Will was talking to her earnestly, wearing a big smile that made hers blossom, and Lyndsay felt another one of those sharp pangs of regret and loss she was becoming too familiar with.

She'd told him he'd make a great dad; she'd told him she wanted kids; she'd told him about Cody. Yeah, that was all going to work out just fine.

He saw her and waved, and he looked nothing but pleased to see her. But oh, she knew him too well, and how good he was at making even those close to him see what he wanted them to see.

Lyndsay excused herself and went to him, a moth to the flame, a glutton for punishment—oh, she had to stop these mental clichés.

"Happy birthday, Livvie!"

Livvie stuck a finger in her mouth and clutched Will a little tighter around the neck.

Lyndsay had to tease Will. "She's a girl; of course she's fascinated with you."

Will chuckled, but he glanced back at Livvie rather than meet Lyndsay's eyes.

"I forgot to ask where the gift table is," she said, holding up her bag with purple and white tissue paper exploding out of it.

He gestured to a table set up next to the barn, where gifts were already piled high.

"Thanks. Do you have a place to sit?" she asked. "Monica and Heather said there was room at their table."

Will frowned. "Sure."

She studied him, unable to stop the surge of sadness that must have shown in her eyes.

"Sorry, just thinking about Chris," Will said. "We got into a little argument yesterday. I don't want everyone to be bothered by the tension."

"What happened?"

"The damned helicopter again. I sort of said if he wanted to use it in search and rescue, he should learn to fly the damned thing, unless he was afraid."

Lyndsay winced. "I bet that went well."

"It did, which made it worse. Chris didn't even take offense, kind of laughed it off and agreed that he just didn't like the idea of doing it himself."

"Sorry."

"Yeah, I just can't seem to get it through his head that—"

He stopped abruptly, as if he'd meant to confide something to her but changed his mind. Her shoulders sagged a little.

"—that I'm just a cowboy."

"It'll sink in eventually." She reached to take Livvie's hand, and the wide-eyed girl allowed it. "So . . . did you see the new flyer?"

He eyed her. "I did. Nice writing skills. So you didn't publish it?"

"It was the widows."

He shook his head. "Guess I'm not surprised. How did they find out?"

She gave him the details, then added, "They insist they want to help me promote but promise not to reveal my name before I'm ready."

"That's nice of them to give you a boost."

She shrugged. "I was pretty worried, but they assure me the reveal is all up to me." After a long sigh, she put on a smile, determined to forget about what she couldn't control. "Can I get you a beer?"

"Sure, thanks. I'll find Livvie's parents or the next admirers and hand her over."

But Livvie's parents, Josh and Whitney, were already approaching, and Livvie reached her chubby arms toward her dad, almost diving out of Will's embrace. Josh took her, wearing a proud grin. Whitney had dark hair styled in a layered cut to her shoulders, and a single dimple to the right of her mouth that deepened as she smiled.

"She's Daddy's little girl, that's for sure," Whitney said. "I've never seen a man buy so many versions of toy horses—stuffed ones, riding versions with wheels, little action figures."

"She's going to be my little cowgirl," Josh said, kissing Livvie's forehead. She burrowed her head under his chin, sucked her thumb, and stared around her with her mom's big gray eyes.

Lyndsay imagined what it would be like to have a child of her own, to cuddle every night, to introduce her to the world, to share her with her daddy.

But not Will.

She gave Will a brief smile. "You stay and chat. I'll get the beer."

In the cooler shadows of the barn, Lyndsay was filling up two Vote Thalberg cups from a keg when a female voice said in her ear, "Love your promo flyers!"

Lyndsay jumped and spilled beer down her hand. Jessica laughed. "Sorry!"

"You're not sorry. You love to startle me. And I didn't do those flyers. I promised you the first exclusive, and I wasn't planning on doing anything for myself."

"If not you . . . ?"

Lyndsay finished filling a cup and started on the second one. "Once I found out, I promised not to tell. It'll come out. I'll be able to talk about it when we do the interview."

"We should do that soon so we're ready to go to publication end of next week."

Lyndsay felt a little thrill at the idea of her first interview as an author—and was so glad that it would be with Jessica. "I'd love that. Give me a call and we'll set up dinner or something."

"How are things with Will?" Jessica asked. "He looks mighty good holding a baby."

"For a man who doesn't want kids," Lyndsay said, then quickly looked around, but they hadn't been overheard. "I shouldn't have said that, sorry."

"It's not like it's a big surprise," Jessica sympathized. "He and I never dated long enough to talk about stuff like that, but obviously you two have been moving faster."

"Not sure it was wise, but it's been fun." It *was* fun, but it was no longer the same. "I knew going in that he wasn't the long-term type. It's just harder than I thought it'd be."

Jessica put a hand on her arm. "I'm sorry, Lynds."

"Thanks."

Lyndsay returned to her table and set a beer down in front of Will, noticing that Brooke and Adam had joined them, too.

Travis took in Lyndsay and shook his head. "So

how do you get your girlfriend of a couple weeks to wait on you, when I can't get mine of a year to do the same?"

Monica and Lyndsay exchanged amused glances as Monica said, "Hey, I can be just as polite as Lyndsay. Taking turns being nice to each other only makes sense. It's just so often your turn," she said smugly.

Adam joined in. "I've been married for almost six months, and I don't think I've mastered this yet either."

"Hey, I'm nice to you all the time," Brooke said, spreading her hands. "Who's doing your chores around here while you and Coach McKee are finishing up the latest house for our returning vets?" Her glance took in the whole table. "And I do it gladly, of course."

"The welcome ceremony for our newest house is next week," Travis said, "so everyone pay attention to your e-mail for the details."

Lyndsay knew that he and Adam, fellow ex-Marines and now good friends, had begun working on the houses together. "Wow, how many houses have we renovated so far?"

"About fifteen over the last five years or so," Adam said. "This newest one will be for a female vet, Sergeant Jamie Knapp, and her family."

"My sister's coming to visit and attend the ceremony," Travis said.

"That's great," Will said with enthusiasm.

Travis's sister was a Marine who'd lost a lower

leg to an IED. She'd fought to prove she could still be effective in her work so that she could keep serving her country. Lyndsay was really looking forward to meeting her.

"So how's it feel to be out of the apartment?" Lyndsay asked Monica.

"It was feeling a little claustrophobic," Monica admitted. "Steph is enjoying it immensely. Every couple days she brings me up to show me another wall she decorated."

Through this chitchat, Lyndsay couldn't miss the obvious way Chris and Will were avoiding each other's eyes. And then the fireworks really began when Chris seemed to almost belligerently bring up a story of Will rescuing a trapped skier after an avalanche. He earnestly talked about his brother's bravery, and he sounded so proud—but Lyndsay had a feeling there was a dig meant there somewhere.

As if to give them privacy, Brooke, Adam, Monica, and Travis went to join the buffet line.

Will rounded on Chris, his eyes stern. "You've got to stop this. We can't be upset with each other—this is the last thing Mom needs, with her problems."

"You don't think I worry about Mom?" Chris demanded.

Lyndsay and Heather gave each other concerned glances.

Chris continued, "I keep balancing how much I talk about the wedding, trying not to stress her, wondering if that just makes everything worse."

"What do you mean, 'stress Mom'?" Steph said, as she came to stand next to her brothers. "What's going on that you haven't been telling me?"

There was an edge of fear to her voice that had her brothers actually looking apologetic toward each other.

Will sighed. "There's nothing major, it's just . . . I started noticing something the last couple weeks, but I didn't want to say much until I was certain."

"Certain of what? Are she and Dad okay?" Steph demanded, her voice getting shrill.

"They're fine," Chris said, taking her arm to draw her into an empty chair between them. "We're just worried about Mom's stress level because we think she's been drinking a bit too much."

Her mouth dropped open and moved silently for a moment. "I wouldn't have moved out if I'd known she was having problems. Wait—could my moving out have caused this? She didn't want me to go. I shouldn't have—"

"Stop," Will interrupted gently, taking her hand. "There is no one thing causing this. And though I talked to her about it, Mom doesn't see what I've been seeing."

But Steph's eyes were brimming with tears. "Oh, God, she wanted to talk to me a couple days ago, and I was rushing to buy a stupid vase before the store closed and I was short with her—"

Will cupped her face. "I'd hug you right now, but we don't want people to think something's wrong. It'll get back to Mom."

Steph nodded like a bobble-head doll and quickly wiped at her eyes. "What do we do? Should I move home?"

"No," Chris said. "That's like asking if I should cancel my wedding. Mom isn't an alcoholic. We're just worried she's starting to rely on wine too much, and it's making her oversleep and miss some ranch duties. But Will talked to her."

Steph turned wet eyes on Will.

"Mom knows we're concerned, and so does Dad," Will said. "Let's give them some time to talk to each other. Now let's go get some food and enjoy Livvie's celebration."

Steph nodded and rose to her feet, followed by Chris and Heather.

After the three of them moved away, Lyndsay looked at Will. "You did a good job with her."

"I should have told her what was going on before," he said, shaking his head. "I'm too used to protecting my baby sister."

"I like that about you."

He searched her eyes for a moment, but only said, "Let's go get some food."

Chapter 18

It was far too easy to discuss his family's most intimate problems in front of Lyndsay, Will thought—and he didn't like it. He stood behind her in line for the food, and he couldn't help admiring the way her short skirt hugged her hips and left her long, slender legs bare. Her strappy sandals practically decorated her feet. He was just raising his perusal to the silky top she wore, when she marched away from the buffet, her plate only half full.

"Mrs. Thalberg!" she called. "Got a moment?"

Knowing they might need a referee—but was he objective?—he followed Lyndsay to where the three widows and her dad were busy eating barbecue.

"Want us to make room for you two?" Mrs. Palmer asked.

Will did a double take on seeing the birthday balloon print all over her dress.

"No, that's okay," Lyndsay said, "but I have a question about . . . something you distributed today."

Mrs. Ludlow regally glanced around. "No one seems to be paying attention. Did you like our second effort?"

"Uh . . . sure. You all know I appreciate your support, right?"

Mrs. Thalberg looked at Will. "So now your young man knows, too?"

Will felt conspicuous, but he nodded.

"Perfect," Mrs. Thalberg continued. "Just wait until you see what we have planned for the day that Lyndsay reveals her secret—you'll be so proud!"

Lyndsay's eyes widened, but Will detected the excitement she seemed to be trying to hide.

"Can't you tell me what it is?" Lyndsay asked.

"We don't want to do that in case there is a technical problem," Mrs. Ludlow said. "You understand."

Lyndsay glanced at him and he shrugged. She put on a smile. "Okay, then, I trust you all. And thank you so much."

Will followed her back to the buffet line, where she finished selecting food, her expression pensive.

"*Do* you trust them?" he asked softly.

"I know they honestly have my best interests at heart." She searched his gaze with her own. "Do you think I'm making a mistake? That I should insist they stop?"

"It's your career."

"But I've connected you to it, haven't I?" she asked sadly.

He didn't say anything.

"We need to talk, Will. After the birthday party, okay?"

He nodded, wondering if she was going to apologize again—which wasn't necessary. But maybe there was no point in delaying his own discussion with her. So they sat through party games, where the adults took turns reading nursery rhymes in silly voices, puppet play for Livvie, and blowing bubbles. Then it was time for the gifts and the cake, and even after Livvie retired for the evening, the party continued, patio heaters lit for warmth, lantern lights glowing softly all around them as couples danced.

Lyndsay met his gaze. "Let's go for a walk, Will, okay?"

They walked side by side, not touching, heading behind the house, where Sandy Thalberg had created beautiful gardens. There were lights strung in a few trees, enough to see by and make things romantic. He gestured to a bench and Lyndsay sat down.

"Lyndsay—"

"Wait, I need to say something first. I've been doing a lot of thinking these last couple days. I know things can never be the same after how I've . . . infringed on your privacy with my book. I've made you uncomfortable, and I'm frankly mortified by it. It's not fair to drag this out any longer, when we both knew where this was headed from the beginning. I think we should stop seeing each other, Will."

She finally paused and took a deep breath. Surprised, Will studied her expression in the gloom of twilight, saw her sorrow, but also her determination. The fact that she beat him to the same conclusion should make him feel better, but it didn't. She was the first woman to really understand him, he realized, to understand what he was capable of—and what he was not. It was a scary moment, this connection deeper than he was used to.

"Okay, so you're not saying anything," she said with exasperation.

The sadness in her voice was like a physical hurt inside him, which should prove this was the right decision for both of them.

"I'm sorry it has to end this way," he finally said, taking her hand.

She looked down at their joined hands for a moment, then gave him a crooked smile. "I'm not sure I know what you mean. How else was it going to end? Unless you mean you wish you would have done the breaking up."

"You know that's not true. I never wanted to hurt you, Lyndsay, which was part of the reason I hesitated about dating you."

"It was worth the risk, at least to me." She squeezed his hand once, let it go, and slapped her hands to her thighs as she rose.

He followed her and took her arm when she

would have walked away. "You may not believe me, Lyndsay, but I'm really going to miss you."

They stared at each other for a long moment.

She cupped his face with a trembling hand. "I'm not just going to miss you, Will. I'm going to ache for you. I've fallen in love with you."

He let out his breath, leaning his face briefly against her hand. That was a stab of pain he hadn't expected.

"I learned things about you that made my feelings change into love," she said. "That you still grieve for a girl who died long ago—"

He stiffened.

"That's a tragedy and testament to your loyalty all at the same time. To people who think you can never love a woman—they're wrong. You loved Brittany. And you care about the kids in your community, even if you don't want kids yourself. You give of yourself even when you don't mean to— which is what your brother Chris keeps pointing out by admiring your rescue exploits. You're loyal to your family; that's why it's so sad that you're trying desperately to never have one of your own. I hope you rethink that someday, Will. I hope you find a way to let Brittany rest in peace."

She stood on tiptoes to kiss his cheek, then walked away, disappearing into the darkness past the house.

Will remained alone for a few minutes, reminding himself that being alone was the choice he made. *Forever* being alone, even when he finally continued dating. It was what he deserved. Lyndsay had it all wrong about Brittany. *Brittany* was at peace—it was he who never could be.

Saturday morning sucked, as far as Lyndsay was concerned. She'd cried herself to sleep after breaking it off with Will the night before—it wasn't as if she'd expected him to beg her to remain his girlfriend, but it still hurt worse than any breakup she'd ever had.

Since her face was still puffy and her eyes bloodshot, she decided to go for a run and get exercise out of the way, only to see Matias Gonzalez riding his bike down the road to the Sweetheart Ranch. This was the Saturday before the science fair—she knew for certain that his poster and display weren't finished. She felt disappointed that Matias wasn't taking it seriously, like all their discussions hadn't meant anything. Will certainly knew how important it was to the boy's grade—Lyndsay had rattled on enough about it. She hoped he sent Matias home.

But she wasn't about to chase after him and find out what was going on.

Her mood improved when she got home to find a large box on her front step. It was from her publisher, and she practically squealed with joy to open it and see her author copies, book after book with her name on it, the title, *A Cowboy in Montana*, embossed and foiled. She had one copy already, but this . . . this was a whole box. She stared at it and let more tears come, but this time they were tears of joy and amazement and pride. She'd written this book.

Fortified and renewed in this new career, she took a shower, then got back to what was once again the most important thing in her life—her writing. Cody's brother needed his own happy ending, even if she didn't see one happening for herself.

Will was limping when he came into his parents' kitchen. It was late afternoon, and he'd spent his day up in the mountains, leading pack horses laden with salt blocks to leave out for the cattle. Silver had been startled by a fox, danced sideways, and hit a fence post, slamming Will's ankle hard. He'd be black and blue for days, he knew, and it was already swollen. Like his mood could get any blacker, considering he should be relieved Lyndsay had dumped him. He'd iced the ankle, showered, but there'd been nothing for dinner in his fridge, so he'd come over to see what his parents had—

And found his mom with a tall glass of wine on the patio, staring out at the mountains, a half-empty bottle next to her.

She saw Will, and her guilty expression was all the evidence he needed. He limped over and sat down next to her.

"What's wrong with you?" Faith asked cautiously when he didn't speak.

"Hurt my ankle up in the mountains. It'll get better. What's wrong with you?" he asked pointedly.

She stared at the glass, swirling it for a moment before taking a sip. "It takes the edge off, and I'm under a lot of stress."

"What stress?" Will asked. "We all want to take the load off you. What can we do?"

"Stop acting like there's an easy fix to everything."

"I didn't say—"

"People told me that parenthood never ended, that little kids had little problems and big kids had big problems."

"What big problems? Chris is getting married, for God's sake. This should be a time to celebrate. We're all healthy."

"Are you? Are you *mentally* healthy, Will?"

He stiffened. "Excuse me? Are *you* talking to *me* about mental health?" And then he spoke without thinking, the last couple days' tension spewing out. "Perhaps if you got your head out of the mystical clouds and maybe got some basic counseling to figure out why you're looking for answers in a bottle—" And then he really heard himself and broke off, horrified.

Faith gaped at him, her eyes bright with tears.

"Mom, I'm so sorry," he began. "I don't know what I—"

"I'll tell you what problems I'm having, and I

don't need a counselor to figure them out," she said. "Do you know what it's like to have one son go on and on about his wedding, a joyous time in his life that'll never come again, while another son decided at *seventeen* that he'd never marry, that a dead girl was the only love he'd ever have?"

Will felt himself pale. "Mom, it's not like that."

"No? Then what's it like? And let's not forget that Daniel is unhappy with his life and I don't know why, that your sister felt like she had to get away from home instead of coming back after she'd been gone nine months at college"—her voice broke on a sob—"which is utterly stupid for me to be so upset about, because she's growing up and needs her independence and wants to share it with me, but I'm wallowing in self-pity and—what did you say?—looking for answers in a bottle." She threw her wineglass, and it shattered on the stone patio. Putting her face into her hands, she wept, her shoulders shuddering.

"Mom."

Will didn't know what to do except drop to his knees and put his arms around her. She clung to him, and they rocked together for a long minute.

He glanced up to see his dad standing in the doorway, face stark white and full of helpless sorrow. Joe came to them and put a hand on his wife's shoulder. When she saw him, her sobs increased anew as she wrapped her arms around his waist, and he bent over her.

Will stood up, letting his dad take over. He backed up step by step, watching them, feeling useless and sorrowful.

Had he really caused his mom such worry all these years?

Chapter 19

Will hadn't meant to go to Tony's Tavern, but he just couldn't sit at the bunkhouse and tell his brothers what had happened. He was still trying to make sense of it all, but right now, all he could feel was his mother's pain.

When he entered the tavern, only fainting limping, Tony nodded his hello, as he was dealing with another customer at the bar. Will looked around and had to admit to himself he was hoping Lyndsay wouldn't show up. Of course, this was her brother's place . . .

He sat down at the end of the bar, and Tony brought him a beer. Will nodded and took a long gulp before wiping the back of his arm across his mouth.

Tony eyed him. "You okay? Was that a limp?"

"It's nothing, just hazards of the cowboy life. We can't all have cushy jobs like bartender."

Tony grunted.

"Guess you haven't heard the news. Your sister dumped me."

Tony's dark brows shot up, although otherwise his expression remained impassive. "*She* dumped *you*? Has that happened before?"

"Sure it has. But not a lot," Will admitted, then took another drink.

"Gotta admit, I saw her face whenever she was with you. Didn't see this coming, not this soon, anyway."

Will shrugged. "She told me about the book, and the truth about the character Cody."

"Aah. Be right back."

Tony stepped away to help another customer, leaving Will to brood over his thoughts. To make things worse, he saw Sean Lighton, the guy with the obvious crush on Lyndsay, watching him from a couple places down the bar. When Sean saw Will notice, he quickly turned away. Will scowled, figuring the guy had overheard that he and Lyndsay were through.

"Well, that's an expression that says it all," Tony said on his return. "You didn't take the book well?"

"I'm really proud of her, of course. What an incredible accomplishment."

"But?"

"But I think the book is evidence that she wants more from me than I can give." She'd said she loved him, told him all the reasons she admired him, while he'd felt undeserving and even ashamed that he couldn't live up to what she needed.

"Lynds always goes all in."

"That's not the only reason we broke up. She wants kids and a commitment, and she knows she's not getting that from me, so she cut me loose."

Tony didn't respond.

"And apparently, those life decisions of mine have helped drive my mother to drink."

Another eyebrow lift from Tony. "You're really having a good couple days, aren't you?" Then he looked over Will's head. "Guess who's here."

Will let out his breath. "Can't be surprised." Maybe he'd even been waiting for Lyndsay. He realized he wanted to tell her about his mom, to ask her opinion, to see if what his mom had said could be true. He'd grown to depend on Lyndsay's opinion, to need her thoughts. But he didn't have the right to ask, at least not for a long time. He wasn't sure they could ever be friends again, which made him so sad that he almost wished they hadn't dated.

But that was a cop-out. He didn't wish they hadn't dated—he'd never forget how alive she made him feel.

Bracing himself, he glanced over his shoulder and saw her with Jessica and Kate. The three of them were laughing, wearing cowboy boots and skirts. Lyndsay's long hair hung in waves down her back, and her bangs sort of stuck out beneath her hat brim in cute tangles.

And then he saw Kate's brother Dave strolling behind them, as if they'd come together.

"Is Kate already fixing Lyndsay up with her brother?" Will demanded tightly. Sean was going to be disappointed, too.

"I don't think so," was Tony's mild response. "Kate and Dave had planned tonight for a while."

Will should have felt relieved, but he didn't. And then Lyndsay moved down the bar and spotted him for the first time. Her stride faltered and her eyes grew wide and a little too bright.

"Hi, Will," she said, but kept going. "Hey, Tony."

Kate stared at Will in surprise, then frowned at Lyndsay's back as she followed her friend. Will turned back to the bar, unable to miss Sean's gaze lingering on Lyndsay's back.

But Tony was watching Will. "What are your plans tonight? I could take a break and we could talk about your mom or whatever. Maybe not so much my sister . . ."

Will sighed. "Thanks. At least you didn't think I was here to pick up a new woman."

"Didn't occur to me."

"Might to Lyndsay."

"I don't think so."

When the three women were seated around a small wooden table in the back room, with the pool table between them and the front room, Kate leaned over it and hissed, "What the heck is going on with you and Will?"

"Oh." Feigning casualness, Lyndsay took a handful of popcorn and ate it before explaining, "I broke it off after Livvie's party last night."

Kate's eyes widened before filling with sympathy.

Jessica whistled long and low, regarding Lyndsay with interest. "Really?"

"Well, I knew going in he wasn't the settling-down type. And I want to find that kind of guy. We had a lot of fun, but it was time to end things and put him behind me."

Kate didn't speak for a moment, just continued to study Lyndsay with growing sadness. "I'm sorry, Lynds. I'd hoped if anyone could turn him around, it would be you."

"Well, you're giving me a lot of credit. I guess loving him wasn't enough."

And her voice broke on that stupid "L" word, and Kate and Jessica took her hands, their eyes full of sympathy.

"I can't believe he had the guts to show up here," Jessica said darkly.

Lyndsay cleared her throat. "He likes to talk to Tony. I never wanted to be a problem that came between the two of them, so I'm glad. It's not like I'll never see him again. We're going to run into each other all the time, so eventually we'll be friends again, I'll make sure of it."

"That's big of you," Jessica said grimly. "Where the heck is Nicole? I'll go get us some drinks. Maybe something stronger than beer."

"Sounds good," Lyndsay said.

When Jessica had gone, Kate dropped her voice. "Did you break up over the book?"

Dismally, Lyndsay said, "Partially. He's a private person, and I intruded on that, even though I hadn't meant to." Her brows drew together. "There's more. I think his whole problem is still about Brittany. He blames himself, even after all these years. I can't be mad at him when he's mourning a dead girl."

"Well, that's tragic, but since he's hurt you, I can be mad."

"Damn, you're a good almost-sister-in-law."

Then Jessica returned, looked from Kate's face to Lyndsay's, and gave a melodramatic sigh. "I missed something, I know I did."

Lyndsay laughed and told herself she would find a better mood if it killed her.

Will's family often had Sunday brunch on the patio after church if the weather cooperated, and it ended up being a beautiful day. Not that his parents had gone to church; Will had professed to being clueless to his brothers about the reason their parents had stayed home. It seemed too personal and private to discuss Faith's breakdown.

Steph, Chris, and Heather showed up, and Will suggested they start cooking even though their mom hadn't come down yet. They all tried to talk normally about the upcoming hay cutting and whether the weather would cooperate. The kitchen was a peaceful place to be, full of white cabinets with a lot of glass fronts showing the antique dishes passed down in their family, gleaming chrome appliances that were a more modern touch.

And then Faith entered the kitchen with Joe. She was wearing a flowing dress in greens and blues over earth mother brown sandals. Will tried not to study them both too openly. Her eyes might have been a little bloodshot, but her grin was welcoming and warm, as always.

"Look at this," she said to Joe. "What a treat to be cooked for. I could smell the bacon up in our room."

"I've set the table on the patio," Steph said. "Orange juice is already poured. Go sit down, and we'll bring out the food and coffeepot."

Faith touched Will's arm as she went past, and she smiled at him. He found the knot in his chest easing. They enjoyed a nice breakfast, talking about light subjects like Livvie's birthday party, the upcoming welcome ceremony for the vet house renovation, and, of course, the historical society vote and election-day volunteering Will's dad had signed up for.

"It's this week," Daniel said. "I, for one, will be glad it's over."

Steph rolled her eyes. "Hey, it's been a lot tougher for Will. His girlfriend is linked to the Thalberg camp."

Will decided it wasn't the right time to clarify

his new dating situation. No one in his family had been at Tony's to see the arctic divide that had separated Lyndsay and him. "Hey, it's been tough for all of us."

"So is that why Dom told me you two avoided each other last night?" Daniel asked.

Will could have kicked him under the table. It wasn't like he could blame Daniel, though—the family always discussed everything.

Now his mom was studying him. "What's wrong, Will? Don't bother keeping secrets. Trust me—that's worse for everybody."

Will hesitated, then gave in. "Lyndsay and I broke up."

Chris shook his head sadly, Daniel gave him a cynical, narrow-eyed stare, and his parents and Heather gaped.

"But—you looked so happy at the birthday party!" Steph exclaimed. "Weren't you?"

"Yes and no. I knew things weren't going well. We broke up right afterward."

"And you're okay with that?" his mother asked.

"We tried it, and it didn't work. We've been friends a long time—I'm sure we'll go back to that. It's not like we spent years together."

When no one said anything, that phrase practically rang across the yard, while his mom stared at him with eyes full of old sorrow.

Okay, so he hadn't dated *anyone* for years, other than Brittany.

Conversation gradually resumed, but never with the same lightness, and he felt exasperated. Why did this breakup bother them all so much?

Probably because it bothered him, and he wasn't being subtle enough about it.

When the siblings got up to remove the dishes, Faith remained seated. "Will, can we talk—privately?" she added.

His brothers and sister eyed him, but between them and their dad, they took all the plates except for the coffee cups and disappeared inside. Will sat down next to his mom's chair, and she took both his hands in hers.

"I am so sorry for how I behaved yesterday," she said earnestly, tears beginning to shimmer in her eyes.

"Mom—"

"No, let me finish. I made it seem like my problems were your fault or your brothers' or sister's fault. That was unfair of me to focus on a simplified answer to a very complex problem. This has *never* been your fault, do you understand?"

"Well, sure, but having kids played a part, and I'm your kid."

"Listen to my words, Will—you are too quick to blame yourself for everything. You have to stop that. Being a parent is never easy, and if anyone had told me that in some ways it gets *harder* as your kids grow up, well, I guess I wouldn't have believed them. But I raised you to be an adult who makes his own decisions. Stepping back and letting you make them—even when you're thirty-three years old and don't need my help—is just plain hard. I think I let the worry eat at me, and when I decided to become a partner at the Mystic Connection, thinking it would distract me, well, it only added to my load."

"Are you regretting that, Mom?"

"No, I'm regretting that I didn't talk to your dad long before now. When you marry someone, they're a sounding board, too, a person who understands you and can help you make decisions."

It was a little weird that he'd just been thinking that Lyndsay understood him in a way no other woman had.

"Mom, you know I always need your help."

"Sometimes it doesn't feel that way, hon. I remember when Brittany died like it was yesterday. You were inconsolable, and I was helpless."

He briefly looked away. "I was young, and it was a terrible situation. Things are better now."

"Are they? Nothing I said convinced you it was an accident. That whole summer—you lost weight, you were hollow-eyed. But gradually you recovered, or I thought you did."

"Mom, of course I recovered. I'm even a productive citizen—and you once despaired about that!"

She smiled, but it was tinged with sadness. "The other day, you helped me to realize that my main problem is my inability to handle stress. I dwell and worry. And then I started telling myself that I needed a glass of wine each night to wind down. Gradually that turned into two, and then three. All my worries seemed to disappear into a mellow haze. I didn't realize how it was affecting me until you pointed it out, how I was getting secretive from your father." She gave a little shudder. "I was totally in denial. But I made an appointment with a counselor, and I've done some research. I'm going to start a stress journal and try to focus on the positive, because always dwelling on the negative leads to stress. I didn't want to bother your dad with all this, and though I thought I was protecting him, he was feeling shut out. And I got rid of all the wine, just gave it away. If I crave it, I promise to talk to your dad. Does that sound good to you?"

"It does, Mom," he said, leaning forward to give her a hug. "I'm proud of you for taking these steps."

She searched his eyes. "I don't know if I ever would have done it without you being brave enough to tell me the truth. Thank you, Will. I love you."

"I love you, too."

Together they went inside to finish helping with the cleanup, and although Will was relieved and happy, he wondered if he was more like his mom than he'd thought—that maybe he was in denial that he had a problem. She thought he blamed himself for things when he shouldn't. But when things were his fault, he couldn't deny it. His breakup with Lyndsay? That was his fault, wasn't it? He couldn't give her what she wanted.

Maybe he was in denial about that, too. But he didn't know how to change, or if he even deserved to.

Chapter 20

Lyndsay almost didn't go to Monday night's softball game. She wasn't going to bring a blanket or have a romantic picnic. She'd have to watch Will use that incredible body in athletic endeavors that did not involve him moving over or under her. It was all so depressing.

But . . . it was election eve, and Mrs. Thalberg and Mrs. Sweet had already spent the final week going door-to-door, talking up Valentine's historical society and the importance of steering it in the "proper" direction—depending on who you supported. Lyndsay couldn't imagine they could come up with something new, but she had to be there to find out.

To her surprise, there didn't seem to be any gimmicks or tchotchkes or beer. Just two elderly women sitting at two different tables, ready to answer questions. Throughout the game, Lyndsay saw people stop to talk to them, but it had been a monthlong election season, and folks probably knew the answers to all their questions.

Theirs was the last game of the evening. By the time it was over—Tony's Tavern defeated the Valentine Valley fire department—dusk had already settled over the valley, and the ball field lights were being turned off. Lyndsay climbed out of the stands and tried to leave quietly. But she had to pass near where the two presidential contenders were no longer talking to historical society members but to each other.

"Eileen, I did not think you capable of it," Mrs. Thalberg said coldly.

"Rosemary, I don't know what you're talking about" was the equally cool reply.

"You're trying to bribe the membership!"

"I am not—I am simply donating something to better explain the history of our town."

"Your mother's memorabilia—the same items you wouldn't donate a few years back. But now you announce it the night before the election?"

Mrs. Thalberg frowned, hands on her hips. Mrs. Sweet looked innocent and cool, her hands clasped genteelly before her, broad-brimmed hat (like the one on the lapel pin) shadowing her face in the growing darkness.

Lyndsay's dad stood away from the candidates, watching impassively, his arms crossed over his chest. Lyndsay went to stand beside him, and he gave her a distracted nod.

"This is just like high school all over again,"

Mrs. Thalberg said. "Don't you remember when you wanted the school council presidency, and your daddy donated money toward the gymnasium renovation?"

"I didn't have anything to do with that," Mrs. Sweet sneered.

And suddenly, behind both their heads, a blaze of fireworks boomed and exploded.

"Where did those come from?" Mrs. Thalberg demanded.

Mrs. Sweet grinned.

And then they went on arguing like they didn't even notice.

"So is my grandma causing problems?" Will asked from behind Lyndsay.

She jumped, startled, then glanced over her shoulder, wondering how long her eyes would get itchy and her throat tighten up every time she saw him. He was studying her too closely, as if he either expected her to break down and beg him to take her back—or missed her.

She gave him a faint smile. "Nothing Mrs. Thalberg can't handle." She turned to her dad. "Has it always been like this? Will told us this started because of a guy in high school."

"Well, it did," Mario said simply. "You never bothered to ask me about it, you know."

"So we're asking now. What do you know, Dad?"

He cleared his throat and rocked once on his heels. "I was courting Eileen when Rosemary caught my eye back then."

Lyndsay gaped. "*You* were the young man Mrs. Thalberg lured away from Mrs. Sweet?"

" 'Lured' is not quite the word," Mario said. He eyed the sizzling white fireworks that haloed Mrs. Thalberg. "It's not like I'd given Eileen a fraternity pin. We were simply flirting, but there was something about Rosemary, feisty even then." He studied his "lady friend" with fondness.

"But you didn't stay together," Will commented.

Mario shrugged. "I admit the feud made it difficult. I didn't like coming between a group of girls. And I was a teenage boy—we don't usually date a girl for years."

Lyndsay glanced hastily at Will, but his expression remained impassive. Her dad probably didn't even remember Will's high school love affair with Brittany.

"And it took you all this time to ask her out again," Lyndsay said, shaking her head.

"The memory of your mother was a strong influence on me," he said softly. "It didn't even occur to me to think of another woman for a long time."

Lyndsay had never thought Will and her dad had lots in common, but there was loyalty to a woman's memory . . .

Will kept his expression impassive as the fireworks went on brightening the night sky and he thought about Mr. De Luca's words. High school wasn't all that different in the late '90s than it had been in the '50s, but still, he himself had been one of those boring guys who'd stayed with a girl for years.

And been loyal to her memory, too.

He'd been in denial about that for a long time, a trait he'd obviously inherited from his mom. Perhaps he was giving it so much thought now for a different reason. It hadn't occurred to him in many years that he deliberately avoided commitment. It was always just something he did.

And now he was trying to avoid Lyndsay, had planned to break it off with her if she hadn't beaten him to it. He missed her already, missed their late-night phone calls, the teasing way she spoke to him, the way she gave him her body and her emotions with abandon.

And her love. She'd given him her love.

And knowing she'd thought so much about him that she'd based her book's hero on him had sent him running. He shouldn't care so much, but he did. Had he been starting to fall in love, too? Maybe he needed to know the truth about what she'd written.

At last the fireworks were over with a final big bang that deafened the ears and faded into a smoky trail. Mrs. Thalberg and his grandma marched away from each other, stiff-backed, and he hoped that tomorrow's election would see an end to the open feuding.

"Dad, I'll leave you to your girlfriend," Lyndsay said. "Have fun."

Mario smiled, but it was hard in the growing darkness to tell what kind of look he threw at Will. Did he know they were no longer together?

"You, too, babes," Mario said.

Lyndsay turned and headed for the parking lot.

Will caught up with her. "Lynds, would it bother you if I read your book?"

She eyed him skeptically, then gave an exasperated laugh. "Okay, fine. I'll try not to imagine you reading it."

"Why not?"

"I don't know. Ever since I found out it would be published, I've felt . . . squeamish. Strangers out in the world will be reading it. I feel squeamish about *everyone* reading it, so don't take it personally."

"Okay, I won't. I'll follow you home and pick up a copy."

"Tonight?" she asked, her eyes gleaming wide in the twilight.

"Is that okay?"

"It's a school night—not like I have a date."

He arched a brow, and she just smiled smugly.

"Oh, but I walked over," she added.

"I'll drive you home, then."

She nodded, but remained silent to the parking lot and the few blocks to her house. It was difficult being in the enclosed cab of his pickup with her, for Will could smell her faint perfume and see her tension by the way she gripped her hands in her lap. Usually, when he ended things with a woman, he was able to put it in the past, to move forward to the next exciting challenge. Not this time. It had been three days of replaying their every moment together in his head and wondering what Lyndsay was doing every hour.

As they pulled up to the front of her house, she reached to open the door. In that split second, he wondered what she'd do if he just grabbed her and kissed her. The feeling was so powerful that he was shaken by it, and he let the moment pass.

She let him inside the house, but he stood by the door, not making himself comfortable, not wanting her to be misled. Misled? She was the one who'd broken things off. And that thought almost made him laugh at the irony. He could hardly act offended, now, could he, not after all the women he'd dumped.

Or was he still riled that she'd seen through his bullshit?

She came out of the small hallway at the back of the house and handed him a book. He studied the beautiful mountain scenery on the cover, the image of the lone cowboy in the distance.

"Doesn't seem like me," he said.

She shot him a look, then reluctantly laughed. "Don't worry, I didn't send your picture or anything. And I didn't name him Will. Kate thinks we'll be okay."

He nodded, seeing her name in big letters over the book cover.

"This is truly an accomplishment, Lynds," he said quietly. "I do know that."

"Thanks," she said, her cheeks tinged with a blush.

For a moment he hesitated, and the air between them seemed fraught with regret and sorrow and might-have-beens.

"Now don't make me autograph the book," she said, her teasing sounding forced. "I wouldn't have a clue what to say."

He smiled, said, "Good night," then turned and walked away.

Lyndsay woke up at dawn, her eyes scratchy from lack of sleep—and probably from the tears that had kept falling from her eyes, through her hair, and into the pillow as she'd stared into the darkness long past midnight.

She was plagued by recrimination. Maybe she'd broken it off too soon with Will—after all, he already wanted to read the book! Maybe if she'd given him some time . . .

No, all she would have done was get even more attached, and he would have been the one to end things. She'd done the right thing for both of them. But it was hard to convince her heart of that.

When she went to leave for school, she found a flyer in her screen door and almost had a heart attack, wondering what the widows had done now. But it was only a reminder to stop by the community center and cast her ballot for the historical society officers. She saw the names of the people running for the other offices—unopposed—and it made her shake her head with amusement.

She glanced at her watch. If she hurried, she could stop there on her way to school and get it over with, because after school was the science fair, and she couldn't wait to see what all the kids—especially Matias—had done.

The community center had once been a brick factory, now remodeled with meeting rooms, an industrial kitchen, a game room, and a banquet hall that had held events of such importance as a speech by the president of the United States, and now something so local as a historical society vote. Valentine Valley took its history as a mining town very seriously.

She saw lots of people she knew as she marked off her ballot and stuffed it in the box. She poured a cup of coffee and stood quietly talking to Will's cousin, Matt, for a few minutes, before they both headed out the door for work. It was two days before the end of school, and the kids were crazed with excitement. She was pretty excited, too—she'd have a summer to finish her second book and start planning her third. She always needed the summer to recover from the nonstop prepping, teaching, and grading whirlwind.

After school, the kids who'd participated in the science fair headed down to the gym, while Lyndsay oversaw the dismissal for the rest of her kids. She spent a half hour grading papers until the fair began, then she grabbed her purse and went to take a look.

Parents and other visitors already wandered the

aisles. Rows and rows of tables were set up with freestanding display boards. Before each stood a proud child, ready to describe his or her work. The judging had already happened, and here and there she could see the occasional blue ribbon of a winner. Standing on tiptoes, she searched for Matias. To her surprise, she saw Will standing with him, hand on his shoulder, talking intently.

The ache of sadness was still sharp and overwhelming, and she had to take a deep breath to control her reaction. Will was such a thoughtful guy with kids. She should walk another aisle, she knew, but she couldn't stop herself from approaching them.

Had Will read the book? It was only the next day—of course he hadn't had time. She was going to have to stop worrying about it. He might never discuss it with her out of embarrassment. And maybe that was for the best.

Matias glanced past Will, and his chubby face lit up when he saw her. "Ms. De Luca, you'll never believe it. I took third place in my category."

She high-fived him, casting a surreptitious glance at Will before saying, "I can't be surprised. That was a great idea you came up with."

"Well, you helped. Check out the charts I drew on the poster. Cool, right?"

Will smiled as he said to Lyndsay, "I was just asking him to explain the experiment to me."

So Matias laid it out, and it was obvious he'd practiced for the judging round, because he delivered it smoothly and with enthusiasm. An older couple, perhaps someone's grandparents, stopped to listen, and as Matias started answering their questions, Will and Lyndsay stepped back and let him take over.

"So I saw Matias biking onto your ranch last week," she said in a quiet voice. "I admit, I was a little concerned that he should have been working on his science poster, but it's obvious he's well prepared for today. What was he doing with you?"

"This wasn't his only project. He wanted to present a poster with the 4-H club at the rodeo later this month. He asked me if he could borrow one of our horses and learn to ride. I've been helping him."

Lyndsay stared at him. "Why didn't you guys tell me?"

He studied her, bemused. "Why should we?"

"Because . . . I don't know. I kind of thought he was getting distracted at the end of the school year, when it's so important to focus on tests."

"You thought I was distracting him?" he asked mildly.

"No—well, yes, but I was probably upset for other reasons. It doesn't matter. In the end, it's kind of funny, because we've both been bonding with the same kid."

He eyed her, then briefly looked down. He had thick eyelashes a woman could envy, and they now seemed to hide his thoughts from her.

"Well, he's the kind of kid you want to help?" he

said. "Unsure of himself—he just needs a little encouragement. But that's what you do as a teacher, isn't it?"

"Yeah, but sometimes that gets lost in the craziness, you know? I enjoy being with kids, especially one on one."

"You seem to like the science fair a lot, even though it's extra work."

"Did you know I got my certification in both math and science? I love science."

"Why didn't you teach it? Heck, why didn't you just major in writing?"

"I wasn't so sure of writing as a career—it took me eight years to sell, and you don't even make all that much money unless your book really takes off. So being a teacher, something else I loved, seemed the safe thing to do to support myself. As for science . . ." She paused and thought back. "I wanted to stay in Valentine Valley, and the only opening was in math, so I thought, what the heck. And I was happy for a long time. But there's just something about the sciences. Talking about it with Matias, googling ideas, it's like . . . part of me came alive again."

"I like seeing you excited about what you do," he said solemnly. "I think it's been missing for a long time. I want everyone to enjoy waking up to the day as much as I do."

"I've always been able to tell that about you, Will. Your love of the ranch is obvious in everything you do. I guess I've been envying that about you."

"Are you going to do something about it?" He faced her, shoulders squared, hands on his hips, challenging her.

Her smile started slow, but she felt it grow until it almost split her face. "Yeah, I think I will. I haven't heard about any science openings here in town, but I'm certified to teach grades seven through twelve. I can check in Basalt or Carbondale, that's not too far a commute. Wow, for a moment I almost felt like I did when I first started to teach—minus the terror of wondering if I could control a class."

Then, to her surprise, he cupped her cheek with his hand. "You're glowing," he murmured.

And he stared into her eyes like he was going to kiss her. Their breakup, the public setting, it all seemed to fall away under the spell of the powerful yearning she felt for him. But it was more than yearning—it was love, making the love she'd thought she'd had in her early twenties pale in comparison. And the heartache—at times like this it seemed unbearable.

He wasn't going to let himself fall in love with her, she knew that. So she gently turned her head away from his hand.

"Thanks for listening, Will," she said, her voice breathless.

He cleared his throat, though he still sounded husky. "Glad to help. Guess I'll say good-bye to Matias and go vote."

"I voted this morning."

"I bet I know who you voted for," he said dryly.

"I bet I know who you'll vote for," she teased right back, reminding herself of the friendship she wanted to salvage if she could. "Who do you think will win?"

"Mrs. Thalberg." He heaved a sigh. "Hope my grandma isn't too unbearable for a while."

She laughed. "See you later, Will."

"You going to the welcome ceremony at the renovated house?"

"Sure."

"Then I'll see you there."

She watched him wave and turn away, and thought it almost sounded like a date. She knew it wasn't though, and he wasn't leading her on. He'd always been a friendly guy. And since his own heart was never touched anymore, he didn't realize how such tiny gestures could wound a woman's breaking heart . . .

Chapter 21

Lyndsay spent the next day going back through the e-mails from her district about fall teaching positions, then scoured the career listings online for science positions. Though there were none at her own school, there were several within the district she could apply for. She felt more optimistic than she had in a long time and positively giddy about revealing her publication news to all her friends. If only Will . . .

No, she had to stop this. She knew it was going to take a while. Running into him everywhere she went wouldn't help, but she had to get used to it. And she had to make it easy for him by not mooning over him, or sighing, or, God forbid, blinking back tears.

But she didn't have to make things worse on herself by attending the 4-H meeting at Sweetheart Ranch. She thought Will was capable of handling it by himself, so she stayed far away.

She parked her car a few blocks away from the welcome ceremony and carried her famous Butterscotch Delight pudding cake for dessert. The volunteers had remodeled an old bungalow-style home, perfect for a recently discharged sergeant and her husband, who were ready to start their family.

Lyndsay set her offering at the dessert table being manned by Mrs. Thalberg. "I saw the big announcement of your win this morning in the *Valentine Gazette*."

Mrs. Thalberg smiled. "Thank you, dear. It was quite an honor to be named president." She leaned over the table and added in a low voice, "And to win with seventy percent of the vote, too!"

Lyndsay grinned. "We all trust you'll do a great job."

"Thank you. And Eileen's input will be just as valued as before. She's still on the board of directors, of course."

"So she won't quit?"

"Heavens, no! That would be cowardly, and Eileen Sweet is certainly not a coward."

"Why, Rosemary, that's the nicest thing you've ever said about me."

Lyndsay turned to see Mrs. Sweet being escorted to the dessert table by Will. She was wearing a flowery dress with a smart little fedora perched above the elegant bun at the back of her head.

And Will—he was wearing worn jeans that hugged him in all the right places, and a bright blue polo shirt that emphasized his eyes, now shadowed beneath the brim of his Stetson. Lyndsay expected those eyes to shy away from her, but they met her gaze openly, frankly.

"Well, I certainly didn't say it just to be nice," Mrs. Thalberg said coolly. "I only speak the truth. I trust you'll remain on the board?"

"Of course. And congratulations on your win."

"Thank you."

"William, shall we go find Travis Beaumont's sister? I'm looking forward to meeting a female war hero. Lyndsay, why don't you accompany us?"

Lyndsay hesitated, then reminded herself for the hundredth time that she and Will would be friends again. "Thanks, I'd love to meet her, too." But she kept Mrs. Sweet between them.

They found Travis and Monica near the front steps of the house, introducing his sister Kelly to Sergeant Jamie Knapp and her husband, Craig. Jamie was in her midtwenties, enough years behind Lyndsay that she recognized her face but didn't really know her, especially since she'd gone into the army right out of high school and spent eight years doing several tours of Iraq and Afghanistan.

But now Jamie was getting a whole new start in life, a home and the beginning of a family, something Lyndsay was starting to worry she'd never have.

Now even her thoughts were sounding pathetic, Lyndsay thought in disgust. The day wasn't about her but a celebration and thanksgiving for what Jamie and other women like her had accomplished.

Kelly, Travis's sister, was one of those women. She had auburn hair the same as her brother, pulled back into a loose knot at her neck. She was wearing a skirt, which made it obvious that her right leg was prosthetic beneath her knee. She and Jamie looked at each other with instant camaraderie, two women in a select group where women were still rare. Lyndsay admired their bravery, their ability to head off into the unknown. They were the stars of the meet-and-greet beneath a tent on the front lawn.

There were tours through the house, appetizers, barbecue, and dessert. Lyndsay felt the soul of the town at moments like this, when everyone came together for a good cause. And to see the tears in Jamie's eyes as she took possession of her house for the first time after risking her own life for the US—it certainly put Lyndsay's problems in perspective.

To her surprise, Will stayed with her as they mingled. She saw members of her family and his eye them surreptitiously, but no one said anything. Occasionally their shoulders brushed, and it was torture and temptation all at once.

As the backyard emptied out after a tour of the house and grounds had finished, Lyndsay stopped Jessica to make an appointment to do the interview, and Jessica eyed Will in surprise.

"He knows about the book," Lyndsay said in a low voice. "We can talk in front of him."

Not that there was much talking, beyond setting

a time and place. When Jessica had gone, Lyndsay forced a reassuring smile for Will and leaned close.

"Don't worry—I will never say anything about you being connected to the book."

"I trust you, Lynds."

"Do you?" She eyed him, trying to find a way to keep things normal. "Well, you know I trust you. I'd even trust you enough to . . . give me a helicopter ride."

His expression grew pained. "I can't do that."

"I was just kidding, but now I'm curious. I knew you wouldn't give the kids a ride, but I'm a consenting adult. What gives?"

They stood alone near a bench in the back corner of the yard, which seemed like it would be a peaceful place, but not with the way Will seemed stiff with tension.

"It was never just about the kids," Will confessed, "although it made me leery even imagining putting them at any kind of risk. I've really liked being with them, and for the first time, it's given me pause about the choices I've made for my future. But every time I think too much about kids, something inside me just shuts it all down." He regarded her solemnly. "I know that's not what you want to hear."

She shrugged. "I knew that going in."

"But as for the helicopter, on our first date, when you hopped in, so confident, I actually *wanted* to take you up," he admitted. "I'd never felt that way about anyone but my family."

"I don't understand."

"Well . . . it was Brittany who first suggested the helicopter. She found a ranch online that used them, and we made all these plans . . ." His expression turned wistful but not sad.

Lyndsay almost didn't breathe, surprised that he'd brought her up—and that he actually kept talking.

"I never forgot the helicopter idea," he continued. "We bought one, and I learned to fly. On my first solo trip I felt . . . connected to Brittany, at peace for the first time. Except for my family, I didn't want other people up there. But I didn't feel that way about you being up with me, and I admit, it kind of spooked me."

"And yet we kept dating."

With his hands in his pockets, he shrugged.

"You've kept yourself connected to Brittany and the accident for a long time."

He put a hand on the back of the bench, his knuckles whitening as he stared into a distant past.

Lyndsay remained silent, and through some sort of magic, no one else came into the backyard. She was able to focus on Will and absorb the ache of frustration and loss. The fact that he was still talking to her about his emotions . . . she didn't want that to give her hope, because it could be all about putting her in the past.

He wasn't looking at her when he said, "Did you know we planned to get married right out of high school?"

She briefly covered her mouth, knowing her eyes still betrayed the surge of sorrow. She didn't know what to say, but he didn't seem to want a response, as the words continued to pour out of him.

"I know what you must be thinking—we were really young, and would have changed our minds, but . . . I never felt that way. Brittany and I would talk about marriage and having kids all the time. I already knew my career—hell, I'd been in training for it my whole life. I didn't intend to go to college, not then. She mostly wanted to be a mom, and being a ranch mom really suited her. She was all about family, you know?"

To her surprise, he turned and actually looked at her, as if he needed her to understand. She nodded, knowing her eyes were big and wet, and she had to bite her lip to keep it from trembling.

"Of course, after she died, I went to college. I just couldn't stay around Valentine and think of everything I'd lost—everything I'd taken away from Brittany. But my heart wasn't in it, which is why I eventually dropped out. It was hard to find a new kind of life, when I hadn't planned one without her." He sighed. "Turns out that I wasn't the only one in my family affected. My mom pretty much admitted that worry about me has stressed her out so much she took to drinking."

Lyndsay gasped. "Will, that seems like too simple an explanation."

"Yeah, it is, I know that. A lot of things have been stressing her out, but I've been one of them.

We had a good talk, and she's glad I told her what I saw, and she's getting help. She and my dad are talking about it, too, since apparently she hadn't even realized she'd been shutting him out."

Lyndsay reached to touch his arm, then stopped herself. "Well, that's good."

"But it doesn't change the things I've done, Lyndsay. I can't ever be the kind of boyfriend or husband you want. I took marriage and babies away from Brittany—I don't deserve to have them."

This time she did touch him, gripped his arm until he met her gaze. "She died in a car accident in a storm, Will. You didn't take anything away from her. It was an *accident*."

She felt him flinch.

"She was waiting for me and I didn't show," he said woodenly. "That's the only reason she took off driving during a storm. I tried to reach her, to tell her I got delayed, but we didn't have cell phones then."

The last was said so roughly that she felt it like a raw scrape across her nerves.

"That doesn't make her accident your fault," Lyndsay insisted. "To continue to blame yourself—"

"I know! You don't think I've told myself this a thousand times?" he asked bitterly. "But it doesn't change how I feel. It doesn't change how sick at heart I am every time I'm with her parents, especially since they're so nice to me."

"Wanting to help them is a good thing, Will, but

it doesn't mean it has to be about guilt."

"I'd do anything for them," he said in a low, angry voice. "I take their small herd of cattle to summer pasture with our own. I help with the branding, the calving, and the haying. But it's never enough to erase how guilty I feel." And then he gazed deep into her eyes. "Thanks for listening and trying to help, but I'm beyond that. I just felt you should know the truth so you can move on, okay, Lynds?"

"But Will . . ." Her words died away. What could she say if he was determined to live in the regrets and mistakes of the past?

With a nod, he left her there in the backyard. Slowly, she sank down onto the bench, then put her head in her hands, the last of her hopes crushed beneath his cowboy boots. Will would never move past Brittany's death, because he didn't want to.

School was finished Thursday, the day before Lyndsay's book publication, as if she'd coordinated it. On Friday morning, her new life as a public figure began. She was giddy with plans to check her retailer rankings every hour all day. She also intended to stop in at the Open Book and have a moment of reverie in front of the display of *A Cowboy in Montana*. To see her book on a store shelf was a dream come true. Maybe she'd call her dad and see if he wanted to go with her.

Jessica's article would appear in that day's *Val-*

entine Gazette, and when Lyndsay got a phone call at 8:00 a.m., she thought for certain it was about that.

She saw Kate's caller ID and answered. "Hi!"

"You've got to get to Main Street right away."

Lyndsay was tempted to pull the phone away from her ear and stare at it. "What? This isn't about the *Gazette*?"

"Great article, by the way. I cried. But no, it's not about that—it's related. Come on down to Sugar and Spice. I'll be waiting. And look good. People are going to be taking your picture."

"Kate, what is this about?"

But Lyndsay heard the beep of the phone disconnecting, and *then* she stared at it. Look good?

Trying not to get overexcited, she took a quick shower and wore a casual blue dress and tan sweater. Public author clothes. She saw a bunch of missed calls on her cell before leaving, but she decided not to answer until she knew what Kate was talking about.

Her shoes weren't conducive to walking, so she drove the few blocks, turned up Main Street—and would have rear-ended a car if there had been one in front of her. As it was, with a screech of tires, she pulled over and just stared.

There was a huge banner strung across the street, with her book cover ten feet high, and beside it, the words YOUR SUMMER JUST GOT STEAMIER . . . THANKS TO OUR OWN LYNDSAY DE LUCA!

She took her foot off the brake, and the car

lurched forward into the curb, since she'd forgotten to put it into park. She did so, turned it off, then slowly got out and leaned against the car just to stare. Her throat got tight and her eyes filled, even as she kept telling herself she couldn't ruin her makeup. But oh, to know how proud her family was of her, and now all her friends would know, too . . . gees, she better find a tissue.

She heard the jingle of a shop door opening behind her.

"I never thought you'd get here so soon," Kate called. "You must have set a land speed record."

"A shower speed record, anyway," Lyndsay murmured, still not taking her eyes off the giant banner that swayed with the brisk morning breeze.

"Well?" Kate asked, coming to lean against the car beside her, eyeing her with anticipation.

Lyndsay felt dazed and excited and scared all at the same time. She turned wide eyes on Kate, and gradually, a grin spread across her face.

Giggling, Kate hugged her. "This is so incredible! Now the world—well, our corner of it anyway—will know how awesome you are. Aren't the widows wonderful?"

Lyndsay let Kate lead her by the hand to the sidewalk. "They said they had something big in mind, but I had no idea . . . They are publicity *machines*."

Inside Sugar and Spice, almost a dozen people were clapping when she came in, and Lyndsay stared around at her brother, dad, and Ethan, at Emily and Nate. Steph and the three widows were all wearing aprons that now sported her book cover.

Lyndsay opened her mouth to speak, but she was so choked up that she couldn't say anything. She ended up in her dad's arms, and she buried her face in his shoulder and tried not to cry.

"Okay, okay, pass her around," Nate said, giving her a hug that lifted her clear off the floor. "We're so proud of you!"

"We can't wait to read the book!" Emily cried, when it was her turn.

The only thing missing was sharing the day with Will. Regret and sadness were a deep ache that might never go away, and she tried to push them into the recesses of her mind.

"I saw your book in the window of the Open Book this morning," Steph gushed. "They have dozens of books on display, a big picture of you and everything. You're doing a book signing there next week?"

Lyndsay nodded, still feeling the silly expression decorating her face.

"Even my grandma must be excited," Steph said. "She called to ask if I'd seen the big banner, so of course I raved about it. She's coming over here to talk about it with you."

Lyndsay blinked at her for a moment. "Coming . . . here? Why?"

Steph's smile faded into confusion. "Well . . . to congratulate you, I bet."

"We're not exactly close, and since I broke up

with Will, why would she care?" A sick feeling roiled her stomach uneasily.

Steph glanced at Emily. "Well . . . she's always proud of the citizens of Valentine Valley. Why would it matter about you and Will?"

"I don't know, but it just seems . . . weird." Lyndsay glanced at the widows, and to her consternation, they gave each other uneasy looks. *Uh-oh.* But before she could question them, the door jingled and the matriarch herself marched inside. The happiness was sucked out of the room like a giant fan in reverse.

"Lyndsay De Luca," Mrs. Sweet said, "I have something to say to you."

Lyndsay took a deep breath. "Good morning, Mrs. Sweet." She tried to brace herself to be scolded. The others continued to murmur to each other, but their gazes remained on the elderly lady.

"I have heard that you've written a book and that my grandson William is featured prominently." Mrs. Sweet came to a stop right in front of Lyndsay.

Lyndsay swallowed even as her eyes went wide. She looked around in disbelief, wondering how the hell her secret had gotten out already. It must not have spread far, because almost everyone else looked surprised or intrigued.

But not the widows.

"Mrs. Sweet," Lyndsay began, "I hope you're not offended, but—"

"Offended? Why should I be offended? Why shouldn't my grandson be the hero of a book?"

Lyndsay felt the heat of a blush steal over her, and she couldn't help wondering if Mrs. Sweet was entirely clear about the sexual content of a romance. She saw the wide, shocked eyes of her friends focus on her—and then her father gave a snort of laughter from behind her, and Ethan playfully elbowed him. Soon, smiles seemed contagious, and relief began to spread through her body like a warm beam of sunshine breaking through clouds. Though she'd dreaded everyone finding out, she was surprised how relieved she felt that she no longer had a secret to keep. She was still worried about how Will would take everyone's knowing, but at least his grandma wasn't humiliated.

Lyndsay wished Will had been at her side, that they could share a smile over this—that he could be a part of this important day. Without him—it wasn't the same. He hadn't called her about the book, so she had no idea if he'd read it so he was at least prepared. Some people might recognize that altered scene as something based on his life with Brittany—hell, Brittany's *parents* might recognize it, and her smile faltered. She wasn't in the clear yet.

"Grandma," Emily said, "we don't understand what you're talking about."

"Some of us understand," Kate said meaningfully, looking directly at the widows. "Don't we?"

"It's our fault," Mrs. Thalberg said, stepping out from behind the counter, hands clasped in front of her apron, where the cover of *A Cowboy in Montana* was prominently displayed.

Lyndsay bit her lip to keep from giggling. Her emotions were veering all over the place. She struggled to sound calm as she asked, "How did you find out about Will?"

Mrs. Thalberg lifted a placating hand. "I'm so sorry, my dear. Once we heard about your book, naturally the three of us downloaded it to our e-readers and tablets. It appeared at midnight, and we stayed up just to get started reading. We think you're a gifted writer, by the way," she said, her smile sweet as she touched Lyndsay's hand.

Lyndsay briefly clasped the woman's hand in return. "Thank you so much. But could you finish what you were saying?"

"I can tell her, Rosemary," Mrs. Palmer said gently.

"No, it should be me, Renee. Lyndsay, we felt free to discuss your book this morning, once your ban on publicity was lifted, and perhaps we should not have been so foolish as to discuss your hero's similarity to Will while we were having breakfast at the True Grits Diner."

Lyndsay briefly closed her eyes. "Someone must have overheard you."

"Our waitress, Harriet," Mrs. Thalberg said, ending the name on a heavy sigh. "I heard her gasp. Knowing her, she didn't keep the gossip to herself."

"It's all my fault," Mrs. Palmer said sadly. "I don't hear as good as I used to, so the girls sometimes have to speak louder for me."

Mrs. Ludlow patted her shoulder, then turned to Lyndsay. "Does Will know about the similarities?"

"Yes, he does," Lyndsay admitted.

"Wait." Emily lifted both hands. "You based the hero on my playboy brother? The ego-stroking must have left him preening."

"Not exactly," Lyndsay admitted. "But he was nice about it."

"Of course he was," Mrs. Sweet insisted. "What man wouldn't be flattered when the lovely girl he's dating thinks so highly of him?"

Lyndsay had to blink back tears at Mrs. Sweet's kindness.

Kate said, "I don't think that most people are going to recognize that there are a few similarities. The widows only speculated, having known Lyndsay a long time. Her admiration of Will shines through every paragraph—"

"Kate," Lyndsay said in a warning tone.

"I mean," Kate hastily added, "that she admires her hero, Cody, who only *begins* with some of Will's characteristics. He's his own man, with different goals and personality. I think, Mrs. Sweet, that you will enjoy the book for its own sake."

Mrs. Sweet eyed Lyndsay over her glasses. "I will read it immediately, and then we can discuss it. Perhaps you'd come speak to my book club."

Lyndsay could only nod and mumble, "Thank you, I would enjoy that."

Mrs. Sweet swept out, leaving a brief, stunned silence in her wake.

"Lyndsay, if you admired my brother so much," Steph said with exasperation, "why did you break up with him?"

Before Lyndsay could answer, Monica and Brooke rushed in, obviously to talk to their best friend, Emily. They took one look at Lyndsay and came to a halt.

"Hi, Lyndsay," Brooke said. She gave Emily a wide-eyed glance.

"We've all been discussing her book," Emily said.

"Good!" Monica said briskly. "Then let me say, Lyndsay, how very proud we are of you."

Lyndsay smiled. "Thanks."

"And is it true about Will?" Brooke asked.

All eyes turned back to her with avid interest, and Lyndsay sighed. "Yeah, it's true—although I swear I didn't realize it when I was writing the book. My cowboy has some of his characteristics. He didn't stay exactly like Will, of course. And Steph, to answer your question, I broke up with him because I knew I wanted more out of a relationship than he did."

"I'm so sorry, Lynds." Emily gently laid a comforting hand on her shoulder.

"Look," Tony said, "don't worry about Will. He'll be fine with everybody knowing the truth— especially since he already knew."

"Thanks, Tony," Lyndsay said, "but you're my brother. Reassurance is part of your job description."

"Well, we'll find out. I just texted him that we're all here. He's on his way."

"Great," Lyndsay said faintly.

Chapter 22

Will got the first clue something was up when he was thigh-deep in an irrigation ditch, trying to pull out a damaged dam and replace it with another. His cell phone kept ringing or beeping with texts, one after the other. When he finally had the dam in position, he waded out of the water, reached for his phone, which was inside his hip boots and deep inside his jeans pocket, and saw the lineup of missed calls and text messages. He swore out loud.

The first was from his brother, Chris, congratulating him on being every woman's fantasy brought to life. Will frowned in confusion. *What the hell—?* Then Daniel chimed in on the same group text, saying he'd just downloaded the story of Will's life and would soon be able to quote the good lines.

Will leaned against the ATV as realization struck. Lyndsay's book was out in public—and so was his part in it. He'd read it the last few nights—

devoured it, really—and the character hadn't turned out much like him besides looks, a little bit of personality, and that one scene. He'd gotten into the story and forgotten all about his connection to it. She really was a great writer.

But apparently the whole world had now found out his "part." He knew Lyndsay, Kate, and Tony wouldn't have released the depths of her secret, so how had it gotten out?

And then Tony texted him, letting him know where they all were. Will hoped Lyndsay wasn't taking the revelation of her secret badly. Just when the most exciting accomplishment of her life should be celebrated, could his part in it be making her into a joke? Well, he wasn't going to let that happen.

He texted his brothers: *Lynds's hero not exactly like me. She took me and toned me down some.*

And there was more he could do for Lyndsay.

Lyndsay paced the bakery, waiting for Will. A few customers came in, including some who knew her and gave her hearty congratulations. She was sure everyone else had lots of questions, but they held back, sensing her uncertainty.

She heaved a sigh. She thought she'd only have to worry about her students' parents finding out she wrote a romance—now they might think she wrote kinky stuff about real-life guys in town. Did she really care so much about what other people thought? Or maybe it was all about Will.

Where was he? She just wanted to get this confrontation over with.

"This is strange," Brooke said from a little table, where she was having coffee with Emily and Monica. "Whitney and Josh are having breakfast at True Grits, and they said Will just brought the house down."

"What?" Lyndsay felt a little dazed. Brought the house down?

Brooke snickered as she read her phone. "Apparently, he threw open the doors, strode inside, and said it was only a matter of time before someone 'wrote about me'—his words. And another quote: 'You can't be this awesome and not expect it.'" She burst into laughter, joined by Monica and Emily.

"What the heck is he doing?" Lyndsay murmured to no one in particular.

Kate stopped Lyndsay's pacing by stepping in front of her. "You told him a while ago, right?"

Lyndsay nodded. "But now it's public knowledge, which makes it different."

"Now Will's at Hal's Hardware," Mario said, glancing at his own phone.

It was still strange how much her dad loved his iPhone. She'd even known him to pin it into his pocket so he wouldn't lose it.

"Will didn't bother eating?" Steph asked curiously.

"He's making the rounds," Mrs. Thalberg said with satisfaction.

Lyndsay didn't get it.

Mario chuckled. "Francis Osborne quotes Will, too. He says when questioned, Will told everyone that he'd always thought his story would be dramatized in a rock song or an epic poem." He gave Lyndsay a comforting look. "Seems to me you don't have to worry about Will's reaction."

"I'm just worried that he's putting on an act," Lyndsay said, twisting her hands together. "He's really good at making people believe only what he wants them to believe."

"Maybe you're worrying for no reason," Mario said gently.

"I'm trying to tell myself that. But Dad," she said, lowering her voice, "part of me is focusing on Will because . . . without him, this day, the proudest day of my life, just . . . isn't complete."

He put his arm around her shoulders. "I'm sorry, babes."

"Thanks. Apparently Will has other plans, so I think I'll just take off for a while."

"Are you sure?" Kate asked. "Do you want company?"

"I'm fine. I'll see you all later."

Lyndsay headed out the front door and onto Main Street, where she saw the banner boldly proclaiming her cover and the promise of a "steamy" summer. It made her smile, but . . . she couldn't forget about Will.

Several people stopped her, and she gladly answered questions about the book. When Will's name came up, she let it go with, "You'll just have to read it and see what you think." She imagined she'd be saying that a lot over the next couple weeks . . .

As she reached her car, Sean Lighton called her name.

"Hi, Sean," she said, smiling.

"Great news about the book." He gestured to the banner. "I never knew you were a writer."

"I sort of kept it hidden until the book sold."

"Never knew you were so shy either," he teased. "Bet you have a lot of parties and stuff planned today."

"Not really. Why?"

"Oh. Well, I had hiking plans and wondered if you wanted to go. Not as a date or anything," he hastened to add, "just friends. But I bet with the book news—"

"That sounds great. I'd love to go." She was surprised when the words tumbled out, but suddenly, getting away from town and her feelings of missing Will just seemed like the perfect idea.

His mouth dropped open for a moment before a big grin split his face. "Well, okay, then!" He glanced at his watch, then at her. "I have everything ready. I was just going alone, but I have enough supplies for two. I bet you need to change."

"Follow me home. I only need a minute."

At her house, Sean waited patiently by his car while Lyndsay changed into hiking pants, boots, and a short-sleeve shirt, then packed a fleece and rain shell. She knew how cold it could get this time of year at higher elevations. After applying sunscreen, she pulled her hair into a ponytail and added a visor, then grabbed her CamelBak and filled the bladder. Sean had said he had everything else they'd need.

When she appeared outside, he looked up from his phone in surprise. "That was quick."

"I do my best."

As she tossed her old duct-tape-covered backpack into the rear seat of his SUV, she saw his shiny new pack and boots.

Sliding into the front, she said, "New gear?"

"Yeah," he admitted.

She knew he was a computer geek trying to fit in with the outdoorsy world of the Rockies, and that made her sympathize. "So what did you have planned for today?" she asked.

"We're going up the main spine of the Elks," he said importantly.

"Ah ha." She tried not to smile. "Which part?"

"The Hell Roaring trail," he said with enthusiasm. "Sounds intense."

"Well, no, it's a good hike, but not that intense. It's named for the sound of the spring runoff on the other side of the ridge. But there's probably snow still up there."

"Only the last bit. We'll be fine."

They drove fifteen minutes on paved roads, then another half hour going up dirt roads, occasionally stopping for meandering cows or slowing down as they passed through cattle guards, a break in the fence where the road was covered by a grate.

At last they reached the trail head for Hell Roaring. Across a valley of pine trees, they could see Capitol Peak in the distance. For a couple of hours, they climbed a trail winding through pine groves and open meadows, stopping to admire the mountains below, and the Continental Divide far in the distance to their east. The way was occasionally muddy, and more than once Sean fell to a knee. It was good to think of nothing but balance and foot placement, feel the air filling her lungs, and savor a deep drag of water from the tube of her CamelBak.

But at last they reached the beginning of snow up above the tree line. Grass spiked from it in clumps, and half-buried rocks showed that there'd be deeper drifts ahead. She hated post-holing, because you never knew how deep your leg would sink or what it would hit.

Lyndsay turned to Sean, who'd fallen a bit behind. "Maybe we should turn back now. It's a bad time of year to be up here without crampons for the bottom of our boots."

"But we're almost to the ridge," Sean protested. "Another hour at most. Your boots can take the mud and snow, right?"

She hesitated, her eyes shielded from the sun beneath her visor. At last, she pulled her gloves out of her pack to combat the cold. "Okay, a little bit longer. But I'm turning back when I want to, even if it means leaving you behind."

"Of course! Let's have some gorp to refuel, and then we can keep going."

"Hmm, good old raisins and peanuts."

"You bet."

"Hand 'em over."

He laughed, and they sat side by side on boulders, admiring the view of the valley below and the peaks of mountains dusted with snow in the distance. It was a couple hours past noon, beginning to verge on being too late to hike this high without overnight gear. She'd just go another hour at most, no more.

Chapter 23

When Will finally arrived at Sugar and Spice, there was quite a crowd gathered, and they eagerly surrounded him. Apparently they'd been getting text updates about his tour of Valentine Valley. Word was getting out that he enjoyed the book and loved being the center of attention—as if that last part was anything new. Heck, maybe he should subtly spread a rumor that "casting" him had been all his idea.

"So where's Lyndsay?" he asked Tony.

Tony and Kate glanced at each other.

"We don't know," Tony said.

Will looked around, then locked eyes with Mario, whose expression was sober.

Kate said, "I've tried to reach her, but she doesn't answer calls or texts." After hesitating, she added, "She was worried about your reaction."

"I'm just fine. She's the one we should be worried about. This should have been the best day of her life. What happened?"

He got the scoop about the eavesdropping that happened at breakfast from the widows themselves.

"I'm so sorry," Mrs. Palmer said.

"Don't apologize," he insisted. "I'm fine with it. I'm just sorry Lyndsay was worried that I wouldn't be."

"Will," Steph said, "through the window I saw her talking to Sean Lighton. Whatever they were discussing, he seemed pretty happy about it."

She would hardly start dating someone so soon—would she? And today, of all days? No way. "All right, I'm going to see her. I'll let you know what I find out."

"For a guy who's not big into relationships," Tony said, "you seem to care an awful lot about my sister."

"Of course I do. That's never changed. And she broke up with me," he added over his shoulder as he neared the front door, "remember?"

But Lyndsay wasn't at home, though her car was. That meant she couldn't have gone far. He drove up and down the main roads, but he didn't see her. He texted her close friends and family, but no one knew where she was. He tracked down Sean's cell from the friend of a friend, but Sean didn't answer either.

And his feeling of distress spread from the pit of his stomach to tighten through his chest.

Where was she?

By midafternoon, just when he was wondering if

the police could help, his phone rang. It was Lyndsay's ID. He couldn't press the button fast enough.

"Lyndsay? Where are you?"

"Will?"

She sounded both frantic and relieved, which upped his own tension. But the sound broke up almost immediately, and he only heard a syllable here and there.

"Lyndsay, I can't hear you!"

" . . . broken leg . . . Mountain Rescue . . . roaring . . . Capitol Cree—"

And the phone call went dead.

His heart raced, and perspiration broke out on his forehead. She wanted him to call Mountain Rescue? She'd broken her leg? Where the hell was she? "Roaring" could mean the Fork, but she'd said Capitol Creek . . . she had to mean Hell Roaring trail.

He tried to call again and again, but she didn't answer. So then he called Mountain Rescue's dispatch, got put through to his buddy, Aaron Epstein, and told him the situation.

"So I think they're somewhere on Hell Roaring," Will finished, talking too fast, he knew. "And I can fly you there."

"Whoa, wait a minute," Aaron said. "I agree that that's where they probably are, but we can hike up there easily enough, take a couple litters."

"No, you don't get it. That's my *girlfriend* up there, and if you try to hike this time of day, you're going to end up there after dark. We don't know how bad her leg is broken—maybe she can't spend the night on the mountain. I'm offering to fly you in—it won't cost you anything, and it won't tie up your helicopter."

"Well, if you put it that way—"

"I'll pick you up at the Aspen airport."

"That's good." With concern in his voice, Aaron asked, "Are you sure you're up to this, Will? You sound shaky."

Will took a deep breath. "I'm fine. Just hurry."

Even as he texted Tony and told him to pass the news that he was off to rescue Lyndsay, all he could think of was that she'd needed to get away because of *him*. He should have just called her instead of trying to save the day—then she'd have known he was okay with their secret being out. Instead, she was in danger. She'd sounded frantic and scared in just those few syllables. He felt sick to his stomach—and Aaron was right. His hands were shaky. He fisted them and told himself to get it under control. Lyndsay needed him.

With snow-dusted Mount Sopris majestically capping the Elks in the distance, Will flew his helicopter above the treetops along the Hell Roaring trail. Aaron was in the seat next to him, headset on over his helmet, his curly dark hair sticking out around the edges and down his neck. Aaron was scanning the countryside as hard as Will was.

"There they are!" Aaron called, pointing ahead. "Just beneath the ridge."

Will's feeling of intense relief was almost dizzying, but he was focused on what he was doing, so he let any emotions slide away from him. Lyndsay was on her feet, jumping up and down and waving a red jacket. Will laughed aloud.

Aaron stared at him.

"Sorry. Lyndsay's okay. I'm just happy."

It was Sean who was lying in the snow-covered rocks. Hopefully he was okay, too, but Will was focused on the sight of Lyndsay. He flew past her, higher up the trail, and landed gently on the flat of the ridge, his skids crunching as they settled into the gravel. Aaron doffed his headset, opened the door, and hopped out. Will wished he could follow, but he had to shut down the engine and rotors first, and that was a process. Frustrated, he gritted his teeth and did his job.

By the time he was climbing to the ground, Aaron appeared over the ridge again.

"Lighton's basically okay, broken leg, not a compound fracture. We'll use the litter to get him up here."

Will followed Aaron across the rocky field, skittering through snow, but the wind had skimmed any deep drifts right off the top of the ridge. Mountains surrounded them on all sides, but Will wasn't paying attention to the view. He was looking for Lyndsay, and when he spotted her on the open trail, crouched beside Sean, he could have hugged her.

He settled for an arm around her shoulders

when she stood up. Sean, his face white, regarded the two of them with dismay, then sighed and relaxed his head back onto his pack.

"You okay?" Will asked Lyndsay.

As Aaron began unbuckling the litter straps, she briefly leaned against Will, then smiled. "I'm fine. I knew you'd find me."

He grimaced. "I barely heard what you were saying when you called. Hard to believe you got any cell reception at all."

She gave a short laugh. "I ran around holding my phone in the air, and when I found one bar, I froze in this contorted position."

"I'm glad you did." He didn't let her go, and she didn't pull away. "What happened?"

As Aaron assisted Sean into the litter, she used the opportunity to back away and lower her voice.

"It was stupid. We shouldn't have climbed up this far without the proper equipment. Sean knows it—he's embarrassed. He didn't even want me to call Mountain Rescue, thought he could limp back down the trail."

"How did he break the leg?"

"We were almost to the ridge. He was just below me when he started to slide twenty feet or so back down the hill. He couldn't self-arrest to slow himself down, and he hit a rock." She shuddered. "I swear I heard the leg snap."

He rubbed her arm in sympathy.

"I handled this whole day poorly," she said,

shaking her head. "I never should have agreed to climb higher without crampons."

"Don't blame yourself. It's all my fault. I heard you were worried about the book secret getting out. I should have called you, let you know I was okay."

She glanced at him in surprise. "Your fault?"

Before he could reply, Aaron called, "Okay, Will, he's secure. Let's get him up to the ridge."

After that, it was all business, carrying the litter the last hundred yards up the rocky slope, then securing it in the helicopter. Sean kept apologizing to Lyndsay over and over, until Will could have told the guy to shut up. But he refrained.

Once everyone was loaded aboard, Will started the engine and eventually lifted off, heading back toward Aspen.

Once they got Sean onto the Mountain Rescue truck, Lyndsay promised him she'd call to check up. Then she headed back toward the helicopter, where Will was still seated at the controls, the blades whirling overhead. She ducked as low as possible, running toward it, then slid into the front seat beside him.

Once she had the headset on, she smiled and said, "Guess I managed to get a ride out of you after all."

He rolled his eyes. "Buckle up. It should only

take about fifteen minutes until we're back at the
ranch."

When he lifted off, she watched him work but
didn't try to talk to him. He seemed . . . remote,
professional. On the trail, he'd kept his arm around
her, comforted her, but that guy seemed far away
now.

The darkness crept up in the east, as the sun
had already set behind the mountains. The sky was
pink and gold, and all around the twilight below
seemed like a dark mist, framing Will. She still
couldn't believe what she'd heard him say—that
this accident, this crazy day, was all his fault.

His fault!

She knew he didn't think himself the center of
the universe—he just took the blame naturally, because that's what he'd been doing since high school.
Well, she had news for him—but she wasn't having
this discussion through headsets.

She wasn't used to flying low over Valentine
Valley, so she took in the beauty of the lights
coming on over the streets, the tower of town hall
lit for the night, the big neon sign on the Royal
Theater displaying a half dozen colors.

"I can see my house!" she called, trying to
lighten the tension.

He nodded but didn't smile.

Ridiculous man.

The ranch was a long stretch of darkness, lit by
few lights except near the buildings. Will had radi-
oed ahead, and his brothers had gotten the landing

site ready, lights lit to guide them in. There was a landing light beneath the helicopter, too, and it helped Will see the ground below.

"You're not landing on the dolly tonight?" Lyndsay asked.

He shook his head. "Too tricky at dusk. No weather approaching tonight. I'll do it in the morning."

They touched down with a minor jolt, and she sat still and watched as Will ran through his checklist to shut down the helicopter.

She didn't want to interrupt him, so it wasn't until the engine was silenced and the rotors still that she said, "You were great up there. Thanks so much."

She could see the muscles in his jaw clench, but he didn't say anything, only took off the headset and opened the door.

Frowning, Lyndsay did the same, then ran around the front of the helicopter and stopped him when he would have headed for the hangar. "So I thank you, and you ignore me?"

She saw one of his brothers come out of the hangar, but she waved him off, and he went back inside.

"I'm not ignoring you, Lyndsay," Will said calmly. "But you've already thanked me, and it doesn't feel right to be thanked."

"Why not? You got my message and you flew to our rescue, when we would have had to spend a night on the mountain—and we were ill prepared for that." She shook her head. "I feel like an idiot."

He didn't say anything, just looked at her.

She threw her hands wide. "Okay—why did you say our hiking accident was your fault? How could you possibly believe that?"

He folded his arms over his chest. "His broken leg wasn't my fault, but it could have just as easily been you who was hurt. If static had captured just one more word of your phone call, I would have had no idea where to find you. And you'd have been stuck up on that mountain because of me, because I didn't tell you I was okay with our book secret being revealed."

"Will, *listen* to yourself! You had nothing to do with my decisions. *I* wrote a book that got published, *I* based a character on you, and *I* panicked when word got out. I didn't check to make sure Sean had the proper equipment for a hike above the tree line at this time of year. It wasn't your fault—just like Brittany's death wasn't your fault!"

He reared back as if she'd slapped him.

"Yeah, I'm saying it, and you're listening to it," she said forcefully. "I made my own decision—and so did Brittany. Stuff happens, and sometimes it's out of everyone's control. You need to find a way to accept that and not blame yourself."

"Accept that?" he echoed. "She's dead. She'll never get married or have kids or any kind of life. And I'm just supposed to do all that when she never will?"

His voice broke at the end. Lyndsay wanted to throw her arms around him, but she didn't, not yet. "Yes," she said softly. "Yes, Will, Brittany—and her family—want you to have a normal life, a good life, a fulfilling life. Do you think Brittany would be happy that you never let yourself find love? Do you think she was that kind of girl, who'd selfishly want the boy she loved to suffer because she died in a senseless accident?"

He said nothing, just stared at her, his eyes narrowed with confusion and pain.

"Stop putting up barriers, Will," she whispered. "I promise to stop, too. I didn't wait for you today—I ran away, rather than see how I'd affected you, rather than face how my success doesn't seem enough without you there to share it with me."

He looked startled, but she plowed on.

"I hid my secret from you until it had to be dragged out of me. Do you think I like that about myself?"

"Lyndsay, you're making yourself sound like a coward, and you're not."

"That's nice of you to say, but I'm feeling like a coward about now. And you—" she broke off, aghast that her throat seemed to close up and her eyes burn. "You'd r-rather live with the ghost of a dead girl than take a chance on a real live one. We're not all fragile dolls. We make stupid decisions—we're human. Don't let that deny us the chance at real happiness. I love you, Will. I think somewhere inside, you want to love me."

"I don't want to hurt you," he said roughly. "It would kill me to hurt you, Lynds."

"Then don't hurt me." She stepped close and put her hands on his warm face, saw the wetness shining in his eyes. "Let's take the chance, Will. I don't want to hurt you either. I want to love you."

She stood on her tiptoes and kissed him, and for too long he remained stiff, his lips unyielding. She thought she'd truly lost him forever. And then, with a groan, he embraced her hard, holding her so tight to him she could barely breathe. He kissed her over and over, her cheeks, her eyelids, her forehead.

Against her ear, he whispered gruffly, "When I thought I could have lost you . . ."

"You didn't, Will. You won't ever lose me again."

It was his turn to take her face in his hands. "I *love* you, Lynds," he said intensely, heatedly.

Her tears spilled over, and she found herself laughing helplessly, this time being the one to kiss every part of his face she could reach. She'd waited a lifetime for those words.

"Say it again," she said against his mouth. "Say it again."

"I love you." He kissed her hard. "I love you." He lifted her off the ground.

She flung her arms wide and laughed into the growing darkness as he spun her around. Will loved her.

Epilogue

Lyndsay's signing at the Open Book on Main Street was the culmination of so many dreams. People were buying her book, and she hoped that she could make them laugh, cheer them up at the end of the day, and sigh with wistful happiness when they got to The End.

Her local readers had a special treat: Will was making his own appearance at the signing. At first he'd stayed in the background with her family until he'd reluctantly agreed to pose with readers buying the book, only getting into the spirit of fun when Lyndsay insisted it was okay. She loved how he was so concerned about her enjoying her big day. When Mrs. Palmer asked him to sign her copy, too, Will gave Lyndsay a concerned look, but she left space for his signature next to her own.

"I'm only signing because you asked, Mrs. Palmer," he said. "We all know Lyndsay's the real artist here."

Lyndsay ran her fingers over both their names side-by-side, then looked up at Will, so close she could see his eyelashes. He was smiling at her with pride, and she'd never imagined feeling so happy, so proud, and so fulfilled. She'd changed her life for the better, had risked everything to publish a book—and found love with Will Sweet, her own personal, real-life cowboy. Heroes existed outside of books, too.

COMING IN 2016

Fairfield Orchard

A brand new series from Emma Cane

The fun doesn't have to end here! Keep reading to explore the rest of Valentine Valley and the people who call it home as they find true love.

A Town Called Valentine

A Valentine Valley Novel, Book 1

Welcome to Valentine Valley—where broken hearts come home to mend, and true love may lie just across the range . . .

Emily Murphy never thought she'd return to her mom's rustic hometown in the Colorado Mountains. But after her marriage in San Francisco falls apart, leaving her penniless and heartsick, she returns to her old family home to find a new direction for her life. On her first night back, though, a steamy encounter with handsome rancher Nate Thalberg is not the fresh start she had in mind . . .

Nate has good reason not to trust the determined beauty who just waltzed into town—he's no stranger to betrayal. Besides, she's only there to sell her family's old property and move back out. But as Nate and Emily begin working side-by-side to restore her time-worn building, and old family secrets change Emily's perception of herself, both are about to learn how difficult it is to hide from love in a place known far and wide for romance, family ties, and happily-ever-afters: a town called Valentine.

True Love at Silver Creek Ranch

A Valentine Valley Novel, Book 2

Welcome to Valentine Valley, where tongues are wagging now that the town bad boy is back—and rumor has it the lean, mean ex-Marine is about to lose his heart! But like it or not, in a town like Valentine, love happens . . .

Adam Desantis is back—bruised, battle-weary and sexier than ever! Not that Brooke Thalberg is in the market. The beautiful cowgirl of Silver Creek Ranch needs a cowboy for hire, not a boyfriend—though the gaggle of grandmas at the Widows' Boardinghouse thinks otherwise. But from the moment she finds herself in Adam's arms, she's shocked to discover she may just want more.

Adam knows it's crazy to tangle with Brooke, especially with the memories that still haunt him, and the warm welcome her family has given him. But he finds himself in a fix, because tender-loving Brooke is so much more woman than he ever imagined. Can a soldier battling demons give her the love she clearly deserves?

Just about everybody in Valentine thinks so!

A Wedding in Valentine

A Valentine Valley Novella

*It's the wedding all of Valentine Valley has
been waiting for!*

Bridesmaid Heather Armstrong arrives
for Nate and Emily's big weekend, only to
discover that one of the ushers is the man
she had a close encounter with when they
were trapped by a blizzard seven months
before—and he's the bride's brother!

Cowboy Chris Sweet never forgot the
sexy redhead, although she'd disappeared
without a trace. At first the secret creates
a divide between them, but as they grow
closer during the romantic weekend, will
Heather dare risk her heart again?

"The Christmas Cabin"

from the anthology
All I Want for Christmas Is a Cowboy

A Valentine Valley Novella

It's Christmas in Valentine, and the Thalbergs remember how their family came to be . . .

Sandy, recently diagnosed with MS and abandoned by her husband, is determined to make Christmas special for her five-year-old Nate. While they're trooping through the woods to cut down their Christmas tree, a snowstorm arises, and a mysterious old ranch hand points them toward an abandoned cabin. Little do they realize, the ranch hand also guides cowboy Doug Thalberg to the same place . . .

The Cowboy of Valentine Valley

A Valentine Valley Novel, Book 3

Welcome to Valentine Valley, where the cowboys have many talents and love is waiting around every corner . . .

Ever since a heated late-night kiss that absolutely should not have happened, cowboy Josh Thalberg makes former Hollywood bad girl Whitney Winslow's pulse beat faster. But when she decides to use his gorgeous leatherwork in her new upscale lingerie shop, Leather & Lace, she's determined to keep their relationship strictly professional . . . even if she wants so much more.

Josh has never met a challenge he isn't up for. Which is probably why he allowed Whitney to persuade him to take the sexy publicity photo that went viral and now has every woman in America knocking down his door . . . every woman except the one he can't get out of his head.

But how to convince a reformed bad girl that some rules are worth breaking?

A Promise
at Bluebell Hill

A Valentine Valley Novel, Book 4

Welcome to Valentine Valley, where love captivates even the most guarded of hearts . . .

As an agent of the Secret Service, Travis Beaumont has become an expert at staying detached. With the upcoming wedding of the President's son to a Valentine Valley resident, Travis can't afford any distractions. But a sexy, local flower shop owner seems determined to push past all of his defenses.

Monica Shaw has always put the needs of others before her own—even if it's meant placing herself in harm's way. For a long time, a simple life running her flower shop has been enough, but when Monica meets a gorgeous, mysterious man who takes her breath away, she suddenly wants more. But can she convince a no-nonsense Travis that love is definitely worth the risk . . . ?

When the Rancher Came to Town

A Valentine Valley Novella

Welcome to Valentine Valley! The Silver Creek Rodeo is in full swing and everyone's talking about the rancher who came to town . . .

Bed & Breakfast owner Amanda Cramer wants nothing more than a quiet, private life. Well, she wants guests too, but after her share of unwanted notoriety she's gotten comfortable hiding out in her inn . . . perhaps a little too comfortable. When her newest guest arrives—tall, dark and breathtaking—Amanda begins to question her self-imposed exile.

Ex-rodeo star Mason Lopez knows all about the limelight. He'd avoid it if he could, but since one last ride could mean saving his family's ranch, he'll go all in. When he gets to Valentine Valley for the Silver Creek Rodeo, Mason checks into Connections B&B and finds himself immediately drawn to the beautiful, reserved woman who owns it.

Mason only has three days in town. Can he convince Amanda to open her heart to him and welcome the world back in?

Sleigh Bells in Valentine Valley

A Valentine Valley Novel, Book 5

Return to Valentine Valley, where Christmas lights are twinkling and first love burns brighter the second time around . . .

When Tony De Luca's ex, Kate Fenelli, waltzes through the door of his tavern and pulls up a bar stool, she turns his balanced world on end. Once they'd been each other's first love, first everything. But then life happened, and they walked away with broken hearts. Now Kate is back in Valentine, and they can't seem to stay out of each other's way. When Tony begins wondering what would happen if they rekindled the sparks, he knows he's in big trouble.

Kate can't believe she's sitting at Tony's bar spilling her life-changing problems to him. He's as gorgeous as ever, and she can't seem to forget how incredible he always made her feel. Still the door on that chapter of their lives closed long ago. Yet with Christmas buzzing in the air, Kate can't help wondering if anything is possible—even a second chance with the only man she's ever loved.

At Avon Books, we know your passion for romance—once you finish one of our novels, you find yourself wanting more.

May we tempt you with . . .

- **Excerpts** from our upcoming releases.

- Entertaining **extras**, including authors' personal photo albums and book lists.

- Behind-the-scenes **scoop** on your favorite characters and series.

- **Sweepstakes** for the chance to win free books, romantic getaways, and other fun prizes.

- Writing **tips** from our authors and editors.

- **Blog** with our authors and find out why they love to write romance.

- **Exclusive content** that's not contained within the pages of our novels.

Join us at
www.avonbooks.com

AVON

An Imprint of HarperCollins*Publishers*
www.avonromance.com